Please return/renew this item by the
last date shown to avoid a charge.
Books may also be renewed by phone
and Internet. May not be renewed if
required by another reader.

www.libraries.barnet.gov.uk

BARNET
LONDON BOROUGH

NP

COPYRIGHT

The Good Heart ©2017 Helena Halme
Published worldwide 2017 by Newhurst Press
Second edition 2017
Previously published as *The Good Officer*

ISBN-13 978-1-9998929-5-1
e-ISBN: 978-1-9998929-4-4

ACKNOWLEDGMENTS

I couldn't have written this novel without the support of my long-suffering husband. The original Englishman is an excellent first reader, but even a better cook. I am also grateful for my editor, Dorothy Stannard, who tirelessly and patiently has worked with me on the many versions of this book. Thanks must also go to my naval expert, Adam Peters, for all his invaluable advice. It goes without saying that all mistakes intentional or not, are entirely down to me, or required for fictional purposes.

ONE

HELENSBURGH, SCOTLAND

I t was a cold morning, on 30th January 1985. There was no rain, and Kaisa could just about make out the faint outline of the sun in the distance, low above the Gareloch. The sight of the opaque light behind a thin layer of cloud made Kaisa feel oddly optimistic. She held on tightly to the cup of coffee she'd brewed and inhaled the familiar, comforting smell. She had decided she would drive them to the community centre on the Churchill Estate, on the other side of Helensburgh, where the court martial was to be held. It was only a quarter past eight, and Peter was already wearing his full uniform, with sword; he looked very smart.

'Do you want something else before we go? More tea, or water?' Kaisa asked. She saw Peter's straight back through the open kitchen door. He was standing in front of the mirror in the hall, adjusting his cap. Without turning to look at her, or speaking, he shook his head.

Peter hadn't wanted her to come to the court. But his lawyer, Lawrence, had told them Kaisa needed to be there to show the court that they were a happy couple. Kaisa had recoiled from the phrase. She didn't know what happiness was anymore.

That morning she'd dressed in the black trouser suit that she kept for job interviews, with an off-white roll-neck jumper inside the jacket for warmth. Pammy, her friend on the married patch, and the only Navy wife who still talked to her, had said it was bitterly cold at the community centre, and that they might have to wait around outside for hours before the proceedings started. Kaisa didn't ask how her friend was so knowledgeable. She wondered if the waiting around was part of the punishment, but there'd been very little information about the day; just the one letter summoning Peter to the court martial at 10 am.

'You are not needed as a witness because you're my wife; you just need to be present,' Peter had told her. His eyes were dark, and as usual when he spoke with Kaisa these days, they displayed no emotion whatsoever.

'I'm going to drive,' Kaisa said to Peter's back. She could see his image in the mirror, but couldn't see his eyes under the black peak of his Navy officer's cap. She thought how handsome he still was, even though he'd lost so much weight. The past few weeks, during the awful state of limbo before the court martial, Kaisa had often coaxed Peter to eat. He'd lost his appetite for food, and life, it seemed. She couldn't pinpoint the time when he had changed; at first, when the consequences of all her terrible actions had played out, they'd been able to comfort each other. They were like two survivors, thrown together in a sinking ship, bailing out water, fighting together to remain afloat. But slowly, Peter had drifted away from her, into his own shell, into his own world. He'd grown quieter, and wanted to be with her less. Now when Kaisa tried to touch him, he flinched.

Kaisa knew it was the impending court martial that was playing on Peter's mind, so she let him be. She understood how much his career in the Navy meant to him, and hoped that when the proceedings were over they would find a way to love each other again.

Outside, braving the strong winds whipping up the hill where the grey pebbledash houses of the married quarters stood, Peter looked thin and gaunt. When he removed first his sword and then his cap and placed them carefully on the back seat of the car, Kaisa saw the dark circles around his eyes.

Kaisa parked on the sloping car park, and pulled up the handbrake hard. Peter winced; he just couldn't get used to her driving. Not looking at her, Peter got out and picked up his sword from the back seat. He fixed it onto his belt and walked across the small yard towards the entrance of Drumfork Naval Club, a low-slung, 1960s building. It was used as a social space for naval families, and as everything in Helensburgh, was run-down and grey-looking. Peter noticed the ice on the ground too late and slipped on the steps.

'You OK?' he heard Kaisa say behind him, but he didn't have the energy to reply to her. Instead, he cursed under his breath and took a handkerchief out of his pocket to wipe the palm of his hand. There were a few spots of blood. 'Fuck,' he said out loud. Glancing down, he saw his uniform trousers had escaped the worst of it and still looked crisp and smart; they still had the deep creases he'd ironed into them that morning.

Inside, it was even colder than on the windswept hill. Peter rubbed his hands together, keeping the hankie between them in an attempt to stem the blood, which was dribbling out of the fleshier part of his right palm. He nodded to the same Wren who'd shown him into Himmler's office three weeks before. She didn't smile as she stood up from the grey plastic chair she'd been sitting on, but her eyes had a kindness to them. Peter moved his face away from hers. During the past weeks he'd heard nothing but condolences, people saying how sorry they were. He didn't need their sympathy – he needed this to be over and to get back to work. Even Kaisa had nothing but sorrow in her eyes and Peter couldn't stand it. What he needed was anger; he needed people to understand how angry he was. Angry at Kaisa, angry at Duncan, angry at the Navy for posting him and his new, young, pretty wife to this God-forsaken arsehole of a place, angry at Scotland and the bloody Jocks complaining in their harsh accents, angry at the drab, ugly married quarters on the hillside, overlooking the steely cold Gareloch, angry at himself for being so stupid as to care that his wife had slept with someone else. He put his handkerchief back into his pocket and told himself to calm down.

The door behind him opened and his lawyer, who had been to see Peter at home, shook his and Kaisa's hand. Peter flinched; the stone steps had grazed his palm and even though the bleeding had stopped it still hurt.

'You OK?' The guy, who was probably only a few years older than Peter, asked.

Peter looked at his hand. 'Yeah.'

The lawyer nodded and turned to Kaisa.

'Perhaps, Mrs Williams, you'd like to go in. Sit at the front – they need to see you together.'

Kaisa nodded and went inside.

When they'd met previously, the lawyer had also immediately said how sorry he was about the 'incident' as he called it. Lawrence Currie was a lieutenant like Peter, but he'd studied law in Edinburgh and had a slight Scottish lilt when he spoke. The accent had put Peter off him at first, but he'd warmed to the man when he'd told Peter that the court martial would 'run its course whatever you or I may think.' He'd said that the panel would have decided what the outcome would be even before Peter stepped inside the room. 'So the best thing is to stand there, reply to any questions as quickly and briefly as possible and get out. You can then get on with the rest of your life.'

'Yes and No responses are the best,' he'd added.

Now Lieutenant Currie motioned for Peter to go and sit at the far end of the room. Out of the earshot of the Wren, Peter supposed.

'We've got a little time to go over everything,' the lawyer started.

He told Peter that he should plead guilty to assault. 'I will then bring in the mitigating circumstances of you being back from your first patrol, the wee shite, whom you'd considered to be a friend, taking advantage of your pretty, foreign wife, and so on.'

Peter nodded. He wasn't looking at the lawyer, but was hanging his head. He was trying not to let the anger rise again.

'Are you OK?' the lawyer asked, again, touching Peter's arm.

Peter looked up. 'I'm not pleading guilty.'

The lawyer was silent for a moment, then sighed and said, 'I strongly advise you to throw yourself at the mercy of the court. They will have sympathy for you.'

Peter moved his eyes away from Lawrence.

The lawyer sighed again. 'Now, don't forget they will take your sword from you. It means as an officer, you are placing your rank, status and reputation on hold for the duration of the proceedings.'

Peter nodded. 'When are we going in?'

'Any minute now. But there's something else I need to tell you. There will be reporters outside with cameras. One is from the local rag, *Helensburgh Advertiser*, but there are also the nationals: *Daily Mail*, the *Sun* and the *Telegraph*.'

Peter put his head in his hands. He thought about his parents, his brother in London, and his sister. They'd all read about his stupid actions, and now they would have to explain it to their friends. Until now he'd been something of a local hero in Wiltshire; his achievements in cricket during his school years had often been written about in the *Wiltshire Times*, and when he passed out from Dartmouth, there'd been a long article about it in the same local paper. That was partly because Prince Andrew had graduated at the same time, so the Queen had also been there. Still, it was a picture of Peter in the freshly pressed naval officer's uniform that had appeared inside the paper. Even when he'd married Kaisa, his mother had sent in a wedding picture of them to the paper, which had printed it with the caption 'Local submarine officer, RN, marries a girl from Finland.' Now they would have something far juicier to write about. Would they dig out the picture of him and Kaisa on their wedding day? Suddenly a phrase he'd often heard came to his mind: 'There's a touch of the pirate about every man who wears the Dolphins.' He grinned and recalled when he had caught the Dolphins, the badge of the submarine service, between his teeth from a glass of rum. It was an old Royal Navy right of passage on qualification and proved that submariners were a bit wild. He immediately regretted such thoughts and straightened his face. Then the door opened and he was loudly called in by a Naval Provost.

TWO

The court martial suite of the Drumfork community centre was a large room at the back of the building. There was a long table at one end, and chairs set out on each side, with a gangway left empty through the middle. Kaisa sat at the front, with her blonde head bent and her hands crossed in her lap as if in prayer. The room was full. Peter recognised Pammy and Nigel but avoided looking at the rest of the crowd. The large table had five empty chairs. Another, smaller desk was set to the side, occupied by a lieutenant, the advocate for the Crown, Lawrence said. Lawrence hurried to the empty seat next to the other lawyer and the Provost indicated for Peter to stand in front of the court. As he passed the crowd, Peter's eyes settled briefly on Nigel, who nodded almost imperceptibly. Moving his eyes away from his friend, Peter saw a colourful round rug in one corner of the room, and on top of it an unruly pile of plastic toys. The room must be used for a play group, Peter thought, and again he felt the urge to smile. 'For fuck's sake, keep it together,' he told himself, and he concentrated on setting his mouth straight.

For a moment the room seemed to sway in front of Peter's

eyes, but he managed to steady himself by closing them for a second. A court official nodded for Peter to remove his sword. With shaking hands, he struggled to unclasp it from its scabbard. He thought he'd prepared himself for this naval tradition, but now when it came to it, his hands wouldn't obey his commands. Eventually Peter managed to get the sword free, and he placed the gold-handled weapon on the table in front of him.

The official, a small man with a serious expression, proceeded to tell everyone to stand. There was a hush as five men, also wearing full dress uniforms, their swords awkward in their hands, walked in and settled down in the chairs facing Peter. The Captain, the President of the Board, who wore small half-moon glasses perched at the end of his long nose, sat down in the middle, with the two commanders on either side. A lieutenant, a submariner Peter had once been introduced to, but whose name now escaped him, went to sit at the far end of the table, and a very young looking sub-lieutenant with a pink face, sat nearest to the lawyers. Neither looked at Peter.

That Peter didn't know any of the Board came as a great relief to him. His mouth felt dry and he swallowed hard. The men gazed gravely at him and then the President asked him how he pleaded. Peter said he was 'Not guilty.' He tried to make his voice as steady as possible, but there was a tremble at the last syllable. He heard whispers behind him, and avoided looking at his lawyer. Lying awake the previous night, he'd decided he just couldn't admit to guilt. Even though he'd punched Duncan first, it was his so-called friend who had done the unthinkable. Even Himmler had said so on that awful day of the fight.

Peter was then told to sit down. The lawyer next to Lawrence got up and told the sorry tale of Peter's 'assault' on Duncan. The Naval Provost who'd been at the pool and the two lifeguards then gave their account of the fight that Peter had started. Peter zoned out, trying to keep his nerves steady.

When the prosecution had finished the President said, 'Over to you Lieutenant Curry.'

Just as he'd told Peter outside, Lawrence spoke about the mitigating circumstances and how Peter 'had been pushed to the edge.' He paused and leaned over to his desk to pick up a piece of paper. 'With your permission, Sir, I'd like to read out a short statement from the other party.' There was a collective intake of breath, then a murmur from the crowd.

'Silence, please,' the Captain said, and nodding at Lawrence added, 'Go on.'

With a clear voice, Lawrence read out a statement from Duncan in which he said he was sorry about his indiscretion against 'his fellow naval officer, and friend, Lieutenant Williams,' and that he had not suffered any long-term medical consequences from the incident. He also stated that he was not planning now, nor any time in the future, to seek any kind of compensation for the actions against his person. After Lawrence had finished reading, the courtroom filled with a low chatter, causing the Captain to raise his head and give the room a stern stare. 'Please, I must insist on silence.'

Looking at Lawrence, he said, 'Is that it?'

'Yes, thank you, Sir,' Lawrence replied. He sat down, giving Peter a glance and a quick nod.

'The court will adjourn to consider its decision,' the President said and everyone got to their feet.

When Peter was called back inside, his eyes shifted to the table, where his sword had been moved so that the tip was pointing towards him. So they'd found him guilty. Peter's feet felt heavy, as if he were in chains, while he walked slowly towards the end of the room. Would they dismiss him from his beloved Navy? He could see Kaisa was again seated at the front, with her head turned towards him, her red-rimmed eyes looking at Peter.

The next part of the proceedings went by in a flash. Peter was told that he could continue to fulfil his duties for Her Majesty's Submarine Service, and keep his rank, but that he'd be fined £500, to be taken from his salary in the next six months. The court was dismissed and the Board, led by the Captain, clattered out of the room; Peter was handed his sword. The court official gave him a long stare as he held the weapon flat in his hands. Peter placed his sword inside the scabbard, attaching it back to the belt smoothly this time. He wanted to smile, but thought better of it. He took hold of the handle, and immediately felt himself stand taller.

Lawrence came up to him and shook his hand. 'You took a chance; that could have been much worse.'

'Thank you,' Peter said. He was a little curious about how the lawyer had got the statement from Duncan, but he didn't ask. He didn't want to know anything about that bastard ever again.

Outside, the reporters ambushed Peter and Kaisa, as they tried to rush to their car. The flash hurt Peter's eyes and he pulled his cap further down.

'Give us a smile, Keese,' one reporter, mispronouncing Kaisa's name, shouted, and Peter could feel Kaisa lean closer to him. He took hold of her hand and pushed past the reporters. He saw Lawrence stay behind to answer their questions.

In the car, Kaisa put her hand on Peter's thigh. She didn't say anything, just stared at the road ahead of them. He looked at her small, slender fingers, with their nails bitten to the quick. When had she started biting her nails? He realised that he felt nothing under her touch. Usually the pressure of her hand so close to his crotch would have caused an immediate reaction; but now there was nothing. She removed her hand to change gears.

'A fine was good, right?' she said and glanced at him.

'Yeah, obviously the best thing is not to be court-martialled at all. It'll be on my record forever,' Peter said drily and watched the still, steel surface of the Gareloch. That should put a stop to her bloody optimism, he thought.

His words had the desired effect, and shut Kaisa up. They drove the rest of the way in silence. Back at the married quarter, Kaisa went immediately upstairs. Peter could hear her crying in the bathroom. He slumped onto the sofa and closed his eyes.

THREE

I n the afternoon after the court martial, Peter had to do something to clear his mind. He decided to go and fetch his things from the base. As luck would have it, the first person he bumped into was his Captain. The old man called him into his office. 'Peter, you're a good young officer, who's had a bit of bad luck. Just do a good job in your next appointment, and this will soon blow over, believe me.'

'Thank you, Sir,' Peter replied.

'Now, there's one more thing. Did you see the reporters in there?'

Peter lifted his head, 'Yes, I did. Lt Currie told me about them,' he said simply. 'And,' Peter felt his voice falter, but paused trying to steady his nerves, 'they took photos,' He looked down at his polished boots and continued, 'to show ...'

Peter couldn't find the words, so the Captain came to his rescue, 'Yes, I understand, to show a happily married couple.'

Peter nodded.

'Well, that's what you two were, and I'm sure will be again.' The Captain went on to tell him to expect some coverage in the local rag. 'There will be something in the national press too,' he said, taking hold of Peter's arm. 'Just hold firm, don't make any comments. If you haven't done so already, it might be best if you tell your family as soon as possible. And take your phone off the hook,' he added.

Peter went home. Kaisa was still upstairs; she had fallen asleep, fully clothed on their bed. Peter didn't want to wake her, so he tiptoed downstairs and dialled the number of his parents' house. It was the most difficult conversation he'd had in his life. His father was quiet, listening to Peter's sorry tale, and when it was over there was a long silence at the end of the line.

'Dad?' Peter said, wondering if the old man had heard any of what Peter had told him.

'I'll get your mother,' his father replied eventually, and Peter heard the phone being placed on the table. He imagined the tidy bungalow his parents lived in now that their three children had grown up and left home. He thought, again, how this scandal would affect the order of their lives. How would their large circle of friends, many of whom were ex-Navy or ex-Army and had fought in the Second World War, take the news? Would they be sympathetic, or would they talk behind his parents' backs and shun their company? He remembered how thrilled his parents and the whole family had been when Peter graduated from Dartmouth Naval College. When the Queen herself attended the passing out parade, they were bursting with pride.

The wait for his mother to come to the telephone felt like an age. He could hear her ask what was up, and the muffled reply from his father, which he couldn't decipher.

'Peter?' his mother said, with a higher pitched voice than usual.

'I'm sorry, mum,' Peter said. He began telling her the whole story, about how Kaisa had been with a friend of his, Duncan, while he was on his first patrol.

'He seemed such a nice young man,' Peter's mum interrupted, and Peter remembered the weekend during their time at Dartmouth when he'd invited Duncan to Wiltshire to stay with his parents. Peter tensed up and formed a fist with the hand not holding the receiver. 'Well, he's not.'

At that moment, he heard a sniffle from the lounge, and saw Kaisa sitting on the sofa, her knees up to her chest, her body balled up tightly. Peter hadn't heard her come down the stairs. She was crying hard now, and Peter wished he could go to her instead of having to finish the conversation with his mother.

But Peter had to continue. He told his mother how he'd found out about the affair on his return, how the bastard had been at the base, talking to Kaisa at the swimming pool, how he hadn't been able to control himself and how he had knocked Duncan into the water.

'I was dismissed my ship,' Peter was hanging his head, the shame of the court martial fully hitting home.

'Oh, Petey,' her mother used a nickname Peter hadn't heard in years, not since he was a small boy. He suddenly yearned to see his mother, to be comforted by her.

'It'll probably be in the papers,' Peter said instead, delivering the final blow.

'Oh,' was all his mother could say. 'What do you mean, in the *Wiltshire Times*?'

'Well, probably not, unless ... it'll be in the national ones, most probably.'

'The *Telegraph*?'

Peter sighed, 'I don't know mum. We'll be down next week, if that's OK?'

There was a pause.

'Mum?' Peter wondered if the line had gone dead.

'Of course, we'd love to see you,' his mother said.

Peter asked her to pass on the news to his sister and brother, and hung up.

THAT EVENING, he and Kaisa sat in their cold house at Smuggler's Way and drank half a bottle of vodka. Kaisa cried, on and off all night. Peter wished he could cry too, but he simply wasn't able. All he wanted was to numb his senses. He couldn't help Kaisa, couldn't bring himself to comfort her.

The next day the story appeared in the *Telegraph*, on page three, where the salacious stories were usually found. It felt unreal to see a picture of him and Kaisa, looking solemn but standing close to one another, printed there, with the headline, 'Two Royal Navy Officers Fight Over Pretty Swedish Wife'. The article was short, but his head was pounding and he felt sick when he saw the words, 'The actions of 24-year-old Lieutenant Peter Williams are believed to have been fuelled by jealousy, after it was revealed his wife, Kaisa Williams, also 24 and originally from Sweden, had been having an affair with a fellow Navy officer while Lt Williams was away at sea.' In the *Daily Mail* Peter's court martial and Kaisa's affair with Duncan was a front page headline, 'Two Royal Navy Officers Brawl In Pool Over Sexy Swedish Blonde'. But the *Sun* was the worst, 'Bomber Boys Battle Over Bonking Blonde Bombshell'. Peter read the articles swiftly. The tabloids he merely scanned, but he read the *Telegraph* in full. It gave the verdict and even described Peter as 'a brilliant young officer' and reported on the 'great interest shown in the case' at the court martial.

Peter put the papers in the bin. His head was hurting from the vodka. He found a packet of paracetamols above the sink and swallowed two with a glass of water, while surveying the grey mist over the Gareloch. When he turned around, Kaisa was standing in the doorway to the kitchen, silently watching him. She moved slowly to the bin and pulled out the papers.

'Swedish!' she said, and Peter, surprised at his own reaction, had to suppress a smile. He wanted to hug Kaisa, it was so typical that her incorrect nationality would be the one thing she commented on, but something stopped him. Examining the paper with her head bent, she looked so tired, her face drawn and the blonde hair hanging limp on her shoulders, that Peter felt a strong urge to protect her, to tell her everything would be alright, and that he loved her. But he couldn't move, nor speak. He gazed at her, willing Kaisa to look up and say she was sorry. Instead, she put the papers back in the bin and, not looking at him, said, 'I think I will go to Helsinki to see mum and Sirkka.'

FOUR

HELSINKI, FINLAND

They were sitting side by side at the end of the jetty, with their feet just touching the water. Peter had rolled his uniform trousers up and Kaisa was wearing a summery dress. The sun glittered on the surface of the lake. For once, it wasn't raining. Peter turned his head towards Kaisa and took her hands between his. His dark eyes under his naval cap looked as sparkly as the surface of the water. Kaisa sighed with happiness. She lifted her chin and moved her head closer to Peter's. As his lips approached Kaisa's, she opened her eyes and woke up with a start.

It was dark, and the heavy, stuffy room was silent, apart from the gentle snoring of her sister, Sirkka. Kaisa turned over and tried to get back into the lovely, summery dream, but she was now wide awake, disturbed by the snoring, which was getting louder. She could have gone and adjusted her sister's pillow, which is what she usually did if the snoring got too loud, but Sirkka was working an early shift at the Intercontinental Hotel on Mannerheim Street the next day, whereas Kaisa could lie in — or sleep all day if she wanted. She looked at the clock with the small reflective dots on the windowsill behind her and saw it was nearly 4 am. The events of the last few weeks flooded back to her, and she wanted to howl with misery. The shame of the fight between Peter and Duncan over her, and Peter's immediate sacking from the bomber submarine, HMS *Restless*; the whispers and looks of the other Navy people, even from their so-called friends, in the shops in Helensburgh, when she and Peter had tried to live a normal life before his court martial; and Peter's visible disappointment at the sudden nose dive his career had taken, made worse by its astronomical rise. His appointment to the Polaris submarine in Helensburgh just a few months after passing his nuclear qualification had been such a coup; he'd been one of the youngest officers of his rank — lieutenant — to be appointed to one of the subs that served as Britain's nuclear deterrent. Not being able to take the covert hostility of her fellow Navy wives on the married quarter estate in Rhu, nor Peter's growing indifference to her, Kaisa had decided to flee back to Finland the day after Peter's court martial.

Her mother and Sirkka had welcomed her with open arms. They had decided that she should stay with Sirkka in her one-bedroomed flat in Töölö to begin with. But during the past days Kaisa had detected a slight change in the way her mother treated her; her own failed marriage to Kaisa and Sirkka's father had at least lasted nearly twenty years, whereas Kaisa's relationship seemed to have broken down before she had even celebrated the first wedding anniversary. Of course, Pirjo hadn't pointed this out yet — but Kaisa was sure it was only a matter of time.

Kaisa had been in Helsinki for nearly a week now. She knew she had to forget the past — and Peter — and focus on the future. She couldn't carry on living in her sister's one-bedroom flat, and sleeping on her (admittedly quite comfortable) sofa bed forever. If she was to stay in Helsinki, she needed to find a job, somewhere to live on her own. She needed some purpose in her life. Unless of course, she decided to go back to Peter. They hadn't discussed the future when Peter had dropped her off at the train station in Glasgow to take the train to Heathrow. Officially, she was taking a little break in Finland with her family. Or that was what they had told each other and their friends Pammy and Nigel.

'Write to me when you get there, eh?' Peter had said at the train station, and he had kissed Kaisa lightly on the lips.

Kaisa had nodded, not being able to hold back the tears. They'd rolled down her face, smearing the mascara she'd put on that morning. But Peter hadn't reacted, or wanted to see Kaisa's tears. Unlike the many partings they'd had before they were married, when Kaisa was still a student in Helsinki and Peter was based in Portsmouth. Then Peter would always wipe, or kiss, Kaisa's tears away, and as a parting gift he'd buy her a single red rose. Today Peter just looked away, with his hands in his pockets, indifferent to Kaisa's emotions.

'I'll let you know when the new appointment comes through, and where I'll be living,' he'd said, glancing sideways at Kaisa. His eyes were narrow, and didn't show any emotion when they briefly met hers. He looked quickly away again, towards the empty track, as if he was longing for the train to arrive, impatient to get rid of his troublesome wife. Kaisa knew all he wanted was to get back to work, to get back onboard a new submarine, to rebuild his career. She didn't seem to feature in his plans for the future.

At the chilly station, where they could hear the rain beating down on the Victorian tin roof, they'd stood facing each other, but Kaisa couldn't bear to see the cold expression in her husband's eyes, so she stared at his hands instead. There were a few hairs growing on them, and Kaisa had an over-whelming desire to stroke them and lace her fingers through Peter's. She imagined that he'd look up, surprised, and that his eyes would light up at her touch, like they used to do. He'd pull her hand up to his lips and give her palm a gentle kiss. How she'd longed for him to say he loved her, but instead, when the train pulled into the station, screeching noisily, he'd said, 'Do you want me to help you with the suitcase?'

Kaisa had just shaken her head. She wanted to hold him, to tell him once more how much she loved him, but no words came out. She was so ashamed, and seeing him reminded her of that shame, and of the hurt she'd caused, not only to him, but to his career. Words, which Peter had uttered to her in the dead of night, a few days after the fight with Duncan at the Faslane base swimming pool, rang in her ears: 'You've broken the two things that matter to me most in the whole world. My love for you and my Navy career.' They were probably the most poignant, and perhaps the most honest, words her husband of only seven months had said to her during their marriage.

FIVE

In just a year, Tuuli had grown into a businesswoman. She swept into the café at the top of Stockmann's Department store, wearing a brown woollen overcoat over a smart trouser suit and pointy flats. She still carried the briefcase the two of them had bought at the beginning of their four-year course at the Swedish School of Economics in Helsinki — or Hanken — as everyone called the low-slung university in northeastern Helsinki. Kaisa remembered that particular shopping trip with fondness; they'd ended up buying the exact same briefcase, in different colours. Kaisa's was brown, whereas Tuuli had opted for black. In those early days of their studies at Hanken, they hadn't realised how similar they looked; they both had fair hair, blue eyes and they were both tall — although Tuuli had at least ten centimetres on Kaisa. Everyone, from their fellow students to staff at the famous flirting place, the university's library, mixed them up. Having similar briefcases didn't help. But Hanken was a place where everyone knew everyone by sight at least, so people soon got used to Kaisa and Tuuli looking the same, though some still thought them to be cousins or even sisters when they graduated.

'How are you?' Tuuli said as they sat down with their coffees and cinnamon buns from the self-service counter. There was concern in her eyes and Kaisa had to take a deep intake of breath in order to stop the tears.

'I don't know,' she said instead. A few days after the incident in the pool, Kaisa had written a long letter to Tuuli from Helensburgh, recounting the sorry tale of her unfaithfulness, the fight between Duncan and Peter, and Peter's impending court martial. The letter Kaisa had received in reply was so supportive and kind that Kaisa had cried, and it had played a large part in her decision to 'take a break' in Helsinki. The fact that both Peter and Kaisa had decided on a one-way ticket, bought over the telephone from a bucket flight shop in London, spoke volumes about how long this 'break' in the marriage might last.

'You need to come out with me,' Tuuli said after she'd heard about Kaisa's living arrangements with her sister in Töölö. Sirkka and her mother rented two flats in the same post-war, stone-clad block on Linnankoskenkatu. Both flats had only one bedroom, with a small lounge and a narrow kitchen at the side, but they were in the city, within easy distance from the centre of Helsinki. Sirkka's flat overlooked a busy crossing, while her mother's flat on the floor above had a view of the peaceful inner courtyard. The two women often shared an evening meal together and went walking in the nearby park or, in winter, skiing on the frozen sea near the shores of the president's summer villa. It wasn't a bad place to be based, and Kaisa was grateful to have somewhere to live.

'That'll be fun. Where do you want to go, the KY club?' she said to Tuuli, without much enthusiasm.

Her friend laughed. 'God, no. Haven't been there for ages. That place is for the kids. No, we'll go to a couple of new bars.

Unless you want to go to Old Baker's?' Tuuli reached her hand out and squeezed Kaisa's arm.

Kaisa shook her head. The two young women were quiet for a moment as they reflected on the first time Peter had come to see Kaisa in Helsinki, six months after they'd met at the British Embassy cocktail party. Peter had been a young naval officer, and had come to talk to them at the party, just as Kaisa and Tuuli were about to leave. On Peter's second visit to Helsinki, after they'd exchanged increasingly passionate letters, Kaisa had taken him to Old Baker's on Mannerheim Street. The place boasted of being an 'English pub', but Peter had been refused entry because he was wearing a pair of cords — deemed to be 'jeans' by the bouncer. 'Sorry, you need to be smartly dressed to come in,' the bearded man with a huge belly and a gruff voice had told Peter. He'd had his hand on Peter's chest and spoke to him in loud Finnish. Peter had turned to Kaisa and Tuuli for an explanation. Kaisa vividly remembered Peter's disdain at being told he — an Englishman, and an officer of her Majesty's Royal Navy — wasn't smart enough to gain entry to a place calling itself an English pub. Kaisa and Peter later suspected the bouncer had simply not liked the look of the dark-haired foreigner. It was the first of many times Peter had been publicly singled out for being a stranger with a Finnish girl. Kaisa and Peter had mostly laughed at the prejudice, but on that first time, it had hurt Peter deeply. Kaisa now reflected on her own unhappiness in England and in Scotland, where she'd constantly felt discriminated against — whether it was in the workplace or among her fellow Navy wives. She now wondered what would have happened if the tables had been turned and Peter had moved to Finland to be with her. Would he have had an equally tough time of it? Or worse? And how would he have reacted? Kaisa looked at Tuuli. She knew that sleeping with a friend of hers would be the last thing Peter would do. Guilt, which wracked her every moment, raised its ugly head again, and for a second, she wished she'd never gone to the Embassy cocktail party, and never met the handsome Englishman.

'No,' Kaisa said. 'I don't think I want to put my foot in that place ever again.'

'I understand,' Tuuli said, and gave Kaisa's arm another squeeze. 'But we'll still go out tomorrow night, OK?'

TUULI HAD a studio flat a few streets south of Sirkka's place. She'd bought a bottle of wine to share before they went out. The price of drinks in bars was so high in Helsinki, it was usual to have a drink or two at home beforehand.

'So where are we going?' Kaisa asked. Tuuli looked very slim and tall in her black satin trousers and glittery gold jumper, with a narrow gold belt tied at the waist, highlighting her perfect figure.

'Oh, definitely start at the Sky Bar, then Happy Days and Helsinki Club. We'll see how long Mrs Williams will last,' she said and lifted her glass in a salute.

'Don't worry about me,' Kaisa grinned. She was wearing trousers too, with boots underneath — it was minus ten outside — but she'd decided on a frilly satin blouse after Sirkka had persuaded her out of the black jumper she'd tried on first. 'You're trying to look like a bloody nun, are you?' Sirkka had said.

Kaisa had acquiesced, though she didn't like the inference that Tuuli was taking her on a night out to find a man. Men had caused her enough trouble as it was. Plus she was still married. But she didn't say any of those things to Sirkka. She suspected her sister all but believed that her marriage to Peter was over.

As planned, Tuuli and Kaisa went to the Helsinki Club after they'd been to three other clubs. In each place, they ordered a *Lonkero*, a bitter lemon and gin drink that they had always drunk in the student's bar, for old times' sake. The place was half-full, and Kaisa wasn't at all surprised to see the old group of rich boys from Hanken there. It was as if time had stopped and her life in England hadn't happened at all.

'C'mon, come and say hello,' Tuuli said and grinned. She walked confidently towards the group of ten or so people, sitting on a dark-blue velvet sofa in the corner of the bar. A few couples were on the dance floor, leaning into each other and moving slowly; others were buying drinks at the bar. The lighting was dim and the music loud. The bar, which was lit from underneath, made the faces of the people standing against it seem unreal and spooky.

Tuuli sat down next to Tom's blond friend, Ricky, and the two kissed each other on the mouth. Kaisa was so amazed that she couldn't move. She stood in front of the group, trying not to gape at her friend.

'You remember Ricky?' Tuuli said nonchalantly — too nonchalantly.

The good-looking blond boy, whom Kaisa knew Tuuli had tried to resist at Hanken, got up and reached out to Kaisa. 'Nice to see you again.' He turned around and pointed at Tom, who was sitting in the middle of the group, next to a dark-haired girl, his arm on the top of the sofa above her shoulders. 'You remember him, don't you?' Ricky's eyes had a mischievous look, which Kaisa could spot even under the dark lighting of the club.

Tom looked up and their eyes locked. He nodded and, removing his hand from the top of the sofa, took a packet of cigarettes and made a gesture of offering one to Kaisa.

'No thanks,' she mouthed and shook her head. She bored her eyes into Tuuli, who was ignoring her.

'Sit down, Kaisa,' Ricky said and he and Tuuli shuffled along the sofa, making a space next to Tuuli.

'Would you two ladies like a drink?' Ricky said.

'Yes, I'd love one. Gin and tonic, please.' Kaisa had decided she was going to have one drink with the group, not wishing to make a fool of herself, and then leave. With Ricky gone to the bar, Kaisa whispered into Tuuli's ear, 'What the hell?' But Tuuli just shrugged her shoulders. 'I'll explain later,' she whispered back.

It was typical of Tuuli to keep something momentous like this under her hat, Kaisa thought, as she sat back against the blue velveteen sofa. A mention that she was seeing Ricky might have been expected, seeing the amount of time the two of them had once spent talking about the group of rich boys. It had been Ricky and Tom who had come onto them in the student's bar during Kaisa's and Tuuli's first week at Hanken, and whose advances they'd repeatedly rejected during their four years there. Or was this a set-up? Kaisa looked along the sofa to where Tom, the lanky boy with a wolfish smile, who'd been interested in Kaisa, sat. His head was bent close to the dark-haired girl's face. No, Tuuli must surely know that Tom, whose only goal in life during his leisurely studies seemed to be to bed as many girls as possible, was the last thing Kaisa needed now? And what was Tuuli doing with Ricky? Was it serious?

THE NEXT DAY WAS A SUNDAY, and the weather had turned even colder. The sun, high in the pale blue sky, nearly blinded Kaisa when she opened the venetian blinds in her sister's living room. It was already noon, so the pale winter light flooded the small flat. Kaisa shivered, even though the flat was suffocatingly warm. She felt sorry for her sister who'd left the flat at 6 am, when it was still pitch black, for an early shift at the hotel. She watched a green tram trundle past on the road below, and a woman, holding the hand of a small child, walk briskly over the road. The toddler wore a pink and white snow suit and a stripey woollen balaclava, with strands of blonde hair escaping over her pale blue eyes. Being dressed in layers of clothing made her shape round and her struggle to keep up with her mother seem impossible. She tried to brush away the hair with one fat mitten. Kaisa's mind wandered to children, and she thought about how different it would be to have them here in Finland. The winter clothing must be a pain, but childcare was easier, she guessed. Plus it was a safer society in which to bring up a child, surely? She shrugged herself free of baby thoughts – she couldn't even keep a marriage alive, how did she think she could look after a baby?

Kaisa was drinking coffee and eating a rye and cheese sandwich for breakfast when the telephone in the hall rang out.

'You want to meet up for coffee later?' Tuuli's voice sounded a bit hoarse, and Kaisa wondered how long she'd stayed on at the Helsinki Club after Kaisa had left, having had her one drink.

The two friends met up at the Fazer café in the centre of Helsinki. Tuuli was wearing jeans and a long mohair jumper under her camel coat. She wore a scarf wrapped around her head to keep the cold out. The sun had gone behind a thin layer of cloud and there were a few sporadic flakes of snow falling. Looking at the glass display of cakes, Kaisa couldn't resist a Berlin bun – a deep-fried jam doughnut covered in pink icing.

'Do you remember how we could just afford one of these for our lunch at Hanken?' Kaisa asked Tuuli when they'd sat down. They both laughed. They'd found a table by the large windows overlooking Kluuvikatu, a road linking the main Helsinki shopping streets of Aleksi and South Esplanade. Kaisa hadn't yet dared to walk along the Esplanade park, where she and Peter had kissed properly for the first time. She could hardly believe it was nearly five years ago.

'So, what's the score with Ricky?' Kaisa said after her friend had been silently munching on her Berlin bun for a while. She'd decided that instead of mooning over her own disastrous love life, she was going to go straight to the point with Tuuli.

Tuuli lifted her blue eyes at Kaisa. 'I'm sorry about last night, but I'd agreed to meet him there and I couldn't say no, and then you turned up and I wanted to go out with you too, and ...'

'That's alright, but you could have told me!'

Tuuli put down her half-eaten bun and looked down at her hands. 'Yeah, I know.'

'So, what's the score; how did you meet up again? Or did you have something going on with him at Hanken?' Kaisa was leaning towards her friend, who was still looking down at her hands. 'Oh my God, he stayed over last night didn't he?'

Tuuli lifted her head up, looking sheepish. 'OK, I've been seeing him for about a month, on and off.'

Kaisa's friend told her how she'd seen Ricky outside Stockmann's department store during her lunch hour one day and how he'd seemed so nice, so much nicer than he had at Hanken. He'd asked for her telephone number and she'd given it to him there and then. He'd called her the next evening, and that same Friday night they'd gone out to eat at a small Italian restaurant near where she lived in Töölö Square. 'One thing led to another and he came home with me,' Tuuli said.

Kaisa was quiet. She wondered how much her own tumultuous time in England had been the reason for the lack of letters between her and Tuuli, and how it had made her blind to the lives of others around her.

'We're not seeing each other, though,' Tuuli now said. 'It's casual, and that's how I want to keep it.' Kaisa's friend closed her mouth and leaned back in her chair. Her face told Kaisa that was the end of the matter; there was no more to be said. But Kaisa couldn't help asking about the other rich boy.

'What about Tom, is he seeing the short black-haired girl?'

'No, I don't think he's attached. He's only just back from Italy. I was as surprised to see him there as you were. You still fancy him?'

'God, no!' Kaisa said and laughed. 'He's the last person on my mind. Can you imagine what trouble he'd cause?'

Kaisa felt her friend's piercing eyes on her. Tuuli's demeanour had changed and she was far more relaxed now the conversation had turned away from her own life. 'You could use him for a bit of fun, though, couldn't you?' she said.

SIX

Kaisa was having breakfast alone at the small table in Sirkka's narrow kitchen when she heard the post thump onto the doormat in the hall. It had become a self-imposed routine of hers to try to get up before the postman began his rounds in the block of flats. She'd make herself read the main broadsheet paper, *Helsingin Sanomat*, to see if there might be some jobs she could apply for. Usually, there was nothing she could even imagine doing. She had her degree from Hanken, that was true, but no work experience to speak of. She got up with a sigh. Three of the letters were for Sirkka, but one, with a postmark from Dorset, was for her. The original address on the thick envelope was for the married quarter in Helensburgh. Just seeing 'Smuggler's Way' written, and then crossed out, on the blue paper made Kaisa shiver. She turned the thing over in her hand, but there was no return address on the back of the envelope. She examined the hand-writing and suddenly knew who the letter was from.

Kaisa dropped the envelope onto the table and stared at it. She went to pour herself more coffee, to buy time. To let her think more clearly, and consider her options.

Why would he write to her? And was she sure the handwriting was his? The upright style was very similar to Peter's; in fact it seemed to be a kind of style most people in England had. But Kaisa knew for sure the letter wasn't from Peter; she'd recognise his handwriting anywhere. So, what did he want with her? Wild thoughts began circulating in her mind. Perhaps he was deadly ill? Or what if the letter wasn't from him, and was from one of Peter's fellow officers? What if something had happened to Peter?

Kaisa tore open the envelope. There were two pieces of paper. She began to read. Kaisa snorted at the words she was reading. She dropped the sheet onto the kitchen table, but curiosity soon got the better of her and she continued reading.

Dear Kaisa,

I hope this letter finds you well.

I wasn't sure if I should write to you at all, but felt I needed to contact you this last time to tell you how sorry I am about everything that has happened. I now understand that, however much I wish it were otherwise, you love your husband, and I wanted to reassure you that I respect your decision.

You may not be aware that knowing you has changed my life beyond recognition. But I wouldn't have it any other way. I still love you, Kaisa, and keep the fond memories of our short, but intense, liaison close to my heart. I have now left the Navy, and am living with my uncle, trying to make a go of it as a farmer. (Address below.) Surprisingly, I'm enjoying life in the country rather better than anticipated. Of course, there is a distinct lack of female company, but I have been assured next month's Young Farmers Spring Ball should rectify that problem! Not that I will ever feel the way I feel about you, Kaisa, for anyone else. But, we must all move on, and rest assured, unless you approach me, this will be my last communication with you.

Of course, I very much hope we can remain friends. I understand if right now, so soon after the terrible events in Faslane, you would find it difficult, but you know, time is a great healer. As an aside, I must admit, I feel a little wronged by the powers that be in the Navy. It was your husband who attacked me after all! But I shall keep to my word and not pursue the matter – if only for your sake, and for the sake of our continued friendship, Kaisa.

It is late here on the farm, and I have to be up early to supervise the milking. We have a herd of 50 cattle, and a few acres of land, and I have grown quite fond of the cows. I call them my 'girls'! So if you are ever in the neighbourhood, you must come and visit me and my girls. It is rather beautiful here, and very peaceful. You know I would welcome you with open arms as a dear friend.

I've rambled on long enough. Please write to me and tell me your news. I cannot wait to hear back from you.

Yours always,

Duncan x

Kaisa stared at the few pieces of paper for a long time. She examined the handwriting on the envelope again. Was that Peter's hand that had crossed out the address at Smuggler's Way, and replaced it with Sirkka's in Helsinki? If so, had he recognised Duncan's handwriting? Oh, that man! Why would he continue to pursue her even after everything that had happened? If Peter was still in Helensburgh, and had seen that Duncan was writing to her, would he think they were still in touch? Her hand holding the envelope began to shake, and her breathing became shallow. She tried to calm down, to take long breaths in and out, but her heart was racing. This was so bad, so bad. If only she knew where Peter was, but she hadn't heard from him since they parted at Glasgow train station. He hadn't replied to the letter she'd sent the day after she arrived in Helsinki.

When she'd first seen the envelope with the British postage stamp on the mat, she'd thought it was from Peter. Even the thickness of the envelope had made her hopeful that he'd written a proper letter, telling her his news, and perhaps that he missed her.

But as soon as she'd seen the crossed-over address, she'd known it wasn't from Peter. Tears began welling up inside of her, but she resisted them. She really must stop crying all the time. She put the letter in the bin, throwing the wet coffee grains over it. She refilled the percolator and stood listening to the dripping water, trying to forget about Duncan. But thoughts of the two of them in bed in the dank, cold flat in Helensburgh filled her mind. She remembered how terrible she'd felt afterwards, and how Duncan had still pursued her even after he'd had his way with her and she'd made it clear she wanted nothing more to do with him. Or had she made it perfectly clear? Perhaps she'd still flirted with him, pleased to have his attention? Kaisa felt her head ache. She needed to forget about Duncan, about that awful night and about all the terrible consequences on her life. When the second pot of coffee was ready, Kaisa poured a cup and, determined to find a job and forget all men, sat down at the table and began reading that morning's *Helsingin Sanomat*.

SEVEN

When Kaisa had spent three weeks sleeping on her sister's sofa, Sirkka came home from work one evening and asked to speak to her. It was just past seven and Kaisa was watching *Coronation Street*. There seemed to be nothing but English programmes on Finnish TV, which reminded Kaisa of her old life in Portsmouth and Helensburgh. It seemed utterly unfair to her, but at the same time she thought it was a punishment she deserved.

'Have you thought about what you're going to do?' Sirkka asked after Kaisa had made coffee for them both. They were sitting facing each other at the small table in the kitchenette. Her sister looked tired; she'd just finished a week-long shift of ten-hour days, two of which had begun at 6.30 am.

'About what?' Kaisa asked.

Sirkka sighed. 'About your future!'

Kaisa stared at her sister.

'It's really lovely to have you here, but you can't stay here forever, watching English soap operas.'

Kaisa tried but couldn't stop the tears that began running down her face.

'Oh, Little Sis, what are we going to do with you?'

'I'm sorry, I just can't seem to ...'

Sirkka stood up and hugged her sister. 'Look, I'm doing this for your own good. I know it's hard, but I think it's time to decide what you are going to do.'

Kaisa cried a little more against her sister's shoulder and then, taking the piece of tissue Sirkka offered, wiped her tears away and blew her nose. 'I've been looking at the job adverts in *Helsingin Sanomat*, but they all want you to have work experience, and I don't have any.'

Sirkka sat down again and took Kaisa's hands in hers. 'Look. You have a good degree from a good university – something a lot of a people would kill for – but you do need to take the job search seriously if you want to stay here.'

Kaisa nodded.

'Mum and I've been talking. There is a chance she could find you a job at Neste. They're growing and need staff, especially graduates.'

Kaisa shook her head, 'Working in the same office as mum? You must be joking.'

Sirkka returned her smile, 'It's vast, their HQ in Espoo. You might never see her!'

'All the same. I think I'll find something myself.'

'There's a girl.' Sirkka yawned again and looked down at her hands.

They were quiet for a moment. The noise from a tram trundling past the block of flats broke the silence between them. Kaisa noticed for the first time that there were faint lines around her sister's eyes and mouth. We are getting older, she thought. We're no longer the youngest girls in the disco, the most fresh-faced and fashionable in a bar.

'There is something else.' Sirkka sighed and lifted her blue eyes to Kaisa.

'What?' Suddenly Kaisa thought about money. Of course,

her sister needs her to pay rent! 'Look, as soon as I get a job, I'll pay you ...'

Sirkka smiled down at her hands and shook her head. 'No, you can stay here as long as you like, it's not that!'

'So ...'

Sirkka took a deep breath in, and lifted her eyes to Kaisa once more. 'Matti has been asking after you.'

'What?' Kaisa couldn't help but raise her voice.

Sirkka took Kaisa's hand into hers once more. 'Look, he comes into the hotel from time to time. I can't stop him now, can I?' she said quickly, and added, 'and tonight, he asked me about you.'

'How ...?'

Sirkka leaned closer to Kaisa. 'It's a small town, and you know he lives quite nearby.'

Kaisa's sister told her how on one night months ago, Matti, Kaisa's ex-fiancé, had turned up at the hotel where Sirkka was working. She'd been helping out in the bar because one of the waitresses had been ill, when she had suddenly been faced with Matti.

'You can imagine, I nearly had a bloody heart attack!' Sirkka said and smiled, but seeing Kaisa's straight face, she continued to tell her that they'd exchanged a few words. Sirkka had told him how she and Pirjo had moved back to Helsinki.

'He's still as annoying as ever,' Sirkka said, 'telling me that he was glad we'd come to our senses and returned to the motherland. He sounded like our father.'

Kaisa couldn't believe her ears, or rather she struggled to hear Sirkka's words.

'Anyway, since then he's been in a few more times, and he always makes a point of saying hello, whether I'm in reception, the restaurant, the bar or wherever. He comes by on his way home from work.'

Kaisa had a terrible thought. She looked at her sister's face, 'Surely you're not?'

Sirkka laughed, 'Oh God, no! Kaisa, for goodness sake, I'm not that desperate!'

Kaisa felt bad, and took hold of her sister's hand. 'Sorry, I'm being impossible. Tell, me what did he say about me?'

Sirkka sighed. 'Well ... he'd seen you on the street, I don't know when. As I said, it's a small town and he must drive past our block of flats every day. He just wanted to know how you were. He seemed genuinely concerned.'

Kaisa gazed at her sister's face. 'What did you tell him?' she asked even though she knew the answer.

Sirkka looked down at her hands again, 'I'm sorry, I blurted it out before I knew what I was doing. I get so busy at the hotel, you know, and ...'

'It's OK,' Kaisa said.

'Anyway, he says he's got something of yours he wants to give back.'

In bed that night Kaisa couldn't sleep. She tried not to think about what Sirkka had told her about Matti. It was just too much.

But after the chat with her sister, Kaisa knew she had to work harder to take charge of her life. It was funny how their roles had changed, she thought. Whilst studying in Hanken, and being engaged to be married to Matti, Kaisa had seemed the one who had a plan in place for the rest of her life. Sirkka, after a string of unsuitable boyfriends, and even after getting her qualification as Maitre d'Hotel, hadn't settled in one job, or one place, but had flitted between Lapland, Helsinki and Stockholm, never wanting to set down roots anywhere. Apart from the mysterious man in Lapland, whom Sirkka rarely spoke of, there didn't seem to be any other boyfriends, unsuitable or not, on the horizon. Again, Kaisa felt a pang of guilt; her preoccupation with her new life in England had made her selfish and ignorant of the lives of her family and friends. Now both her friend Tuuli and her sister Sirkka were getting on with their careers and appeared to be so much more in control of their love lives, too. To think she'd been the one with a clear head about what she wanted out of life!

Just look at her now. She had no idea if there still was a marriage to be saved with Peter. She had no idea what he was thinking. She had fled Scotland and left Peter to fend for himself, when it was her who had caused his present troubles. And now Matti wanted to meet her. Tossing and turning in bed, Kaisa thought how she had used Peter to disentangle herself from Matti, and how she had never really explained to Matti why she couldn't be with him anymore. Kaisa thought back to her behaviour after she'd met and fallen head-over-heels in love with Peter. Had she even told Matti that it hadn't merely been Peter, or meeting another man, that had made her relationship with him impossible? Had she ever told him that she'd been doubting their engagement even before she met Peter, worried about their seven-year age gap, and how young she had been, only fifteen, when they'd first made love? She knew she'd never told him how his domineering mother had made her feel trapped and inadequate. She shuddered when she remembered those long weekends in the cottage by the lake, when she had spent hours standing in the hot, stuffy kitchen preparing food and washing up, while Matti sat reading a newspaper or one of his firearms magazines in the shade of the porch outside. Whatever the rights and wrongs of their relationship, surely Matti deserved to know why she had ended it so abruptly? She decided to phone the number her sister had given her and agree to meet him. But as Kaisa thought about what she would say to him, she realised she couldn't imagine facing her ex-fiancé now. Now that she had another failed relationship behind her. Now that she had abandoned another man. Betrayed another man with someone else. Oh God, it was as if there was a string of men lying in Kaisa's wake, men whom she had betrayed and stopped loving. Perhaps there was something wrong with her?

Matti was already sitting at a table at the far end of the café when Kaisa arrived. It was a smallish place on Runeberg Street where, Kaisa remembered, they would sometimes have coffee and cake after a film in the Adlon cinema next door. As she walked past the small movie theatre, Kaisa saw it was closing down and felt a surge of melancholy. She remembered the last film they'd seen there – *Autumn Sonata* by Ingmar Bergman. It was about a complicated relationship between a mother and daughter, and Kaisa recalled that while she had loved the film, Matti hadn't liked it at all. Afterwards they'd sat in this same café, not talking, after Kaisa had – in vain, as it turned out – tried to convey the brilliance of Ingrid Bergman's performance as the famous concert pianist mother, and how good Liv Ullman had been as the long-suffering daughter.

The café hadn't changed; it was still a dark room, starkly furnished with small black round tables and French-style chairs with curved backs. There was a large window overlooking the street, and Matti must have been watching her walk up to the door, because he was looking straight at Kaisa when she entered. He was standing by a table in the far corner, and when Kaisa reached him, she was surprised to find he was a lot shorter than Peter. She knew he was only slightly taller than her, but the difference seemed significant now. He still had the dark hair, though she noticed it was thinning a little at the top. Kaisa couldn't believe she had spent so many years with this man. He seemed like a stranger to her now. And he was so much older. Kaisa did a quick calculation and realised he would be 31. The age her mother had been when they all moved to Sweden! It seemed inconceivable to her that she'd kissed and made love to him. Kaisa shuddered at the memory of their life together.

Matti and Kaisa stood awkwardly for a moment, not knowing how to greet each other. Eventually Matti reached out his hand. 'Hello Kaisa,' he said and indicated for her to sit down.

Matti's grip on her hand was firm, and warm, but Kaisa removed her fingers from his as soon as politely possible.

'I haven't ordered anything yet,' Matti said. 'Would you like a cake, or a cinnamon bun?' His unsmiling eyes were steady on Kaisa and she wondered if he was still angry at her. Suddenly she remembered that you could never tell with him unless he was really enraged, when his brown pupils would expand and his cheeks would get a slightly flustered pink hue.

Kaisa looked at the counter a few tables away, and spotted some *Aleksanterinleivos,* her favourite jam-filled cake with pink icing, in the glass cabinet.

Matti offered to go and get the cakes and coffees, and while he was safely out of the way, Kaisa removed her coat. She'd thought long and hard about what to wear to this awful meeting that she didn't really want to have, and had eventually decided on a cream jumper and jeans. She certainly didn't want to wear anything sexy, or feminine. Now she remembered that Matti hated jeans, but it was too late. Besides, she could wear what she liked. Her heart raced and she felt dampness in her armpits under the jumper. She sat down and tried to calm herself. She suddenly remembered that Sirkka had said Matti had something for her. What could it be? She tried to smile when she saw Matti walk towards her with the tray of coffees and cakes. He, too, had chosen an *Aleksanterinleivos.*

'So, you're back in Finland,' Matti said while he was

munching on the sweet cake. He glanced pointedly at her left hand where she still wore her engagement and wedding rings.

'Yes, but I'll be going back soon.' Kaisa was surprised at her own lie, but she didn't want to give Matti the satisfaction of thinking her marriage was over. She began fiddling with her rings, turning the diamonds the right way up. 'Peter is away at sea, so I thought I might as well come over and stay with my sister and mother for a while.'

Matti had stopped eating. Another thing Kaisa had forgotten was how straight he held his back, even when sitting down. Even here in a café, enjoying a cake, he was behaving as though he was on some army parade ground. He now looked at Kaisa and said, 'That's not what your sister told me.'

'Really?' Kaisa tried to keep her voice level, but she heard the shrill tone. She couldn't look at Matti.

'Sirkka thinks you're getting a divorce,' Matti said and touched Kaisa's hand.

EIGHT

That night in bed Kaisa cried, silently without waking Sirkka. Her sister had been working late, and when she came in around midnight Kaisa had pretended to be asleep. She couldn't believe Sirkka had actually told Matti about her troubles. She had no right!

But Matti knowing about her separation, however temporary, hadn't been the worst of it.

Kaisa couldn't believe how stupid she had been. She thought of how in love – or lust – she must have been to have done what Matti had asked her. And how even more stupid to have forgotten, or pretended to have forgotten, about the existence of the photographs. A cold wave had run through her body when Matti had brought out the worn-out yellow folder and handed it to her.

'I have a new girl now, so I thought you'd like to have these back,' he'd said, grinning. 'She's sixteen. Innocent and pure just like you were.'

Kaisa hadn't listened to Matti as he told her about this new conquest. As if in a dream, she saw him lift the flap and look at the first photo in a stack of some ten, fifteen prints. In the photo, Kaisa was lying on a bed, in her old room in the small flat in Lauttasaari that Pirjo had rented after the divorce from Kaisa's father. Kaisa was naked, apart from a pink silk scarf tied around her small waist, and lying on her tummy. Her upper body was lifted, with her arm supporting her head, revealing her small, pert breasts, her pink nipples echoing the colour of the scarf. Her expression, looking straight at the camera, was the same she'd seen on the sex magazines she'd so eagerly, but with a huge feeling of shame, studied while working at the R-Kiosk the summer she'd been seduced by Matti. Her face showed pure lust. But that wasn't the worst of it. The worst of it was what was showing in the lower half of her body. Her bottom was slightly lifted, and with her left knee pulled towards her tummy, Matti behind the camera had had an uninterrupted view of her most private parts from behind.

In the café, Kaisa had quickly put the photos away, and buried the packet deep inside her handbag. Soon after this she'd left, trying to stop the tears of shame just behind her eye sockets.

She now remembered vividly the day Matti had convinced her to pose for the photos. He'd been telling her how beautiful she was, like a model, and during a weekend when both her sister and mother were away, they had spent the whole two days in bed. Matti had taught Kaisa things she'd never heard of, how she could satisfy him, but also herself. Something inside of her had flipped; she'd been a different person, she'd imagined herself as one of the women in those magazines, full of lust, just thinking about how best to be fucked, how best to suck, lick and bite to arouse Matti, her new grown-up boyfriend. All she had wanted to do was to please him, and pleasing him had felt good. When Matti had brought out the camera, she had felt even more aroused, and had done everything he had asked of her; posed in every way he had wanted her to. Even the scarf had been his idea.

Afterwards, during the four years they spent together, Kaisa had felt embarrassed each time Matti had shown her the photos, which he kept in a locked drawer in his bedroom. Once, as a joke, he'd said, 'You shouldn't be ashamed, they're so good they should be in a magazine.'

Kaisa had been horrified and had made him promise never to show them to anyone.

How could she have forgotten about their existence?

Now, lying in bed she knew that if she was honest with herself, she hadn't forgotten, but with the love she felt for Peter, the love that was so different from anything she'd ever felt for Matti, she'd stopped thinking about them. The idea of asking Matti to give the photos back, or even of discussing them with him, was so repulsive that she'd let it be, hoping he – in his rage – would have destroyed them himself.

That was obviously not what had happened. Kaisa felt sick thinking that he would have been looking at them during all the years she'd been with Peter. She felt violated by Matti. Thinking back, she had been so young, barely sixteen when the photos had been taken. Whereas Matti had seemed like a grown-up, at 23. He'd certainly been more experienced, in sex, as in everything else. Had he taken the photos as some kind of insurance, to have something hanging over her if she changed her mind and didn't marry him after all? Kaisa shook her head. No, if nothing else Matti was honourable. Besides, surely he would have used them against her when she fell for Peter? And why give them back to her now? Suddenly Kaisa thought of something. He had given her the prints, but what about the negatives? Were they tucked inside the sleeve of the packet as they sometimes were? With her heart thumping, Kaisa got out of bed, picked up her handbag, and tiptoed into the kitchen.

She found the packet, took out the photos, and not wishing

to look at them, turned them face down on the kitchen table. She spread the photos, feeling between them, but there was nothing there. Next her fingers searched through the paper sleeve, looking for a strip of black film, but there was nothing inside the envelope, and the see-through pocket on the side of the packet was empty. The negatives had been taken out.

AFTER THE DISCOVERY of the missing negatives, Kaisa hardly slept. She lay awake, trying to make herself have sweet dreams by thinking of other things, of Peter, and how wonderful their love-making had been. But it seemed he no longer loved her. Rather than cry, again, and feel helpless, she suddenly realised, in the dead of night, that she must take charge of her own life. Never again would she be taken advantage of in the way Matti had, and even Peter had, not understanding how difficult life as a Navy wife would be for her. Hadn't he just left her to it, expecting her to cope with his absences, and the different language, culture and people in Britain, on her own? Always just worrying about his own career, not taking into account her ambitions for a meaningful job of her own?

Kaisa still loved Peter, she knew that, and she also knew she'd do almost anything for him, but she also needed to live her own life. She decided she'd start applying for jobs in earnest, and find a place to live. She'd stop waiting for a letter from Peter, and ask Tuuli if there were any jobs in the bank where she worked. She needed to get out of Sirkka's flat, and out of this area, where she might bump into Matti any day. Kaisa turned over and punched her pillow hard. She had wanted to scream at Sirkka for talking to him; for telling him anything about her present life. She wanted to go back in time and not be so stupid as to agree to be photographed naked and full of lust. But she couldn't. What would Sirkka have done in a similar situation? Not that she could imagine her in a similar situation. Apart from one boyfriend, who always drank too much, Sirkka kept in touch with all her exes. For Kaisa, just seeing Matti in the flesh was repulsive. Besides, her current situation would bring nothing but pleasure to her ex-fiancé. Hadn't he predicted as much when she'd left him for the Englishman?

'It won't last,' he'd said when he'd phoned her the last time. She'd still been living in the flat in Lauttasaari, the small apartment belonging to Matti's aunt, which Kaisa had eventually been unable to afford. She'd spent all her small student loan on expensive telephone calls to England, mooning over Peter's letters and failing her exams, so much so that the university had stopped her grant.

Kaisa opened her eyes and looked at the shadows the streetlights painted on the wall of the darkened room. This had to stop. She would have to stop running her life according to the men in her life. The thought sent a current through her body. She flung off the duvet and sat bolt upright in bed. She listened to see if Sirkka was asleep in the room next door, and heard the faint sounds of steady, sleepy breathing. Slowly, so as not to wake Sirkka, she got out of bed again and tiptoed into the kitchen. She shut the door gently behind her and in the light coming from the streetlamp outside wrote on the notepad that her sister kept for shopping lists:

> To Do:
> 1. Find a job
> 2. Find a flat
> 3. Forget about men

Kaisa looked at the piece of paper and immediately did the opposite of the last item on the list: she thought about Peter. She could almost feel his strong arms around her, and hear his husky voice murmuring 'I love you,' just before falling asleep after making love with her, his arm heavy on her waist. The last time they'd made love was on the day of the fight between Peter and Duncan. Their bodies fitted so well together, it was almost mechanical, had it not been so wonderful and awful at the same time. Kaisa had wanted to hold onto Peter tightly, wishing the love-making would last forever, wishing they could shut out the rest of the world and stay in bed, entwined in each other's arms. Afterwards Kaisa had cried silently into her pillow, while Peter turned over and fell sleep. She hadn't been able to settle and had marvelled at Peter's capacity to go into a deep slumber so quickly, so effortlessly. Now, after four weeks of not hearing from him, she began to wonder if her initial worries, long before they married, were justified after all. Perhaps he couldn't *really* commit, couldn't *really* care about her.

Kaisa looked at the note again and shook her head. What had she just written? 'Forget about men!' She tiptoed back to bed and willed herself to sleep.

The next day Kaisa received another letter. This time she recognised the handwriting straight away.

Dear Kaisa,

I hope you are keeping well and enjoying having some time with your mother and sister. Life here in Helensburgh hasn't changed much; spring is on its way, they say, but the slightly warmer temperatures seem to have brought us even more rain! There is the odd daffodil out in our garden, bravely fighting the wind and rain, but otherwise the landscape is as miserably grey as ever. Nigel is away again – you perhaps know that the boat is on patrol now until who knows when? I have been told that we might see the boys sometime early summer in June, but you know how it is, 'I have to kill you if I tell you' and all that. My pregnancy seems to be going well, the due date is June 22, by which time Nigel should be back.

Wish me luck that everything goes well this time! Especially as I don't have you to look after me and lean on if the worst happens again.

A new family has moved into your old married quarter, but the wife, Phyllis, is utterly dull. She has a little girl of three and a boy who's just about to start school. All she talks about is which public school is best and how her son is allergic to nuts. Oh, how I miss you, Kaisa!

I hear Peter is doing alright in Plymouth. I hear he's living on the base, which I presume is a temporary solution until he finds you two a married quarter down there. Nigel and I had a very happy few years down south – Plymouth beats Helensburgh hands down, I tell you.

But the reason I wanted to write to you is that I have heard some disturbing news. Now, this may just be gossip, and most probably is, but I really felt that as your good friend I ought to tell you. Before he went away, Nigel heard a chap say in the wardroom that Peter is seeing someone. Of course, he told the guy off, and said not to spread silly gossip like that, but the fellow was quite certain. You see, he is a distant cousin of this girl, Jackie, and he said he'd heard straight from her at a party in London that she and Peter were an item. I've been really disturbed by this piece of stupid gossip, and didn't know what to do, but felt that you should know. I'm not sure who this Jackie person is, and if there is any truth in it (which there most probably isn't!), but if I were you, I'd get myself back to Plymouth sharpish.

Sorry to bring you such silly gossip, and I hope I haven't done the wrong thing by telling you.

Your friend,

Pammy xx

KAISA LOOKED at the heavy yellow Basildon Bond paper, where Pammy had, with a neat hand, written the deadly words. Had Kaisa understood the English correctly? To be sure, she reread the letter three times, and each time she scanned the paper her chest grew tighter. At the end of the final read she was struggling to breathe, and got up to get a glass of water. She was on her own in her sister's flat. Sirkka had gone to see a friend – it was her day off.

Kaisa sat down at the kitchen table and put her head in her hands. Peter with Jackie? It couldn't be true. But she was reminded of the time early on in their marriage when Peter had taken her to a party at Jackie's beautiful apartment in London. She'd asked Kaisa how it was to be married to Peter in a way that had made Kaisa suspicious and jealous. She'd also told Kaisa that her hard-won degree from Finland would be worthless in England. It was obvious the girl didn't like Kaisa, and thought Peter had made a mistake by marrying her. Of course, Jackie didn't say as much, but as her cold eyes peered at Kaisa, her manicured red nails holding a cigarette, Kaisa knew immediately that Jackie had history with Peter. Peter and Kaisa had had a fight later, during which Peter admitted that Jackie used to have a crush on him. He'd not admitted to a relationship, but now Kaisa wondered if he'd lied to her then? Had Jackie and Peter been together before he'd got to know Kaisa – or even when they'd decided to be 'free to see other people' while Kaisa was finishing her studies in Helsinki? To have an open relationship, Kaisa reminded herself, had been Peter's idea, and his suggestion had nearly broken her heart.

Kaisa looked at her sister's wall calendar, pinned above the kitchen table. She'd been in Helsinki just over four weeks. In just one month Peter had already found himself a girlfriend.

It was also news to Kaisa that Peter was in Plymouth – he hadn't even bothered to write to tell her where he was living.

Kaisa slumped down at the table and cried. She was sobbing when she heard the doorbell.

Outside stood her mother.

'What's the matter?' She walked through the door and past Kaisa.

'Why aren't you at work?' Kaisa managed to blurt out between sobs.

'I have the day off, you know, because of the conference this weekend.'

Kaisa nodded. She'd forgotten. Her mother had said she'd be at home on Thursday and then travel to some work-related weekend in Eastern Finland on Friday. She was wearing smart white running pants and a matching jacket with red and blue stripes on the side of the trousers and top.

'I came down to see if you fancied going for a jog.' Pirjo's clear blue eyes were on Kaisa, 'But what's happened?'

Kaisa made some more coffee, sat down and translated the letter for Pirjo.

'And this Pammy, who is she?'

Kaisa glanced at her mother. She noticed that Pirjo was wearing make-up to go for a run, and in spite of the hollow feeling she had in her stomach, and the utter despair she was feeling, her lips lifted into a smile.

'She's a friend, a good friend.'

'You sure about that?'

'Yes!' Kaisa said impatiently.

Her mother straightened her back. 'No need to be so irritable. I'm just saying that good friends don't usually ...'

'She's a really, really good friend!' Kaisa tried to keep her voice level, 'that's not the issue here. Peter has found someone else!'

Pirjo was quiet, and put her arms around Kaisa.

Kaisa allowed herself to be hugged and comforted by her mother for a while.

'The worst thing is, I think they've been together before,' she whispered.

Her mother let go of Kaisa. 'What?'

Kaisa told Pirjo about the breakfast party, and about Peter's confession that she'd had a thing for him.

'That doesn't mean that they've been together,' Pirjo said. Her eyes were kind, and she took the tissue from Kaisa's hand and wiped away her tears.

Kaisa let herself be comforted by her mother. She put her head on her shoulder and Pirjo hugged her hard. 'I know Peter. He is a very good boy and he would most certainly write and tell you this himself.'

Kaisa didn't say anything. She wanted to believe her, but she also knew Peter. Hadn't he left the girl he was seeing when they'd first met simply by ignoring her letters? And that girl-friend hadn't committed the ultimate sin and been unfaithful to him.

NINE

Since being in Helsinki Kaisa had avoided the bank on the corner of South Esplanade and Erottaja, where the ladies had followed the long-distance romance between Kaisa and Peter closely. It'd been one of her former colleagues who'd organised the invitation to the British Embassy party where Kaisa had met her Englishman. But now that she was looking for a job, a natural place to start was the KOP bank. She'd telephoned her old bank manager and he'd agreed to see her.

'So when did you come back?' Mr Heinola's handshake was firm. Kaisa felt her resolve to appear confident and ambitious about a career in the bank melt under her old boss's direct gaze. Kari Heinola wore clear-framed glasses over a round face. He was slightly shorter than Kaisa, and she noticed his fair hair was thinning on top. He asked her to sit down on the opposite side of his large desk.

'About a month ago.' Kaisa looked at her hands.

'And you're settling back here?'

'Yes.' Kaisa's voice broke, even though she'd tried hard to keep it level.

The bank manager leaned back in his leather chair and placed his hands in front of his face, fingers tapping against each other.

Kaisa kept her eyes on Mr Heinola, and waited.

'It was hard going in England, was it?'

Kaisa found herself telling her old boss how difficult it was to get a job, not just as a foreigner, with a foreign qualification, but also as a Navy wife. She poured out the frustration she'd felt during the long six months she'd spent, bored and frustrated, looking for jobs, first in Portsmouth and then in Scotland, where her career prospects were even worse. She told him about the job at DMS, and how her duties had increased there, but how she had then been refused a permanent job merely on the grounds of her marriage to a Navy officer. She also told him about the job offer on a magazine in London, and how she'd had to turn that down due to Peter's job on a nuclear missile-carrying submarine.

'Leave it with me, Kaisa.' Mr Heinola got up and reached out his hand. 'I'll see if there are any opportunities within our bank. You've always been a smart girl, and a good worker, so although I can't promise anything, I will try my best.'

Kaisa left her old boss's office the same way she'd entered, by the staff door on the side of the building, which led straight onto Erottaja. She'd not been brave enough to go downstairs to the banking hall to meet her old colleagues. Explaining how she'd ended up back in Helsinki to her old boss had been demanding enough for one day; she couldn't go through it all again with the friendly ladies.

Still, Kaisa felt jubilant that she'd managed that much. For the first time since her short-lived marriage ended on the day of the fight in Faslane, Kaisa felt in charge of her own life. This was, after all, what she had envisaged she'd do before she met Peter. Kaisa decided to celebrate with a coffee at the nearby Fazer café. She walked briskly across the Esplanade Park, not looking at the statue of Eino Leino, where Peter had given her sweet kisses and she had fallen firmly in love with him. Peter was now history; whatever her feelings towards him were, they could not be together, Kaisa could see that clearly. She needed to sort her life out, move on, get a job. Besides, she was fast running out of money. She was ashamed when she thought of the £100 Peter had insisted she take with her when he left her at Glasgow station. At first, Kaisa wouldn't hear of it, but Peter had insisted, saying, 'It's my duty to look after you. You're still my wife.' But everything in Helsinki was much more expensive than in Helensburgh. She'd calculated that if she continued to spend at the same rate she'd run out of money completely in a matter of days. Luckily, Sirkka had refused to take any money for rent, but Kaisa felt she needed to buy the odd bag of groceries, even though Sirkka often brought food home from the hotel.

Inside the Fazer café, while waiting to be seated, she stopped to dig out her purse from her handbag, to make sure she had enough money to pay. When she looked up, she saw the smiling face of a man looking down at her.

'Hello,' Tom said, 'lost something?'

Kaisa had forgotten how tall Tom was. The guy was positively towering over her. His eyes were dark and his light brown hair was a little shorter, and tidier, than she remembered. He was wearing an expensive-looking dark grey overcoat, which was open, revealing a suit underneath.

'No,' Kaisa felt suddenly as flustered as she had at Hanken when the two of them had played their cat and mouse game. 'This is ridiculous, pull yourself together,' Kaisa thought, straightening up.

For a moment neither said anything. Kaisa had turned away from Tom to watch a waitress clearing a table that had just been vacated by an older lady in a fur coat. The waitress was wearing a black dress and a frilly white cotton pinafore with a matching head band. The Fazer uniform. The whole place looked as if it was from the 1930s, which is why it was popular with the Helsinki upper classes. It made sense that Tom would come here for his lunch; it was one of the most expensive places in town. Kaisa cursed her frivolity; really, she couldn't even afford a coffee at the cheaper Happy Days Café opposite. There was, after all, no guarantee that her old boss would find a job for her. She should have gone straight home to Sirkka's flat after the interview and raided the fridge there. Now she was stuck here, having to deal with this rich boy. Although he looked like a man now, Kaisa still thought of him as a spoiled brat. He'd only ever been interested in her because he couldn't have her. But she couldn't leave now; behind Tom the queue had increased; if she left, it would look as if she was running away from him. She didn't want him to think he had such an effect on her.

'Here you are, a table for two,' the waitress said, looking at Tom and Kaisa.

'Er, we're not ...' Kaisa began, but Tom said, 'Thank you,' and indicated with his stretched arm for Kaisa to go first.

'So, you're back,' he said after they'd given their overcoats to the waitress and been handed menus in exchange. They were sitting opposite each other in a corner table. Kaisa had been looking down at the small card, but now lifted her eyes and replied, 'Yes.' Kaisa examined Tom's face. She wondered how much he knew of her situation. Surely Tuuli wouldn't have told Ricky anything? This must just be the rich boy fishing.

Tom smiled, 'Well it's nice to see you.'

Kaisa didn't have time to reply before the waitress was back, with her pad and pen poised for their order. Kaisa hadn't even had time to read the menu properly, but Tom said confidently, 'I'll have today's special.'

'Same for me, please,' Kaisa said and hoped the bill wouldn't come to more than she had in her purse.

'And we'll have two glasses of the Chablis,' Tom added.

Kaisa didn't have time to protest. The waitress had taken the order and disappeared.

'Aren't you working?' she said simply, but Tom just laughed. Reaching into his pocket, he took out a packet of cigarettes and offered her one. As he brought the lighter – silver and engraved – close to her face, she saw something surprising in his eyes. A kind of gentleness that she'd not noticed before.

'What are you up to in Helsinki? Visiting?' Tom leaned back in his chair, and took a long drag from his cigarette.

'Well, yes, I suppose, a long visit.'

'Good, I'm in luck then,' he said and smiled. 'I'm just back myself.'

'Really?'

Tom told Kaisa that he'd been living in Milan with his parents for the last few months. 'My dad got me a job in a bank there, but it didn't work out.' He said, giving her one of his infectious smiles.

Kaisa couldn't help but smile back at him. These were more words than the two of them had exchanged during the whole of the four years they'd known each other in Hanken. Yet now it felt as if they were old friends.

The waitress came back with their wine, and Tom lifted his glass to hers. 'To you and me in Helsinki!'

Kaisa raised her glass too and they laughed. When the food came, they chatted some more. Tom said he wasn't working at the moment, but was 'meeting someone later, hence the suit.' Kaisa told Tom she'd probably be staying in Helsinki for a while. 'Perfect,' said Tom.

Kaisa grew serious at that remark, and a for a while both of them were quiet.

'Let's have another glass, my treat.' Tom said when the waitress came to collect their empty plates. The mystery dish of the day had turned out to be rather wonderful arctic pike with a parsley sauce. Kaisa just smiled. She couldn't resist this friendly rich boy. Her grin widened.

'What's so funny?'

'You know what we called your lot in Hanken?'

'No?'

'Oh, I don't think I should say.'

'But you have to now! You can't just give me that gorgeous smile of yours and then not say what brought it on.' Tom stretched over the table. His face was so close to Kaisa's she could have kissed those full lips.

Kaisa grew serious and leaned back in her chair, away from Tom. 'Rich boys,' she said quietly.

WHEN KAISA GOT to Sirkka's flat, there was a letter on the mat. This time she recognised the writing immediately. She picked up the blue Basildon Bond envelope and rubbed her hands together. She was frozen. She'd taken the wrong tram from Mannerheim Street, which meant she had to walk two blocks to Linnankoskenkatu. She'd been so confused after the lunch with Tom, which he'd insisted on paying for.

'I am the rich boy, after all,' he'd said and grinned.

His comment and the whole of the situation had made Kaisa feel very embarrassed, and she'd laughed nervously. All the same, it was a relief, because she wasn't sure she would have been able to pay the astronomical prices the place charged for food, or the fine wine. When Tom had asked for her telephone number while they waited for his change, she wrote down her sister's number. Tom then gave Kaisa his number. He was living in a flat in Ullanlinna, he told her. It was in the southern part of Helsinki, where the beautiful

Jugend houses from the turn of the century were. It was Kaisa's favourite area of the city, and naturally the most expensive. Not a surprise that Tom would be living there, she thought.

She turned the envelope over in her hands. It was very thick and she wondered what that meant. Was he writing her a long letter of goodbye, or a long love letter? Perhaps the stories of Peter and Jackie were just rumours after all. Suddenly Kaisa was afraid to open the envelope. She gazed down at the cold street below. It was two degrees below zero, she read on the little thermometer attached to the outside of the kitchenette window. While she'd been walking from the tram stop, it had started snowing, the light white flakes falling gently onto the ground. An opaque carpet of snow was now covering everything outside, the tops of the street lights, the sand box by the side of the road, even part of the roof of a tram trundling past. It was getting darker, even though it was barely three o'clock, and the snow glimmered here and there against the steel grey sky. Kaisa sighed, sat down at the small table and tore open the blue envelope. Out fell British bank notes, and one sheet of written paper.

Kaisa,

Hope you are keeping well. Please find enclosed £200. I will send you this each month after I get paid.

Send my regards to your mother and sister,

Peter

Kaisa stared at the ten pound notes, scattered on the table in front of her, then re-read the letter. At the station in Glasgow Peter had promised to send her his new address, but week after week, there had been no correspondence from him.

After Pammy's letter, Kaisa understood why; he'd moved on. She didn't want to be the one to ask him about Jackie, because that would make it official in some way, so she hadn't written to him either. She still hoped it was mere gossip; she knew how easily stories like that began in the Navy. With bitterness, she remembered how Maureen had phoned to accuse her of having an affair with Jeff, Peter's best friend and best man. Remembering that ridiculous telephone conversation with one of the other Navy wives in Portsmouth had given her hope in the last few days.

But now this – just three cold sentences and money. The ten pound notes looked dirty to Kaisa. In addition to the detached tone of the letter, they added an extra layer of hurt to the lack of warmth, or love, in Peter's words. Kaisa looked at the handwritten lines that Peter's favourite fountain pen had made. At least he had taken that much care, to use his good pen, the one he saved for official Royal Navy correspondence and his love letters to her – when she had deserved them. But this time there were no kisses. How she now missed that little cross, which had been so puzzling when Peter first wrote to her, after their romantic meeting at the British Embassy in Helsinki. After he had explained the tradition to her, that little 'x' gained so much importance. She would often kiss the letters on that spot, hoping Peter had done the same before putting the sheet of paper in the envelope and posting it. But now, only eight months after their dream wedding, the kisses had disappeared from Peter's letters. Kaisa put her head in her hands. What had she done? How could she have been so stupid to spoil their love for each other? It was obvious now that she had lost him forever.

She examined the letter again. The address in the top right-hand corner was new: 'HMS *Orion, BFPO Ships, London.*' That must mean Pammy was right; he was living in the wardroom, on the base in Plymouth. Poor Peter, he didn't even have a home to go to. But then, she thought, he would have all his mates around him, drinking beer every night, not having to worry about a home, or a wife — a foreign, trouble-some wife, who was always unhappy with something or other. And he could go and see Jackie whenever he was free.

Suddenly Kaisa felt anger. He could have written a few words to say where he was, and how he was. He could have said he was seeing someone else and made their split official. They were still married after all, and what had happened wasn't all her fault. Kaisa had entered the marriage not under-standing that she would have to give up her career and follow her husband from one port to another, often at very short notice. Or that even if she'd chosen to stay put in Portsmouth, to pursue a career, and not move up to the isolation of Faslane, she'd have to accept that she would see her new husband only a few times a year. Or that most employers didn't understand — or value — her Finnish degree. And even if they had, many employees still didn't want to give jobs to Navy wives, because they knew they'd up and leave as soon as their husbands were posted elsewhere, whatever the wives said in job interviews.

Kaisa sighed. She did need the money, however. She counted the notes, picked up her coat and took the tram to the centre of town again. She walked up to a different bank on Alexi, and changed the Sterling notes to Finnish Marks. At least she had money again, she thought, as she slipped into Stockmann's department store and found a pay phone. She took out her diary and dialled a number.

'Hello,' the man at the end of the phone said.

'Hi, it's Kaisa. I just wanted to call and thank you for the lunch.'

TEN

DEVONPORT, PLYMOUTH

Peter sat on his bunk and looked at the letter he'd just picked up from his pigeon hole in the cold and deserted hall outside the wardroom. Without thinking, he did what he always did when he saw Kaisa's handwriting on top of the envelope: he held it up to his face and breathed in the scent. A long time ago, it must have been their second or third meeting after the Embassy cocktail party in Helsinki, he'd asked her to put a little bit of her perfume on the sheets of paper before slipping them into the envelope. He remembered how Kaisa had been puzzled by his request but had promised to comply. After that, all her letters were soaked in perfume, so much so that he'd been teased about it as a young sub-lieutenant onboard his first submarine.

How long ago those heady and carefree days were now. But as he became aware of Kaisa's fragrance once again, he breathed it in all the same and carefully opened the seal. His heart began beating a little harder as he saw what Kaisa had written.

Dear Peter,

Thank you for your letter and the money. I will pay you back every penny once I have a job. There may be one in my old bank here in Helsinki. I went to see the manager yesterday and he seemed hopeful.

It's still very cold here. It snowed yesterday and overnight, and the ground is covered in a white blanket, making everything look pretty and clean.

Kaisa

PETER REREAD the letter and stuffed it into a drawer of the desk by the window of his cabin. He sighed, picked up a thin but clean towel, and headed for the showers.

An hour later, he was drinking a pint in The Bank, a pub in the centre of Plymouth. It was Friday night and, as had become his custom, he was going for a few beers with the young, single, Part Three. The term used for a trainee officer onboard a submarine suited Simon particularly well, because he was a round-faced, pimply 19-year-old, and prone to taking things too seriously. He'd fallen for all but one of the practical jokes the others had played on him, including the old favourite 'Spar Lash'. Peter, too, had fallen for it on his first ship. In the joke, the Part Three is sent to look for a piece of wood and when he finds it, is asked to throw it overboard, at which point the Senior Officer says, 'Here you go, Spar...lash.' Of course the whole of the ship's company is in on the joke, and in the course of looking for the 'Spar Lash' the Part Three is sent around the boat several times, before someone hands him a piece of wood suitable for throwing overboard.

Peter would have preferred to spend his weekends with an officer more his age and rank onboard HMS *Orion*, the diesel boat he'd been demoted to after the disastrous events in Faslane, but apart from Peter, Simon was the only one who wasn't going home to a wife or girlfriend at the weekend. Peter liked Simon well enough and had become a bit like an older brother for him, dragging him home when he'd had too much beer, and making sure he wasn't picked up by any of the working girls along Union Street. And to be fair, Simon was good fun. For one thing, he didn't want to talk about Peter's court martial, a subject the other officers onboard never forgot to mention.

As usual, The Bank was heaving on a Friday night. There were a few sailors from HMS *Orion* there, too, and Peter lifted his pint in a greeting to the group of men standing and drinking a few feet away from him, their tight T-shirts displaying impressive sets of tattoos. Peter often wondered what made sailors think it a good idea to go through the pain of carving the name of a sweetheart on their flesh. Just as well he hadn't had the crazy idea of carving Kaisa's name on his biceps, he thought, and immediately decided to pull himself together.

He saw Simon emerge from the gents. 'Another round?' Peter asked. He'd have to cheer up before going to the Plymouth Yacht Club, a disco down The Barbican otherwise known as the 'Groin Exchange' (or 'the GX' for short).

By the time Peter and Simon had finished at The Bank there was a small queue outside the glass doors leading to the Yacht Club. The GX was downstairs, and as usual there was a fair number of local Plymouth girls there, but this time Peter also noticed a group of Wrens standing by the bar at one end of the dimly lit room. He recognised a shortish blonde girl who worked in the office at the base. She'd smiled at him when they'd passed each other in the corridor, and he seemed to remember talking to her on one occasion. But he couldn't remember her name. Did he even know it? She was wearing a pair of jeans and a light blue satin blouse, revealing the contour of her full breasts. Not bad for a split-arse. He lifted the glass of beer that Simon had given him towards the Wrens.

'You really that lazy?' Simon shouted into his ear, and Peter grinned. Yes, tonight he really did feel that lazy, he thought, and walked towards the group of girls.

Sam, or Samantha, had a rippling laugh, or a giggle really, and this was her reaction to almost everything Peter managed to shout into her ear in the loud club. Soon he took her to the dance floor, and during Alison Moyet's *All Cried Out*, he pulled her close and moved with her to the music. He kissed her and found she tasted of bubble gum. She let him put his hand on her round, firm buttocks, and then move it up to her back, feeling for her bra buckle. It was the traditional kind, not a front fastener, with just one hook. 'That'll be easy to deal with,' he thought. Removing his lips from the girl's mouth, he pressed himself harder against her. She responded by pushing her soft breasts against his chest. 'You're lovely,' he whispered in her ear. He moved his hand to her neck and she let out an involuntary sigh into his ear. Peter could feel himself harden, but he knew he must be patient. When the track finished, he pulled himself away from Sam and gave her a smile. 'Would you like a drink?' He went to join the crowd trying to attract the attention of the barman, who'd now been joined by a thin, pretty girl, with dangly earrings and short black hair. When she looked up from pulling a pint for a guy standing next to Peter, her eyes met his, and for a moment the two looked at each other. She had bright blue eyes, which contrasted with her black hair. Not her real colouring, Peter thought, and found himself wondering what hue her pubes might be.

'So, what will it be?' she eventually said and Peter gave her his order: 'A pint of Bass and a G&T.'

Peter couldn't take his eyes off the barmaid. When she bent down to get the small bottle of tonic from the other side of the bar, Peter noticed she had a tattoo of a swallow on the small of her back. Her arse was the shape of a heart, 'What's your name?'

The girl looked up. 'For me to know and you to find out. Two pounds, please.' She had a London accent.

'Daylight robbery,' Peter grinned and gave the girl the money.

She shrugged and moved to the next punter. Peter stood for a moment and watched her, but he was pushed away by other men trying to get to the bar.

Peter danced with Sam for the rest of the evening, and Simon got together with one of Sam's friends. At 1 am, he paid for a cab to the base, having made sure that Simon and his Wren were safely in a taxi of their own. Sam and Peter kissed in the back seat and when they arrived at the residential quarters they tiptoed across the linoleum floor towards the officers' cabins. It was obvious the Wren had done this before. As soon as they entered the hall leading up to the new wing of the Victorian building, where one corridor led to his quarters and another to that of the Wrens, she removed her shoes, grinned at him, and took his hand. But Peter didn't mind; it was better that way. As soon as they were inside his cabin, Sam removed her top and began kissing him. He took off his shirt and kicked off his trousers. As they kissed, Peter undid the clasp of her bra and, taking a step back, admired her large round breasts. He cupped them in his hands, noticing the unusually large areolas, before removing her jeans. She was wearing small, pink, lacy knickers. Sam took hold of him, and Peter groaned. She moved her hand up and down, and Peter had to think about Mrs Thatcher to stop himself from an embarrassing early loss of control. It had been too long. Sam wasn't a true blonde after all, Peter found, when she pulled down her own pants, but she wasn't too hairy. Peter pushed her gently onto the bunk and parted her legs. She made the right noises when he touched her between the legs, and when a few moments later Peter came on top of her, she responded with soft moans of pleasure.

Afterwards, when Peter was lying on his bunk watching

Sam getting dressed, he reached out and took her hand. 'Come and sit down for a minute.'

'I've got to be off, I'm on duty tomorrow am.'

'Yeah, I know, but I just wanted to say ...'

'What?' Sam had brown eyes, Peter noticed and felt bad he hadn't seen them properly before.

'I'm married, you know.'

Sam looked down at her hands. She was buttoning up her now wrinkled satin blouse, 'Yeah, I'd heard.'

'And you know about the court martial, right?'

'Yep.'

'So, my life is pretty complicated at the moment.'

Sam didn't say anything.

'I'm sorry, but this can't go any further.'

She stood up and said, 'Sure. We had fun.'

'Definitely,' Peter said and kissed Sam quickly on the lips.

THAT MORNING AT BREAKFAST, Sam was in her uniform, sitting in the middle of the wardroom with three other Wrens. She gave Peter a quick look, and he heard some muffled giggles when he walked past their table. Peter nodded to the group and went to sit on his own in the corner of the large dining hall.

The Devonport wardroom was a large space in the old part of the Victorian building. When Peter had first entered the room after his appointment to HMS *Orion*, and seen the oil paintings of famous sea battles on the walls and models of ancient sailing ships hanging from its ceiling, he immediately wanted to show the place to Kaisa. But that wasn't to be.

The steward brought him a cup of tea and he ordered a full English. Opening that morning's copy of the *Telegraph*, he began reading an article about the housing market when two older officers from HMS *Orion* joined him. It was Saturday, and Peter wasn't on duty, and not in uniform, but the engineer and his oppo were wearing their ribbed Navy jumpers with the Lieutenant Commander's rank visible from the golden braid on the shoulders.

'Trapped last night?' James, the engineer grinned, nodding at the corner table where the Wrens were still making a show of Peter by nodding and grinning in his direction.

'Wouldn't you like to know,' Peter said. He turned back to his paper. James Sanders (his nickname was Sandy onboard, but Peter never used it to his face because he thought the guy was a complete prat) and his best mate onboard, Malcolm 'Mac' Rowbottom, sniggered. Peter knew both men had unattractive wives. He had met them at a 'families day' during the half-term holiday. Peter remembered how he'd walked into lunch that day and was faced with a noisy room full of wives and kids. He'd thought of Kaisa then, knowing how much she would have hated a 'families day' had she been with him, which, of course, she wasn't.

'You went to the GX last night, the Part Three told us.' Sandy wouldn't let it go.

Peter nodded. Luckily his breakfast had arrived and he began eating as quickly as he could.

'No water sports this time, eh Bonkie?'

Peter lifted his head up and looked at the man. Mac was sniggering next to his oppo, trying to hide the laughter in his linen napkin. James Sanders was the one officer onboard who kept reminding Peter of his sordid past. Every few days he came up with a new joke about it. This week's jibe was 'water sports', a reference to Peter's fight with Duncan at the Faslane base swimming pool. Peter suspected the engineer was bored with his own life, and jealous of Peter's (if only he knew). Still, he was becoming a nuisance. Once Peter had been appointed to *Orion*, and knew his career in the Navy wasn't over, that he'd been given another chance, he'd decided to put up with the inevitable jokes and jibes. Black humour was the life blood of the Navy, after all. If you couldn't joke, you shouldn't have joined. And he deserved it; he'd messed up. He'd even thought the nickname, 'Bonking Boy', shortened to 'Bonkie', was quite funny. But after a couple of months most of his fellow officers had let it be. (Although he was still known as 'Bonkie'.) Everyone except Sandy, that is. Peter wondered whether he lay in bed at night, thinking of new ways to torment Peter?

Now Peter gave Sandy a grin. 'Very funny.'

As Peter walked back to his cabin, his thoughts once again turned back to the events of the last few months. How he'd been standing in the cold community club in Helensburgh, in front of the Captain of the base at Faslane, and the President and the Sub-Lieutenant. How he'd been taken aback by the similarity of the court martial to court room dramas he'd watched on TV. And how he'd felt as if he was watching the proceedings rather than being part of them. In the end, he'd been found guilty of causing grievous bodily harm to a fellow officer and fined. Of course, even before the court martial he'd been dismissed his ship. And as Lawrence, his lawyer, had said outside the office afterwards, he'd been 'bloody lucky'.

PETER DIDN'T SEE the dark-haired barmaid at the GX again until several weeks after he'd first spoken to her. He and the Part Three had been to the club a few more times, and Sam had been there too. Peter had taken her back to his cabin twice since the first time. He had to watch it, he told himself now, as he scanned the dark room at the Plymouth Yacht Club for the group of Wrens. It seems they'd given the club a miss this Saturday. Suddenly Peter remembered that Sam was going to see her parents in Yorkshire for the weekend. As his eyes moved along the room, he spotted the dark-haired girl smoking a cigarette on the other side of the bar.

'Back in a minute,' Peter said to Simon, and he made his way smartly towards the girl.

'Do you come here often?' he said, leaning towards the girl. He noticed she was a fair bit shorter than him. She was wearing a dark top, off one shoulder, revealing creamy white skin. 'No bra,' Peter thought and gazed at her small, perky breasts, which were visible under the thin fabric. Her skirt was short, and she was wearing thigh-length cream boots.

He'd taken her by surprise. She turned her face towards Peter, and smiled, getting the joke.

'I'm Peter,' he gave her his hand, taking advantage of the smile.

The girl considered the outstretched hand for a moment, and eventually slipped hers into it. Peter held onto her a moment longer than necessary, enjoying the feeling of the slender fingers in his grip. 'And you are?'

She told him her name was Valerie, 'Val for short.'

'Can I have my hand back now,' she said. Her face was unsmiling but there was a flicker in her dark eyes that Peter liked.

'And what do you do?' Peter said. She'd found the formal style funny, so Peter decided to carry on with the same tone.

Val told him she was down from London, 'Helping my uncle with this place.'

'And what do you do in London?'

'You are a nosy beggar, aren't you?' Val said and took a long drag on her cigarette. But she was smiling.

'So if you don't want to talk, how about a dance?'

Val displayed great style on the dance floor. Her slim body moved slowly, but rhythmically, with the music. Peter wondered if she was a dancer. When a slower piece by Phil Collins came on, she took Peter's hand and moved away from the dance floor. She leaned against the bar, where Peter had first seen her.

'You're a great dancer,' Peter said into her ear.

Val grinned and lit another cigarette.

'Would you like a drink?'

Val eventually told Peter that she was studying History of Art at Saint Martin's College in London. Her family was from Plymouth, and she'd come down for the weekend.

'You've got a real Cockney accent going on there,' he said.

Val laughed for the first time, 'Yeah, I share a house with a couple of Cockney rebels, and it's catching. But I can do Plymouth too.' Val launched into a West Country accent, and Peter replied in his best Wiltshire drawl. 'Got to get tis straw out of mi mouth and get mi tracktoor,' he said, and again Val laughed.

At the end of an evening spent dancing and talking, Peter asked Val if he could see her again.

'Sure,' she replied and they agreed to meet up the next day. Knowing everything would be shut in Plymouth centre, he suggested they drive out to one of the village pubs for Sunday lunch.

'Ok,' Val said and they exchanged telephone numbers.

Peter scooped up Simon and they took a taxi back to the base. Peter wondered why Val had asked so little about him. He'd said he was in the Navy, which virtually went without saying at the GX. When he'd mentioned he was in submarines, she hadn't seemed interested. He supposed that, as a Plymouth girl born and raised, Val knew all there was to know about the Navy and its officers. The locals had a name for the Navy – 'fish heads' – and most of the Union Street working girls were supported by the Navy. The Navy's reputation could certainly have been better with local girls. At least the GX only admitted officers; still, as Peter knew full well, that was no guarantee of good behaviour.

ELEVEN

HELSINKI, FINLAND

'I need to see you,' Kaisa said, trying to sound as matter-of-fact as she could.

'Hello, Kaisa,' Matti said. Kaisa could hear him purring like a satisfied cat at the other end of the line. So this *was* a game to him, she thought.

'You know why. Same place today at 5 pm?' she said.

'If you insist.' Matti said.

KAISA HAD DISCUSSED the photos with her sister, who had laughed at first. Obviously she hadn't shown them to her, but she'd told her the worst of it with as little detail as possible.

'Well little Sis, I didn't think you'd get up to something like that!' They'd been sitting in Happy Days Café, having a beer after Sirkka's shift. Sirkka was smoking, taking a deep drag out of her cigarette and making rings out of the smoke.

'I thought you'd stopped,' Kaisa said, picking up the packet of Marlboro Lights, and taking one for herself. 'Can I?'

Sirkka nodded, watching her sister carefully. 'So he gave you the photos, but kept the negatives.'

Kaisa nodded.

'Bastard,' Sirkka said. Kaisa looked at her and smiled; Sirkka had cut her hair short and the new style made her look younger. Sirkka's short blonde curls and make-up tonight reminded Kaisa of the times they used to go out together in Helsinki, after their parents had taken them back to Finland from Stockholm in the seventies. She wanted to talk to Sirkka about those times. How they had used fake IDs to go to night-clubs like TF and Botta, where the lower age limit was at least four years older than they were. How had they managed to keep their fake IDs and nights out at grown-up discos a secret from their parents, Kaisa wondered. Then she remembered how their mother and father had been too busy fighting, even-tually leading to a second separation and divorce.

'I'm following in my parents' footsteps,' Kaisa thought bitterly. Their parents had always been too preoccupied with their own unhappiness to notice that their daughters were running wild. Their father had tried, she guessed. He'd constantly nagged Sirkka to do her homework, and he'd have fits of rage when she came home with a poor school report, or discovered that they'd stayed out far longer than they should have done. He never told Kaisa off, which Sirkka felt was a complete injustice. This had make Sirkka even more deter-mined to do as she pleased.

'He might have destroyed them, of course,' Kaisa said, forcing herself to think of her present, much more pressing problem. Hearing herself utter these words, she knew she was being naïve, deluding herself once again. She was too preoccu-pied with what Peter was doing. For the past two nights she'd not slept for dreaming about Peter and Jackie entangled between white sheets.

'Yeah, right.' Sirkka said, and with her face serious, added, 'You need to see him. I'm sure he's still in love with you, so use that to get them back.'

Kaisa had stared at her sister, 'I'm not ...'

Sirkka placed her hand on Kaisa's arm. 'No, silly. I'm not telling you to go to bed with him. I mean, just charm him a little, you know, with your look of pure innocence. Flutter your eyelashes and tell him you want the negatives.'

'You make it sound so simple.'

Sirkka put out her cigarette and took a swig of beer. 'It is simple. I'm sure if you really try, he'll do anything for you.'

Kaisa laughed.

'And what about Peter,' said Sirkka. 'Do you really think he is seeing this Jackie person?'

Kaisa nodded. She didn't dare look at the kind expression on her sister's face. She was so tired, she knew she'd begin crying again.

'Well, it might just be a revenge fuck.' Sirkka took another drag of her cigarette. Her eyelashes looked very dark and long, and Kaisa absentmindedly wondered if she'd changed her mascara. 'It's what men do; it makes them feel better,' Sirkka added and smiled.

THIS TIME KAISA made sure she was the first to arrive in the café, so she got there a full fifteen minutes early, got herself a coffee and sat down at a table by the window. She wanted to see Matti on the street before he came in.

Kaisa had taken the photos with her, to make her case more forcefully, she guessed. But she kept the envelope in her handbag, planning to bring it out at the right moment. While waiting, she looked around: only two other tables were occupied in the small room. Of course, it was a Monday, and the weather had turned that morning, with cold rain, occasionally changing into sleet, falling steadily. Everyone apart from a crazy person like Kaisa would be rushing home after work, not stopping for a coffee with an ex-fiancé. Kaisa let out an involuntary snort. Once again in her life, she wondered how she'd got herself into such a bloody mess.

A man sitting at a table on the opposite side of the café looked up at Kaisa. When Kaisa responded to his stare, he averted his eyes and went back to reading the evening paper, *Iltasanomat*. That's what she should have done, to distract herself, picked up a newspaper from an R-Kiosk on her way down from Sirkka's flat. But she'd been too preoccupied with trying to keep dry. The rain had been so heavy that her winter boots were soaked. As she sat and waited to confront Matti, she realised that the other customers would be able to hear what she had to say. Of course, she should have suggested somewhere like The Happy Days Café, which was always bustling whatever the time of day – or weather.

As planned, Kaisa saw Matti as he parked his car on the other side of the street. He had no umbrella and the rain, which had now turned into hail, was settling on Matti's fur hat. He hadn't worn the hat the last time they met, though Kaisa remembered him often wearing it when they were together. It was nicknamed the Russian, because all the Soviet leaders wore one in winter, and the Finnish politicians copied them. It had become a popular hat in Finland. After her year in Britain, seeing so many men wearing them made Helsinki look like a Soviet bloc country in Kaisa's eyes. She remembered with fondness how Peter had made that same comment to her the first time he'd visited Helsinki. Kaisa had been very upset with him because of it. Of course, she'd not been angry with him for long; they were so in love then.

Kaisa sighed and watched Matti as he made his way towards the café. In spite of the weather, he didn't seem to rush. After patiently waiting for the traffic lights to turn green, he walked with a steady pace across the wide road, which the tramlines divided into two. Kaisa's mouth felt dry and she fought an urge to leave unnoticed before he got to the other side.

It took a while for Matti to get himself out of his coat and hat, both of which were covered in hail, which seemed to melt as soon as you saw it, leaving a puddle on the floor of the café. But all the while, as he shook himself like a wet dog, his eyes were on Kaisa.

'Nice to see you again,' he said. He was beaming, as if this was a meeting of two old friends. 'I'm getting a coffee and a Berlin bun. Can I get you anything?'

Kaisa shook her head and waited for Matti to go up to the counter and order.

'I want the negatives too,' Kaisa said as soon as Matti returned with his coffee and the large bun topped with pink icing. While he was getting his coffee, she'd taken the photographs out of her bag and placed them on the table between them.

Matti was quiet for a while, studying his hands, but not looking at Kaisa or the photos.

Kaisa glanced around the café to see if the man with the newspaper was listening. To her relief, he seemed to be engrossed in his reading. The girl serving at the counter had disappeared, and the café was now almost empty except for Kaisa and Matti, and the man behind his evening paper.

'The photographs are mine, so it's only fair I should have the negatives,' Matti eventually said.

'Why?' Kaisa said, and when Matti didn't reply, she leaned across the table and whispered, 'So that you can develop another set and ogle at them while you're ...' Kaisa glanced in the direction of Matti's crotch.

'Don't be so crude,' Matti spat out the words. His eyes had a look of pure hatred, just as they had when she'd told him about Peter, in her bedroom in Lauttasaari. She'd found Matti waiting for her when she got back from her secret meeting with Peter the day before he sailed back to Britain aboard HMS *Newcastle*. Kaisa had been in a trance from the Englishman's kisses and his promises to write and see her again. And then, bang, a confrontation with Matti had brought her back down to earth. His eyes had had the same dark threat to them then as they did now.

Kaisa lowered her gaze and said, 'But it's not fair. These pictures, they're of me. Me before ...'

'Not fair!' Matti had raised his voice, and both Kaisa and Matti glanced briefly around the café in embarrassment. But the place was empty. The man with the newspaper had disappeared without Kaisa noticing.

'Is it fair that you left me for some foreign sailor, who has now, by all accounts, left you. As predicted by me. I was good to you, Kaisa, as was my mother.'

'Don't talk to me about your mother!' Now it was Kaisa's turn to raise her voice. 'You should have heard the names she called me after I broke up with you.'

'Well, didn't you deserve those names, the way you cheated on me?'

'I didn't ...' Kaisa began, but a sudden sense of hopelessness overwhelmed her and she felt tears well up inside. She must not cry, whatever happens, she told herself. Snatching the photographs, she placed them back in her handbag and got up.

She put her coat on, not looking at Matti, who had also got up and now took hold of Kaisa's arm. 'Please Kaisa.'

Kaisa lifted her eyes to him and said, as calmly as she could, 'I think you are being horrible. Those pictures are of me, and you should not have them anymore. We were engaged to be married, that's true, but you know as well as I know that I was only 15 and you were 22 when you seduced me. By the way, I believe that is illegal now.' Kaisa held her gaze steady on Matti. His eyes were still dark, but his mouth twitched at the word 'illegal'. 'With that in mind, I had every right to change my mind as I did.' Kaisa paused and was about to leave it at that, but added, 'And you know full well that I was never unfaithful to you. On the contrary, after we broke up I still slept with you for months, out of pity, even though I had already promised myself to another man. And that, as well as falling for you when I was only 15, I regret bitterly.'

Matti opened his mouth, but nothing came out.

'You can post the negatives to Sirkka's address, or even give them to her at the hotel. When I get them, and only then, will I reconsider my decision to report you to the authorities.'

Kaisa left the café, and not caring about the rain outside, ran along the street towards Sirkka's flat.

TWELVE

Tom's flat on the top floor of a Jugend-style house on Neitsytpolku, had a sea view towards the small islands in the Gulf of Finland. The name of his street, 'Virgin Walk', wasn't lost on Kaisa, especially later in the evening, when she walked along it to the nearest tram stop, on her way home.

The meal Tom was preparing as Kaisa stepped into his beautiful apartment, with its bay widow overlooking the sea, was pasta bolognese (his mother was Italian). He'd brought some cured bacon back from Milan.

'It's called pancetta,' Tom said, and smiled at Kaisa. In Italian, he sounded even more charming, and Kaisa was tempted to ask him to speak Italian to her, but felt silly. She didn't know him well enough, yet.

The wine, too, was from Italy, a deep red that warmed Kaisa's throat as she drank it. The first kiss happened in the kitchen, when Tom was cooking. He'd asked Kaisa to come and taste the sauce. They stood very close to one another by the stove, gazing at the boiling red mass of the meaty sauce, and Kaisa could feel his taut body tense as her thigh touched his. She felt Tom's eyes on her when she licked a small spoon clean of the sauce.

'It's good,' she smiled, and when she gave the spoon back to him, he grabbed hold of her hand. She felt his hot breath on her.

'Come here,' Tom said. He pulled her towards him and bent down to kiss her mouth.

His lips were fuller than Peter's and he squeezed Kaisa tightly, while he pushed his tongue into her mouth. Kaisa was tense, but she tried to relax, tried to feel something. Tom didn't seem to notice her lack of commitment, and pulled away only in order to see to the cooking. He gave Kaisa one of his wolfish grins and put a little of the pasta water into the sauce. 'This thickens it,' he said.

The food Tom had prepared was delicious, although Kaisa had no appetite. She had great difficulty eating the long strands of the special pasta – also brought back from Italy, and Tom, laughing, showed her how to twist the pasta in a spoon with her fork. But she didn't mind not being able to eat; she didn't want her tummy to be bloated. They finished the bottle of wine while talking about music, about their respective friends in Hanken and what they were doing now. Kaisa skipped most of the story of her short marriage. She simply said, 'It didn't work out.' Tom didn't ask her to explain further. He told Kaisa just as little about what he had been doing in Italy for best part of a year, and Kaisa in turn didn't ask him to elaborate.

When the wine was finished, Tom asked if she'd like to move to the sofa in the large main living area. He locked his eyes with Kaisa's and she nodded. She knew what was about to happen, as did he.

Tom put some music on his brand-new record player. The steely stack of equipment stood alone in one corner of the room. When Kaisa saw him open up the cover of *Faces*, by

Earth, Wind and Fire, her heart beat faster. The first track transported her back five years to the first time Peter had come back to Helsinki to see her, and they'd listened to almost nothing else. Perhaps if Kaisa had said something then, had told Tom to choose another record, things could have been different.

While the first track played, Tom came to sit next to Kaisa and started to kiss her again. Trying to push the music and memories of Peter away, she pressed her lips against Tom's. He slid his hand underneath her mohair jumper, and started to fondle her breasts. Kaisa hadn't worn a bra on purpose. She wanted Tom to see that she was prepared to go to bed with him. Under her jeans, she was wearing a pair of lacy French knickers. Earlier, getting dressed in Sirkka's flat, she'd considered wearing a skirt with stockings and suspenders, but thought that would be over the top. She didn't want to appear too prepared, or too easy. Besides, the weather had been awful all day, with a combination of rain and sleet beating down the windows in the small flat in Töölö. Kaisa couldn't afford a taxi all the way to Ullanlinna, and would have frozen to death waiting for the tram in such skimpy underwear.

She felt a pleasant excitement from Tom's hands exploring her body, and for a moment, Kaisa relaxed. Tom pulled away, gazed at her eyes and silently led her to his bed – a mezzanine built into one end of the large room. Not letting go of her hand, he coaxed her gently up the wooden ladder. Once there, he pulled his T-shirt over his head and took his jeans and pants off.

Kaisa gazed at Tom's muscular torso, not daring to look down. Not yet. Instead, she too pulled off her jumper and jeans.

'Nice,' Tom said when he saw her knickers.

But when Kaisa moved her eyes down from Tom's handsome face and broad chest, she was surprised to see that he wasn't ready.

'Just play with me for a bit,' Tom said in a hoarse voice, and Kaisa did, but there was no change. She kissed him on his lips, moving to his neck and chest, but Tom pulled her up again and hugged her, 'I'm sorry,' he said.

WHILE KAISA HAD BEEN up in Tom's flat, the temperature in Helsinki had dropped again and a blanket of fresh snow covered the city. It muffled all sound and made the streets artificially quiet. As Kaisa waited for the tram on Tehtaankatu, she felt as if she was in a magical place. This was in such contrast to the embarrassing events of just a moment before, adding to the weird times she felt she was living through. In the tram, her sense of being an actor in a surrealist play continued. The streetlights along South Harbour cast a magical glow against the white landscape as the tram trundled past the now empty market square and towards the imposing view of Helsinki Cathedral. Sitting in the empty tram on the way home, viewing the impossibly beautiful snowy scene, she wondered what had gone wrong with Tom. They had both vowed not to breathe a word to anyone about what had happened, but she now thought she must have done something wrong. Perhaps if she'd asked him to speak Italian to her, things would have gone differently. With everything that had happened to her in the past few weeks, she knew she'd been tense, and perhaps Tom had sensed that.

In a way Kaisa was relieved. She realised going to bed with Tom wouldn't have helped. It would only have made her more confused, would only have complicated her life further. What on earth had she been thinking?

'Oh, my God!' Tuuli exclaimed. 'But good for you for facing up to him. Let's just hope he is as honourable as he always made out and gives you back the negatives.' She clinked her glass with Kaisa's and they both laughed. Although Kaisa had no desire to laugh.

Kaisa had decided to tell Tuuli about the photographs. Or rather, the words just tumbled out of her while they shared a bottle of wine in Tuuli's minimalist apartment in Töölö. Her friend asked how she was and what she'd been up to. It was almost too good a story not to share, although Kaisa still felt the shame of her behaviour. How had she been so stupid to let Matti take those images?

'It was terrible. He was so smug with his Russian fur hat and army posture.' Kaisa said.

They both laughed again, and Tuuli poured Kaisa more wine.

'It's good to have you back,' she said, and examining her friend's face, added, 'I always wondered what you saw in him.'

'Yeah, well, I was young and with my parents' divorce, I guess he was a father figure.'

Tuuli nodded and grew serious. Again they were quiet for a while. Kaisa looked around the small flat. It was a studio, with one large room, a separate kitchenette and an alcove, which was entirely taken up by Tuuli's bed. In the hall, there was a small bathroom. It was exactly the kind of place Kaisa wanted. It had high ceilings, and the window in the living room overlooked an internal courtyard, formed by two L-shaped 1950s stone buildings. Although the flat was close to the tram, and the main Helsinki thoroughfare, Mannerheim Street, none of the traffic noise reached this side of the block. Tuuli had bought the place six months earlier, and she'd told Kaisa the mortgage was killing her. That was the reason for the sparse decoration, Kaisa supposed, but she loved the simple style; there was a standard lamp, a small desk and one print hanging above the sofa – the same sofa Tuuli had in the flat she'd rented during her studies at Hanken. Her old apartment was just a few streets away. Kaisa remembered the place – and the sofa – where she'd crashed so many times after missing the last bus to her own place in Lauttasaari, or later Espoo, the commuter town West of Helsinki, when she was living with her father. The walls were white and a single piece of light fabric hung on one side of the window. Venetian blinds fitted inside the triple-glazed windows, a standard feature in all flats and houses in Finland. Curtains were just for decoration here – unlike in Britain, Kaisa thought, where you needed heavy drapes to keep out the light and noise, not to mention the chill from drafty windows.

'I'm pleased to see you still have the same sofa,' she said and smiled at Tuuli.

The two friends began to talk about 'the good old times' when they were studying at Hanken, before Kaisa married Peter and left Helsinki for Portsmouth.

'So what's really going on with you and Ricky,' Kaisa said. Tuuli was a very private person and although they told each other everything, Kaisa always felt Tuuli was more reticent than she was. Kaisa felt another pang of guilt; she hadn't written to Tuuli many times during her short marriage. Again, she'd been too self-obsessed to think about her friends. That must stop now, Kaisa thought as she waited for her friend to open up.

'I told you, we have occasional sex!' Now Tuuli giggled.

'And you aren't hooked on him?'

Tuuli took a large gulp of wine, 'No!' she exclaimed, but Kaisa wasn't convinced. She knew that Tuuli had been hurt badly by a boy in their second year at Hanken, just when Kaisa's relationship with Peter had got more serious and he'd asked her to marry him. Although they never discussed it,

Kaisa knew Tuuli was afraid the same thing would happen to her again.

'He looks pretty smitten with you,' Kaisa now said.

Tuuli grew serious, 'You think so?'

Kaisa nodded.

'Hmm,' Tuuli said and added, 'No more talk of old flames, what about we go out this weekend and *don't* go to the Helsinki Club afterwards?'

Kaisa smiled and agreed; nothing would convince Tuuli that men were trustworthy. Perhaps she was right.

'But before we drop the old flames altogether; what about you. How did your date with Tom go?' Tuuli said, and nudged Kaisa's knee with her toe.

Again Kaisa found it impossible to keep a secret from Tuuli. And so, making her friend swear to secrecy, she recounted her disastrous attempt to have sex with Tom.

'Wow, that's a surprise!' Tuuli said, but now she wasn't laughing.

'Remember you mustn't tell anyone, especially Ricky!' Kaisa said.

Tuuli grew even more serious, 'Of course I won't!'

'It was so embarrassing,' Kaisa said. 'It seems he doesn't fancy me after all, if he can't even get it up.'

Tuuli looked at her friend, and leaned over to touch her arm. 'Kaisa, you must know that had nothing to do with you! It's his problem. Probably just all that drinking they did in Hanken.'

'Yeah,' Kaisa said, but she knew she didn't sound convincing, because she wasn't even convincing herself.

THIRTEEN

irkka and Kaisa got off the bus near a cluster of newly built high-rise houses. To get to the suburb of Soukka in Espoo, they'd taken the tram to the bus station in the centre of town, and then a coach. Sitting in the bus, Kaisa had been flooded with painful memories of the time she lived with her father. Not that it'd all been unhappy, but for the most part she'd been desperate to finish her studies. She'd longed for Peter, and had been fearful of her father's sudden mood changes. Her father could be pleasant to be with, or a drunken bear with a sore head. She'd never know which version of him she'd find at home.

'I can't believe he's still living in Espoo,' Kaisa said, as they made their way past a children's playground, a covered cycle store, rubbish bins and the traditional carpet airing stand common to all blocks of flats in Finland. The developers had left a rocky mound in the middle of the utilitarian looking houses, where a couple of boys were climbing up and down a slippery rock. Kaisa was transported back to her own childhood; she remembered how she often played alone in the small courtyard outside their block of flats in Tampere.

This was Sirkka's second visit to the four-bedroomed flat that their father had bought with his girlfriend, Marja, a few months back.

'And I can't believe Marja is still with him,' Kaisa added.

Sirkka said nothing. Inside the block of flats, they entered the lift and Sirkka pressed 10 for the top floor.

But as they waited for the lift to make its way up the many floors, she looked gravely at Kaisa. 'He's very keen to see you.'

'Really?' Kaisa said. Sirkka had changed her tune, she thought. She'd always been the one to be the most critical of their father. For many years the two hadn't seen each other, so Kaisa had been surprised when Sirkka had not only suggested going to see their father and his girlfriend on Sunday but also admitted that she'd been there once before.

'He just called on me at work one day and asked me to come over the following Sunday,' Sirkka had told Kaisa.

'And you just went?' Kaisa had asked.

'Yes, well, I like Marja, besides, I was curious.' Sirkka had regarded Kaisa for a while. 'He was OK, you know. Since the accident he's been a lot more ... I don't know, softer somehow.'

Kaisa remembered being told about the accident the previous winter. His car had veered off the icy Lauttasaari Bridge. She'd not even contacted him afterwards. Again, Kaisa felt she'd been selfish. But she'd still been angry with him for trying to stop her mother from attending her wedding to Peter. In the end, Kaisa's refusal to bar Pirjo had led to her mother paying for the wedding instead. The person absent from the reception had been her father. He'd come to the church, but her uncle had given Kaisa away, not him. How could one forgive a father that?

KAISA'S HEART was beating hard and she noticed that her palms were damp when she and Sirkka rang the bell outside her father's flat. The hall smelled of fresh paint. The bell didn't make any sound, so after a few minutes, Sirkka knocked on the door instead. Almost immediately, Marja opened the door. She flung her arms open and hugged the two girls hard. Kaisa was unprepared for the gesture and could feel her body tense.

'Come in, step in,' Marja said. She was wearing one of Kaisa's old jumpers. When she saw Kaisa looking at it, she said, 'Oh, you remember this?' She pulled at the picture of a deer, rendered with old-fashioned stitching on the front. Kaisa remembered that she'd bought the jumper at Hennes and Mauritz in Stockholm during one of the trips Sirkka and Kaisa had made to their old home town when they were first living in Finland. That was at least ten years ago. Before she left for Britain, she'd filled a bag with old clothes for the Salvation Army, which Marja had promised to deliver to the charity.

'This was such a great jumper, I couldn't give it away. I decided to keep it for myself. So many of the clothes that you discarded were perfectly fine! Waste not, want not,' she said and opened a door into a large living room.

Kaisa was so surprised by this thinly veiled criticism of her spendthrift ways that she said nothing. She turned to face Sirkka, raising her eyebrows. Her sister made a face, crossing her eyes and pursing her lips. Kaisa stifled a giggle, and followed Marja.

Her father was sitting in one of the large comfy chairs she remembered from their old house. He was wearing dark navy cords and a navy jumper with a light blue Marimekko shirt underneath. These were the clothes Kaisa had helped him choose when she was still living in Lauttasaari. Kaisa could see he had lost weight. He looked tanned, and combined with the colour of the shirt, his eyes seemed bluer. There was a healthy glow about him. He opened his arms and Kaisa rushed to hug him. Swallowed by her father's bear hug, Kaisa let her body relax. She fought back tears, sensing the old feeling of security that her father's embraces had given her as a child. When he eventually released her and hugged Sirkka in turn, Kaisa stepped aside and, turning her head so that Marja's beady eyes couldn't see, wiped the corners of her eyes with her fingers.

Marja had prepared coffee with bread, cheese, gravad lax and ham for them. But before they were allowed to tuck into the spread, proudly presented by Marja, their father showed his daughters the various rooms in the large apartment. The rectangular lounge overlooked a wooded landscape and had a glimpse of the sea on the far horizon. The rays of the early spring sun glittered on the steel-blue surface. The ice had all but gone, but the sea still looked cold and uninviting.

'Not bad, eh, for your old man?' Their father grinned.

Sirkka nodded and Kaisa made a show of looking at the view, 'That's wonderful.'

'The flat is on the top floor and occupies one whole corner of the building, with two aspects. This is the biggest flat in the whole of the block!' their father continued. Kaisa could see his chest fill with pride. As he took them from room to room, she made the 'ooh,' and 'aah' sounds she knew he expected. Sirkka, however, remained impassive, seemingly unimpressed by the place. Kaisa nudged her, as their father led them to each bedroom in turn. Having been so keen on this visit, Sirkka now appeared to be bored by the flat and their father. But Sirkka gave Kaisa a quick smile.

'Enough room for grandchildren to come and stay!' their father said, turning around to face his daughters.

This last comment at least made her sister react. She said, laughing, 'You've got a long wait for that!'

'On a sunny day you can see all the way to Björkö island!' their father continued, as he brought them back through the lounge and ushered them onto the wide balcony. It was a sunny but cold day, and at this height the wind was stronger, making their father's thin hair stand up. He looked a bit like a friendly professor rather then the Jekyll-and-Hyde character Kaisa had lived with a year ago. He offered Kaisa a pair of binoculars that he kept on the windowsill. Not knowing what she was looking for, but seeing the contrast of colours between the dark wooded forest, the pale blue sky with fluffy white clouds, and the cold grey colour of the sea on the horizon, she nodded appreciatively. She saw no island, and had no idea what, or where, the place he was talking about could be. She assumed the island was much further away, towards the Gulf of Finland.

'Can we go inside, it's too cold out here,' Sirkka said and rolled her eyes at Kaisa. It was a look Kaisa remembered vividly from her childhood and it sent her into a fit of giggles that this time she couldn't contain.

Her father gave Kaisa and Sirkka a look of impatience, a carbon copy of the encounters between Sirkka and their father when the sisters were growing up.

'Oh well, you girls are too young to appreciate a good property deal. But there will come a time when you do. Let's have something to eat – and more to the point something to drink!' he said, seemingly determined not to spoil the good mood of the occasion.

Marja, who hadn't joined them on the tour around the flat, was sitting at the round kitchen table, looking very satisfied with herself, wearing Kaisa's discarded, ten-year-old jumper. Suddenly Kaisa wondered whether there had been any underwear in those bags of old clothes, and if her father's girlfriend was at that very moment wearing her old knickers. She wracked her brains, fighting off another fit of unexplained laughter, but decided such things had probably gone straight out with the rubbish. She hoped so.

When they opened the *Lonkero*, which Marja said they'd bought 'specially for you, Kaisa', a comment that caused Sirkka to snort, and Kaisa to kick her shins under the table, Marja suddenly said, 'So, Kaisa have you left the Englishman?'

On the way back to the city, Kaisa was fuming.

'She's unbelievable!' she said to Sirkka as soon as they'd sat down in the empty bus. The bus driver, who seemed to be in a hurry, had not bothered to wait for Sirkka and Kaisa to sit down before pulling away from the bus stop, making both girls lurch along the gangway. The smell of the bus reminded Kaisa of Peter's visits to Espoo when she was living with her father, and those happy memories somehow made her even angrier.

'Who?' Sirkka said.

'Marja, of course. First she takes my stuff, and then wears my jumper in front of me. Can you believe that!'

Sirkka sighed, 'Well, she's very tight with money.'

'And then that comment about Peter and our marriage. Where did she get the idea that I'd left him?'

Sirkka looked out of the window. Kaisa stared at the back of her sister's head.

'Sirkka?'

Her sister looked at Kaisa. 'What should I have told them? You've been living with me for over a month. Marja asked me how long you'd been in Helsinki, and I told her, so she must have put one and one together.'

Kaisa examined her sister's face. Was she lying? But why?

'You didn't say anything about me leaving Peter, did you?'

'No,' Sirkka exclaimed loudly. The bus stopped at a set of traffic lights. Hearing Sirkka's raised voice, the driver gave the two young women a cursory glance through the rear-view mirror.

Trying to keep her voice low, Kaisa said, 'So what did you tell her exactly?'

'That you've been here for over a month. She asked me when are you going back to England and I said I didn't know.'

'Oh, Sirkka!'

Her sister straightened herself up in the seat. 'You wanted me to lie to her?'

Kaisa looked at her sister, but didn't reply. She was still angry, but she realised how difficult her situation was for Sirkka too.

'Look, I didn't know what to say. You know how Marja is, she is so bloody nosy. I was only phoning them to say you were here, since you hadn't done that yourself. You know Helsinki isn't such a big place. What would have happened if you'd bumped into one of them in town? I didn't expect her to give me the third degree on the phone!' Sirkka looked upset. Her eyes were pleading with Kaisa.

Kaisa took hold of her sister's hand, and said, 'Sorry, I'm being a bitch, aren't I?'

Sirkka squeezed Kaisa's fingers. 'No, I know it's difficult for you, but it's not easy for me either. The amount of times even people at work ask how long you're going to stay, what your plans are ...'

'I know, I know. And I will sort myself out, I promise,' Kaisa said, interrupting her sister. 'I'm going to phone Mr Heinola tomorrow to see if they've got anything for me in the KOP bank. And if he doesn't have anything, I'll go around to Stockmann's. You never know, they might have something for me. Then I can start looking for a flat for myself.'

'That's not what I mean. You can stay with me as long as you like,' Sirkka said, holding Kaisa's hand as if she was ill.

Kaisa smiled at her sister. 'I know, you've been incredibly kind and patient. It's time I moved on with my life.'

FOURTEEN

Kaisa had been in Helsinki for six weeks, and still didn't have a job. Every day, including Sundays, when *Helsingin Sanomat* was full of job advertisements, she'd look through the pages and think about applying for something. Despite her promise to Sirkka, another week had passed without her plucking up the courage to phone Mr Heinola at the bank. She kept putting it off, thinking she shouldn't appear too keen. But none of the jobs advertised in the paper seemed right for her either. On a Sunday in late March, when the snow had all but melted from the little patch of grass at the edge of the block of flats, Kaisa was sitting alone in the kitchen, nursing a hot cup of coffee. When the announcement caught her eye, she dropped her cup on the floor. Absentmindedly, as if it was happening to someone else, she saw the black-brown liquid spread in mid-air then fall to the tiled floor, followed by the shards of the broken china cup. She felt the coffee burn her toes and the lower part of her right calf, and yet she was numb; her senses seemed to be suspended.

Beloved
Matti Johannes Rinne
B 10.02.1953
D 20.03.1985
Taken away from us too soon.
Service and burial 27 March 1985
at Hietaniemi Chapel

SIRKKA RUSHED INTO THE KITCHEN, her short blonde hair standing up, and her eyes large and wide.

'What are you doing?'

Kaisa looked at her sister but she seemed to have lost the ability to speak. She was still holding the newspaper in her hands, open on the first page, where the death notices were prominently displayed. What had made her look at them, she wondered? She felt as if she wasn't really in the room. Even her sister's dishevelled form, with her dressing gown open and her hair looking as though she was in a wind tunnel, seemed to be far away. She moved her eyes back to the notice, and with great difficulty, because her limbs seemed to have lost their ability to move, lifted one heavy hand and pointed at Matti's name.

'Oh, my God,' Sirkka said. She put her arm around Kaisa, and gently took the paper from Kaisa's hands to reread the notice.

Kaisa looked down at the floor. Seeing the mess of the broken coffee cup, she thought she ought to get up and clear it away. She tried to move, but couldn't. Instead she felt something wet on her cheeks, and realised she was making muffled noises.

'Oh, Kaisa, I'm so sorry.' Sirkka pulled Kaisa towards her

and suddenly Kaisa felt a piercing pain reach inside her chest. She leaned against her sister's shoulder, trying to breathe, so that the pressure would go away. Sirkka rocked her back and forth, making soothing sounds, but nothing, nothing stopped her sensation of being suffocated.

'I'M COMING WITH YOU,' Sirkka said.

'Really?' Kaisa glanced at her sister. She was standing in the doorway to the kitchen wearing a pair of black trousers and a black shirt. 'I thought you were at work today.'

'I've taken the day off.' Sirkka stepped inside the kitchen and put a hand on Kaisa's shoulder. 'I don't think you should go on your own. You never know what that mad old cow will get up to.'

'Please, Sirkka, don't say that. She's just lost her only son.' Kaisa bit the inside of her cheeks and took a slow breath in and out. She didn't want to start crying again.

It was two days after Kaisa had found out about Matti's death. After crying for so long that she no longer could, she'd decided she would be brave and phone Matti's mother. She remembered their last conversation vividly. Mrs Rinne had accused her of being a common whore because she had left her son and fallen in love with the Englishman. Kaisa had been upset at the time, but now she understood. Kaisa had broken a promise made to her son and Mrs Rinne had only been protecting him. Besides, none of that mattered now. But instead of Mrs Rinne, the telephone had been answered by a young-sounding girl.

'Just a moment,' she'd said and then Kaisa recognised the voice of Aunt Bea, Mrs Rinne's sister.

'Ah, Kaisa,' she'd said and her voice had sounded deep, and serious, but normal under the circumstances.

After Kaisa had expressed her condolences, Aunt Bea told Kaisa that Matti had been killed in a hunting accident. She said that Mrs Rinne wasn't taking any calls.

'Of course,' Kaisa had replied.

'Are you coming to the funeral?' she had then asked, taking Kaisa by surprise. 'Yes, of course I am,' Kaisa said.

Now, getting ready, she was regretting her rash promise.

'Thank you,' she said to her sister and hugged her. 'I thought I'd be OK to go on my own, but I don't think I am.'

The day of Matti's funeral was bitterly cold, but sunny. Sirkka and Kaisa walked slowly inside the walls of Hietaniemi cemetery, where bare trees flanked the paths between the headstones. The ground under their feet was sanded, but it was hard and Kaisa could still spot traces of snow here and there in front of the headstones. Some of the graves either side of the main thoroughfare leading up to a chapel were large, important-looking plots, separated from the others by chains. Some had just a small stone at the head of the plot. They passed a beautiful statue of an angel, set on a tall plinth, and Kaisa glanced away, trying to keep her mind on getting through the day. Against another large headstone, there was a statue of a mother and a child. The child had her head on the mother's lap, while the mother caressed the child's head. Kaisa swallowed hard; she must control herself and not cry. She took a handkerchief out of the pocket of a black overcoat her mother had lent her, and dabbed at the corners of her eyes.

'Are you OK,' Sirkka whispered, and squeezed Kaisa's arm.

She nodded. When they approached the pale yellow chapel built on a small hill, they saw a group of people, all dressed in black talking in hushed tones, outside the large wooden doors. Kaisa took hold of Sirkka's arm, and as they got closer she saw there was a woman with white hair, looking frail, but wearing bright pink lipstick, in the middle of the group. She was sitting in a wheelchair. Kaisa looked at Sirkka and said, 'I have to go and say hello.'

Sirkka nodded and let go of her sister. She remained still, standing a little away from the group, while Kaisa moved forward. She recognised Matti's Aunt Bea straight away, but she didn't know any of the other mourners standing around Mrs Rinne. She nodded to Bea, and went up to Mrs Rinne. She'd decided to just say, 'My condolences,' and then step back and wait for Sirkka to accompany her inside the chapel. But when she got up to the wheelchair, Mrs Rinne lifted her eyes towards Kaisa.

'You!' she said. Her eyes were dark and surprisingly clear.

Kaisa took her gloves off and reached out her hand: 'My condolences.'

Mrs Rinne took Kaisa's hand. Her bare fingers felt fragile; thin and bony. Kaisa squeezed her hand gently, and then went to pull away, but Mrs Rinne, her dark eyes boring into Kaisa, kept a firm grip on her. The old woman's nails dug into Kaisa's hand, hurting her. Kaisa tried to pull away again, but in vain.

'You bitch,' Mrs Rinne said under her breath and pushed her nails deeper into Kaisa's flesh. Then, as suddenly as she'd set her eyes on Kaisa, she let go of her hand, and turned her dark gaze away from her.

A young girl with long, straw-blonde hair took hold of the wheelchair. Whispering something to Mrs Rinne while glancing disapprovingly at Kaisa, she pushed her into the chapel. The rest of the mourners, without so much as a look in Kaisa's direction, followed Mrs Rinne and the girl inside.

Sirkka appeared at Kaisa's side.

'Are we going in?' she said, looking at Kaisa's face.

'Yes, we must.' Kaisa replied. As they walked into the dark and cold interior of the church, Kaisa glanced down at her hand. Mrs Rinne had drawn blood from her palm.

INSIDE, the chapel was half full. Kaisa followed Sirkka, who chose an empty pew at the back. Kaisa was glad. They were two rows behind the others mourners, so if she needed to cry, she could do so unnoticed. The service was short; only three hymns, and apart from the pastor only the young girl with blonde hair spoke. To Kaisa, she didn't look any older than sixteen, and until she began reading from the single sheet, her small, thin hands trembling, and her hair covering half her face, Kaisa had no idea who she was. She presumed it was one of Matti's cousins, one of Aunt Bea's daughters.

'I wanted to say a few words,' the girl began.

Before continuing, she lifted her head and looked straight at Kaisa. Her pale blue eyes had such coldness in them that Kaisa forgot the burning sensation in her right palm. Kaisa quickly lowered her eyes. It had been a mistake to come to the funeral.

'Matti and I were engaged to be married,' the girl said.

Kaisa lifted her head and stared at the girl. So Matti hadn't been lying; he had found someone else. Another young woman to control. Involuntarily, Kaisa's hands formed into fists, but she winced when she noticed the pain in her right palm.

While the girl spoke, saying how little time they'd had together, and how Matti had 'been taken away far too soon', Sirkka held firmly onto Kaisa's left hand. Kaisa wanted to get up and tell the girl how wrong this was, how a 32-year-old man, tragically dead or not, shouldn't be engaged to a 16-year-old girl. But as the blonde girl stepped down from the pew and sat next to Mrs Rinne, Kaisa thought it really didn't matter any more. Matti was gone, gone with the help of his own gun. The guns, which Kaisa had always felt uneasy about, and even afraid of, had been his own undoing in the end. For the umpteenth time Kaisa wondered how he could have accidentally shot himself. After Kaisa had got over the initial shock of his death, she had stayed awake wondering how it had happened. Of course, there was no one she could ask, and really, it had nothing to do with her.

Still, the night before, Kaisa had had the awful realisation that Matti had deliberately shot himself. That he'd committed suicide and that it was Kaisa's sudden appearance in Helsinki that was the reason. Or the confrontation about the negatives, about their relationship and how she'd been only 15 when he'd seduced her. Had he believed her when she threatened him with the police? In the morning, getting ready for the funeral, she'd chided herself for being too melodramatic, for imagining she was the centre of everyone's universe. After all, Matti and Kaisa had met just twice since she'd returned to Helsinki, and to Kaisa her old fiancé had seemed perfectly happy, perfectly normal, perfectly himself. Kaisa wanting some old photographs back couldn't have upset him that much, could it? She'd decided not to breathe a word of her mad theory to anyone, not Sirkka, not her mother, not even Tuuli.

And now? With all that hostility shown to her by Matti's new girlfriend, and Matti's mother? Kaisa shook her head, and whispered to Sirkka, 'I can't go to the grave.'

Sirkka nodded and when the pallbearers had taken the coffin out of the chapel, followed by the family, with Mrs Rinne, Aunt Bea and the girl in the lead, Sirkka and Kaisa, the last to leave the church, walked in the opposite direction to the other mourners. Passing the beautiful headstones, they walked quickly out of the cemetery, towards the tram stop.

'Wait, Kaisa!'

Kaisa and Sirkka stopped when they saw a woman, heavily pregnant and wearing a black fur hat and a short swing coat, running towards them.

As the figure moved closer, Kaisa saw who it was. 'Vappu?' she said.

The woman was out of breath when she reached them. Kaisa supported her arm with her hand, 'Are you OK?'

'Yes,' Vappu said between pants, 'I just didn't want to miss you! I thought I saw you come into the church but only knew for sure it was you just now.'

Kaisa regarded her old friend for a while, 'Congratulations!'

Vappu smiled up at Kaisa, 'Thank you.' Then her eyes moved back toward the slow-moving cortège on the other side of the church. 'I have to go, but ring me. I want to see you before you disappear again.'

Vappu pressed a piece of paper firmly into Kaisa's palm, 'Promise to call me.' Vappu's pale blue eyes were serious, and although the pressure of the hand made Kaisa wince, she closed her fingers around the piece of paper and nodded, 'I promise.'

Vappu turned on her heels. Not looking back, she began walking at a fast pace towards the far end of the cemetery.

'What was that all about?' Sirkka asked as they began making their way toward the tram stop again.

'Don't you remember my old friend from Lauttasaari?' Kaisa said. 'I didn't think she'd be at the funeral, but of course she would. It was at her family home that I first met Matti.'

'Of course. I'd forgotten all about that.'

Both Sirkka and Kaisa were quiet as they walked along the hard sanded path towards the entrance of the cemetery. Kaisa was thinking back to when she was 14, and a new girl at Lauttasaari school. She'd made friends with Vappu on her first day and had spent more time in her large house than she did at home.

'What really happened to him?' Sirkka said once they were sitting inside the tram and moving north towards Linnankoskenkatu.

Kaisa shook her head. She was too upset to speak. The

tears that she'd managed to hold back inside the chapel, were now flowing freely.

'Oh Kaisa,' Sirkka said and put her arm around her sister's shoulders.

FIFTEEN

For nearly two weeks after the funeral Kaisa hardly went out. She saw Tuuli for lunch at Stockmann's but refused to go on a night out. She wore black, or dark clothes, as if she was in mourning for a close relative. Sirkka didn't comment on her outfits, neither did her mother, even though Kaisa could see they both glanced at her black jeans and T-shirt, when, two Sundays after the funeral, they sat down for a traditional Easter lunch in Pirjo's smartly decorated flat.

'They have no right to be angry with you,' Pirjo said and patted Kaisa's arm.

Kaisa fought tears; she'd done so much crying, not knowing for whom or for what.

'I know,' she said. In her mind, she was aware that she wasn't to blame for Matti's death. And she knew how impulsive and vindictive Matti's mother could be. Besides, Mrs Rinne had looked ill, and losing an only son must be completely devastating. Whether she deserved her wrath or not, Kaisa didn't blame Mrs Rinne for any of her feelings of hostility, or her actions. Instead, Matti's death, and the awful funeral with the young girl in tears and Mrs Rinne scratching Kaisa's hand, had made her realise how much damage she had inflicted on the people around her. In a way, she was mourning her own life so far.

Even before the funeral, she'd felt helpless and insignificant after Scotland, her failed marriage, and her infidelity. Now that Peter had found a new life without her, and Matti had gone, Kaisa thought she might as well be dead herself.

This was partly why she hadn't phoned Vappu even though she had promised. The crumpled piece of paper was still in her handbag, where she had placed it after the funeral. How could she see her old friend, whom she had more or less abandoned after she'd got together with Matti? Besides, Kaisa couldn't even remember when she'd last seen Vappu before the funeral. Seeing her open face, the same vibrancy in her pale blue eyes that she remembered from their school days, had made her long to talk to Vappu, but what would she say? How would she be able to explain why she was back in Finland? Kaisa assumed Vappu had heard all about her affair with the Englishman from Matti, or from her brother Petteri, whose best friend Matti had been. Kaisa wondered if the whole family had been at the funeral and seen her skulk away. How ashamed of her behaviour she now was! She should have faced up to them all, and gone to the graveside to do her duty as Matti's long-term girlfriend and former fiancé. Suddenly she felt a great urgency to leave Helsinki again. There were too many skeletons here.

KAISA HEARD the telephone ring in the hall before she was awake. It was eight o'clock on a Monday morning and Sirkka had already left for work.

'Hello,' Kaisa said trying not to sound sleepy. She hoped it might be Mr Heinola from the bank.

'Kaisa, I found you!'

For a moment Kaisa wanted to put the receiver back on its base, or pretend she was Sirkka, a game the sisters had played as teenagers, but she couldn't do it.

'Vappu?' she said.

'Listen, I'm in the telephone box outside your flat. Can I come up?'

'Now?' Kaisa looked at the clutter in the small flat. Her bed was unmade in the lounge, and from the hall Kaisa could see the plates and cutlery from last night's dinner, as well as her sister's breakfast dishes, piled up in the sink. Her own clothes were scattered around the lounge, on chairs and at the foot of the bed.

'It's bloody cold in this phone box and it stinks of wee,' Vappu said.

'OK, I'll buzz you up,' Kaisa said.

She put the phone down and pulled on a pair of jeans and a jumper. She made the bed as best she could and rammed her clothes inside her suitcase, which she pushed into a hall cupboard. She opened the venetian blinds and the room flooded with light. 'That's a bit better,' Kaisa thought, but she didn't have time to assess the state of the kitchen before Vappu was ringing the doorbell.

Her friend's belly was even larger than Kaisa remembered, and it was hard to hug her. Vappu smiled and said, 'I know, I look like a bloody beached whale!'

'When is it due?'

'Oh, today, actually,' Vappu said and, added, 'but don't worry, I'm sure I'll be late.'

Kaisa couldn't help but smile at her old friend. Her shape was completely different, with the pregnancy, and Kaisa spotted a few lines around her eyes, but otherwise she was the same lanky 14-year-old that Kaisa had met at her new school in Lauttaaari all those years ago. As she made the coffee, Vappu looked up at Kaisa from the small kitchen table. With a serious tone of voice, she said: 'I wanted to see you before I get busy with this little one.'

Kaisa nodded. She had no idea what her friend was talking about, or why it was so urgent for them to see each other.

Vappu gazed at Kaisa, 'You know that I'm married, right?'

Kaisa shook her head, 'No, but I sort of guessed ...'

'Well, while I've been with Risto, I've come to realise that what happened to you with Matti, when you were so young, it wasn't right.'

Kaisa stared at her friend.

'The thing is, Risto is a policeman. That's how I found you, just as well I remembered your maiden name and that your sister is called Sirkka.' A quick grin passed over Vappu's face.

Kaisa nodded, but couldn't return her friend's smile.

'Anyway, he's worked on an underage sex case before.' Vappu's blue eyes were steadily gazing at Kaisa. She was wearing a colourful long blouse over a pair of black pants. Her legs were spread wide and she was leaning onto the kitchen table for support. Kaisa realised it must be very uncomfortable sitting with a large belly like that on the small kitchen chair.

'Do you want to go and sit in the lounge? There's a comfy chair there.' Kaisa held her hand out and helped Vappu up to her feet. Once they were both settled in the room next door, Kaisa asked, 'When you say cases like these, what do you mean?'

'Well, you were underage, weren't you, when Matti and you ..?'

'Yes, but he's gone now, so ...'

'But he has – had – photographs, didn't he?'

Kaisa was stunned; how did Vappu know about the awful

pictures Matti had taken of her? 'Yes, but what, how?' Kaisa stammered. She put her head into her hands in shame. Had Vappu seen the images of her wanton and smiling like a whore into the camera? To calm herself, she slowed her breathing. Looking down at the floor, she continued, trying to steady her voice. 'How do you know about the photos and what do they have to do with anything?'

'Matti gave me the negatives before he – before the so-called accident.'

Kaisa found herself staring at Vappu's face again. She was thinking hard. Was her awful fear that he'd taken his life true after all? 'You mean he?' Kaisa couldn't bring herself to say the words, 'Did he?'

Vappu nodded. Her face was serious, and her gaze was steady. 'He gave them to me for safekeeping, and so that I could give them to you.'

'Oh, my God.'

'He couldn't live with himself. He asked Risto if you were right to say it was illegal. And,' Vappu eased herself out of the low-slung chair with difficulty and put her hand on Kaisa's knee. 'You know that girl, Satu, he was about to marry. She was just fourteen when they met two years ago. He told Risto he had no idea it was against the law. But Risto said he must have known.'

Kaisa couldn't speak. Why hadn't she kept her big mouth shut? Why had she gone and stirred up everything? Again ruining other people's lives.

'Risto blames himself,' Vappu said.

Kaisa pressed her hands together, trying to hold herself still. She had a great desire to stand up and howl. She was feeling dizzy.

'But we've only been together two years ourselves, and Risto had no idea how young Satu was. She is like you used to be; she acts a lot older than she is.' Vappu took a white envelope out of her handbag and handed it to Kaisa. 'Anyway here you go. Do whatever you want with them.'

Kaisa opened the flap of the white envelope and saw a set of dark films inside. She got up and hugged her friend.

'Look Kaisa, this is not your fault. Remember that.'

SIXTEEN

Kaisa woke up late. She'd heard her sister get up and go to work, but had fallen asleep again, only to have another wonderful dream about Peter. But after that she'd had a nightmare in which Matti rose from his grave, walked into the chapel in a black suit and was met by the sixteen-year-old girl in a white gown. Auntie Bea had smiled at Kaisa, who was one of the guests, and said, 'Isn't it wonderful that they can still get married even though Matti is dead?'

Kaisa shook her head and tried to tell herself it was just a dream. She stretched her neck to look out of the window. It was Sunday and she'd promised to go for a jog with her mother. She saw it was a sunny and relatively warm April day. The winter was finally giving way to spring. Couples were walking hand in hand, or with their children between them, wearing light overcoats or macs. It had rained heavily the night before – probably why she'd had such an awful night's sleep, Kaisa thought – and the side of the road was running with water. The temperature on the side of Sirkka's living room window showed 10 degrees Celsius; Kaisa decided she'd wear a padded jacket over her jogging clothes.

She walked up to the next floor of the block of flats and, using the key her mother had given her the day she'd arrived in Helsinki, opened the door.

'Hello,' she called out. Kaisa was still not used to the emptiness of her mother's flat. Each time she stepped through the door, she expected to be greeted by Jerry, the cocker spaniel they'd got after their parents' divorce. He'd died just before Kaisa had left Faslane and Peter. If she was truthful, the dog's death had touched Kaisa deeply, and was one of the reasons she wanted to come home.

Neither Sirkka's small flat below, or her mother's roomier apartment on the third floor of the five-storey block, felt like home to Kaisa. After two months on her sister's sofa bed, Kaisa was desperate to find a place of her own.

'I'm not ready yet,' her mother called from the bathroom, and Kaisa stepped into the kitchen. Seeing there was freshly brewed coffee in the percolator, she took off the padded coat she'd borrowed from her sister, placed her scarf and gloves on the kitchen table, and poured herself a cup of strong black coffee. She ran a little bit of cold water from the tap over the cup. While she'd lived in Britain, she'd got used to weaker coffee, a fact that neither Sirkka or her mother let her forget. 'You've become an Englishwoman,' they'd laugh, but Kaisa knew behind the joking there was hurt. They didn't want her to change, nor lose her to England. Well, they've got me back now, Kaisa thought. She sighed and sat down to gaze at the view of the inner courtyard while she waited for her mother to get dressed.

'It's still cold out there. Are you sure you have enough on?'

Kaisa nodded, 'I've got Sirkka's jacket.' She surveyed her mother, who sat down opposite her at the kitchen table. People said Kaisa looked just like her, and there was no denying it. Often, especially recently, in Helsinki, the face looking back at Kaisa from Sirkka's bathroom mirror was a younger version of her mother. It was a more modern version of the woman who smiled happily from the framed black-and-white wedding day portrait that her mother still displayed on her dresser in the living room. Pirjo had always looked younger than her age. Now, at 49, she sported curly, mid-length, blonde hair. Today (for a jog!), she'd made her face up with light blue eyeshadow that went with her shiny jacket and pale pink lipstick that matched her nails. She looked good, and the only difference in their appearance, apart from the make-up, was that Kaisa's mother was a couple of kilos heavier and a few centimetres shorter. People often – no, always – thought they were sisters when they were out and about, a compliment her mother revelled in. However, such comments made Kaisa feel invisible; the thought of her mother appearing to be in her twenties rendered Kaisa's existence insignificant, or even impossible.

The two women jogged along the now quiet Linnankoskenkatu towards the sea. In that morning's *Helsingin Sanomat* there had been an article about the ice no longer being thick enough to support people's weight. The two women therefore decided to run on the path along the shore. You could make out dark patches in the middle of the sea where the ice was melting.

'It's very late for the sea to be iced over, isn't it?'

'Hmm,' Pirjo said.

Kaisa looked at her mother. The sun was high up in the piercing blue sky, but there was a harsh wind, which made running more difficult than usual.

Instead of replying to Kaisa's comment, Pirjo lifted her eyes to her daughter. 'So, Kaisa, have you come to a decision about what you are going to do?'

Kaisa had anticipated this question, and thought it to be the reason she'd been invited on this Sunday jog.

'No, not yet.' She didn't want to tell her mother about the meeting with the bank manager, nor her lunch and failed date with Tom. Both of these things were just what her mother wanted to hear. She wanted Kaisa to make a life for herself in Helsinki, near to her and Sirkka, but Kaisa still wasn't sure she wanted to stay in Helsinki. After Vappu's visit, and the revelation that Matti had taken his own life, all Kaisa could think about was fleeing the city. But where to? England? Where would she live?

At least she now knew the awful pictures that Matti took would never be seen by anybody. Right after Vappu's visit, she'd cut the negatives into tiny pieces and put them in the bin. When she'd dropped the plastic bag into the large container in the courtyard she'd felt a huge weight lift off her chest. Her life with Matti was history, and her marriage with Peter was history. She knew she shouldn't care about Peter anymore, but she couldn't stop loving him. She was still his wife – for now at least – and obviously Peter thought that too. Even though the letter had been cold, or positively chilly, it was a letter. With money. The cash had angered and saddened Kaisa at first, but afterwards she wondered if that was Peter's way of saying that he still loved her?

'Oh,' Pirjo said.

'It's difficult, because I don't really know what Peter is planning, or thinking.'

'I know, darling, but it's been two months now, and ...'

Kaisa said nothing. It was upsetting to say the word, 'divorce', even though she needed to face it. Really, she thought it was too soon, but how could she explain this to her mother?

'Did Sirkka tell you her news?'

Kaisa stopped and turned to face her mother, 'No.' She was panting, suddenly feeling very out of breath.

Her mother took hold of Kaisa's arms, and said, 'You know that man in Lapland? Jussi?'

'Yes, but I thought that was over?'

'No, it isn't. He's coming to see her for a weekend.'

Kaisa stared at her mother. 'Did she ask you to tell me this?'

'Er, no, not really, but ...'

'So why did you?'

'Well, I thought you needed to know. I mean, the flat isn't big enough for two, really, so when Jussi is there ...'

Kaisa began jogging again. Her mind was in disarray; why hadn't her sister said anything about this development in her on-off relationship with Jussi?

THE NEXT MORNING Sirkka was fast asleep when Kaisa heard the post fall onto the mat in the small hall. She got quietly out of bed, listening to her sister's gentle snores coming from the open door to her bedroom.

There was the morning paper, *Helsingin Sanomat*, which Kaisa usually read cover to cover, soaking in the news and studying the job adverts, although there weren't many positions advertised in the Monday edition. But on the mat, together with the newspaper, was a letter. It was a large brown envelope, addressed to her in Smuggler's Way, but someone had crossed out the address and put Sirkka's address on the side. She scanned the writing, but it wasn't Peter's hand. Kaisa tore open the letter. There was a magazine inside, and a single sheet of handwritten text.

Dear Kaisa,

I wanted to write to you to tell you how sorry I am about all that has happened. I feel responsible for some of my cousin's behaviour, and feel that my involvement encouraged

him. You must believe me that I had no idea of his true
intentions towards you. Had I known, I wouldn't have met
up with you in London. Duncan merely told me that you
were the wife of a good friend, smart and talented, and
looking for a job. Of course, as soon as I met you, I realised he
was right, and purely because of that I offered you the job.
Please believe me, I had no ulterior motive, other than
wanting to employ a talented person.

You must also know that I am not speaking to Duncan,
and will not do so until he apologises to you fully.

Kaisa thought back to the letter she'd received from
Duncan, in which he'd apologised for his behaviour but in the
same breath invited her to see him in the country, so she didn't
really think his apology was sincere.

But I am also writing to let you know that I have left Sonia
magazine to work in an exciting venture that I have known
about for some time. Your situation did, I admit, play a part
in my decision to leave commercial magazine publishing and
enter more serious journalism. I am proud to tell you that I
am now Chief Editor of Adam's Apple, *a feminist*
publication, produced since 1973 by a women's commune
whose work I admire. We carry stories of oppression against
women from around the world, but also give advice to women
on how to be a feminist today.

I am writing to ask you if you'd consider coming to help
us in this cause? I cannot promise a large salary, but it will be
a worthwhile job, a chance to play a role in an important
publication. The Scandinavian countries are so much further
ahead in the cause for equality, and we would be delighted to
have you onboard to share your knowledge and enthusiasm. I
know you are a fellow feminist; I remember our discussions.
And I remember you telling me that you wanted a job where

you could make a difference. Well, here I am offering you one. I've enclosed the latest issue of Adam's Apple, *so you can see what kind of magazine it is.*

Please think about my proposal and write to me.

Yours sincerely,

Rose

Kaisa reread the letter three times before she could quite comprehend what it meant. She began leafing through the copy of the magazine, which to her looked very left-wing. The cover had a picture of three women against the backdrop of a coal mine, with the caption 'Women Winning the Strike'. So they were pro the miners.

As a Finn, having lived all her life in the shadow of the Soviet Union, she was naturally sceptical about communism, but as a student of Political Science, she knew that the left-wing in the UK had about the same ideologies as the Coalition Party in Finland, which was the right-wing party. And Rose was right, she wanted to make a difference, and she was passionate about women's rights. She felt the familiar butter-flies in the stomach: a *real* job in London! A job where she could make a difference to women's lives. Rose had said in her letter the magazine was produced by a women's commune. What, she wondered, was it like working in a women's commune in London? Did they all live where they worked, and was it a squat? She imagined a derelict old Victorian house without plumbing, cold and damp, with a garden full of faeces. No, she couldn't imagine Rose in an environment like that. They must have proper offices if Rose was part of the organisation.

Kaisa looked at the magazine again, and found that the address was Clerkenwell Close, London EC1R. Kaisa tiptoed back into the lounge, aware of her sister's gentle snoring as she passed her bedroom. She found the *London A-Z*, which she'd sentimentally packed in her suitcase when leaving the married quarter at Smuggler's Way. She found Clerkenwell Close and saw it was just a little north of Fleet Street, the area where all the newspapers were produced. Surely that was respectable enough?

SEVENTEEN

LONDON

L ondon was drizzly, but Kaisa was surprised by how much warmer it was by the end of April than Helsinki. She was too hot in her new thickly-lined winter coat, which her mother had bought for her at Stockmann's after hearing about the job in London. It was camel wool, and far too warm, plus the rain made a special pattern on it, as if it was made out of leopard skin. For her mother, Kaisa had put a slightly more glamorous spin on the job offer than was the truth, and hadn't shown her the copy of the magazine that Rose had sent. Pirjo hated communists: something to do with Kaisa's grandparents and the Winter War when Finns fought the Russians. Kaisa didn't want her to think she was going to be working for a left-wing publication.

The offices of *Adam's Apple* were on a side street a few minutes' walk from Farringdon tube station. Kaisa spotted the office instantly, because there were piles of magazine stacked on the pavement, and people milling outside talking and smoking. She was greeted with waves and smiles when she asked for Rose, 'She's upstairs, third floor.'

'Kaisa, how lovely to see you!' Rose gave Kaisa a hug, and added, 'I am so glad you could come.'

The first thing that hit Kaisa when she stepped inside the office was the smell of printed paper. It was a strange combination of a Finnish forest, chopped wood and glue. The inside of *Adam's Apple* looked a lot more chaotic than *Sonia* magazine, where Rose had worked before, but the chaos seemed friendly. The business of producing the magazine seemed to take place in one large room, lined with desks. Rose had got up from her position at the back of the room, where she'd been sitting typing. Behind her was a tall bookcase crammed with books with different coloured spines.

Rose took her hand and smiled, 'Welcome to London!' she said.

Kaisa saw a completely different woman in front of her. Instead of the Princess Di-like, upper-class, well-spoken, carefully put together woman, she now saw a carefree, passionate Rose who was almost make-up free. She'd let her highlights grow out, and Kaisa saw her hair was greying at the roots.

Rose introduced her to the other three women in the office. Rachel was sitting on a table, scribbling something on a notepad. She was a dark-haired girl, about Kaisa's height and build, with a long back and long legs. She had short, choppy hair, and wore a white shirt buttoned up at the neck and loose-fitting black trousers. 'Hi' she said to Kaisa and went back to her writing. On the other side, two women were reading. They smiled and nodded briefly when Rose introduced them as Barbara and Jenny.

Kaisa suddenly felt overdressed. Most of the other women were wearing casual jumpers and trousers, or even jeans, whereas Kaisa wore her black trouser suit under the warm camel coat. She'd have to remember to wear something more suitable for the next day.

"You might have seen Jack, our driver, and the others outside? We've just got delivery of this month's issue, so it's an exciting day for us!' Rose immediately took one copy of the latest issue and gave it to Kaisa. On the cover it said, 'Sex, Drugs And Rock and Roll' in red ink over a black and white picture of a woman.

'Looks great,' Kaisa said.

Rose began talking about the articles, what socio-political issues were covered by the latest magazine (which was Rose's first) and what they were planning for the next. She was so enthusiastic, her face shone.

But Kaisa was worried about money. She was excited by Rose, and about the prospect of working on a magazine in London. She couldn't believe she'd have an opportunity to further the feminist cause, but she was concerned about how she was going to support herself in London. In her letter, or in the expensive phone calls Kaisa had made from her mother's telephone to agree a start date, Rose hadn't made any mention of Kaisa's pay.

Rose had, though, arranged a cheap bed-sit for her in Notting Hill, in a large white-clad house on a road called Colville Terrace, a few streets away from the tube station. She'd left Kaisa some bedding, a kettle and even an ironing board and an iron, set neatly on the single bed of the large room. She had a small kitchenette arranged against one wall of the room, with a large bay window overlooking the street. But the night before, Kaisa's first night back in England, she had slept badly. The street had been noisy around 11 o'clock, with people spilling out of the nearby pubs. It was also cold, and by the time the street had grown quiet, Kaisa had needed the loo. The carpet on the wide wooden stairs was so threadbare, that when Kaisa climbed the stairs to the bathroom on the floor above, her footsteps echoed through the house. Now, as she listened to Rose, Kaisa wondered if she'd been foolish to take a job without knowing any of the details. She'd been too keen to leave Helsinki, what with all that had happened with Matti, her mother's constant queries on what she was going to next, and the visit from her sister's boyfriend from Lapland looming on the horizon. Kaisa had missed his arrival by two days, something she was sure had been carefully arranged by Sirkka. Still, both her mother and sister had shed a few tears when they'd said goodbye at Helsinki airport. There was no going back to Helsinki now.

Her old bank manager in Helsinki had let her down too; he said jobs were hard to come by, even with Kaisa's degree. The job in London was her only chance to move on, to make something of her life. Plus being in England meant she was closer to Peter, even though she knew she was a fool to think they'd patch things up again. Kaisa was still getting money from Peter, but she knew it was wrong of her to keep taking it, and besides, there were no guarantees that this would continue. Especially if he heard she was working for a publication like *Adam's Apple*. Kaisa didn't even have to ask if the magazine was against the Polaris missiles – it was written all over the women's faces.

'Take it, and read it later.' Rose added, 'Listen we're all going to the pub, you wanna come?'

'Sure,' Kaisa said. 'But, I need to know about the job ...'

Rose looked at her, and laughed. 'Oh my, of course.' She pulled out a sheet of paper which had a carbon copy behind it and handed it to Kaisa. 'There's a café around the corner. Go there and read this through, and if it's all OK, come back and sign it, and we'll be all set.'

Kaisa found the café. It was empty apart from an older woman wearing a coat tied up with a piece of string and surrounded by plastic bags, all filled to the brim. The place smelt of fried food and had heavily steamed up windows. Kaisa ordered a cup of black coffee and sat down at a table covered with a red-and-blue checked cloth. She began reading her contract.

~

Rose had insisted Kaisa should come to the party, which was being held in a disused warehouse near the offices of *Adam's Apple*. Kaisa knew she was worried about her.

'You spend all your time just working and sleeping. You're a young woman, you need a sex life!'

Kaisa had blushed; even after six weeks at the magazine, where sex was talked about as if it was as normal as eating bread, she still hadn't got used to discussing freely what people got up to in their bedrooms. Or in public toilets, or parks, or stationery cupboards, or wherever. (In London in summer, anything went). Two of the women working at the magazine were lesbians, and due to the lack of a boyfriend, she assumed, she'd been asked many times if she was one too. Kaisa always vehemently denied it, but the truth was that she really didn't have any appetite for sex at all. With either a man or a woman.

Whenever she thought about sex, her mind wandered back to her last two meetings with Matti, and the photographs, then his death, and the awful funeral. Then she thought of Tom, and his flaccid manhood, and she wanted to cry. If she couldn't have Peter, she didn't want anyone, she decided. She'd been surprised by how little she'd cried since being in London. She'd got herself a little portable TV in the bedsit, and spent most evenings watching English TV, which was so much better than the programmes they showed in Finland. Only on her two wedding anniversaries had she shed a little tear. On the first one, a year after their shot-gun wedding in Portsmouth – hastily arranged after Peter failed to get a certificate in time for their planned marriage in Finland a month later – Kaisa had bought herself a red rose and a bottle of white wine. She'd finished the whole bottle watching *Coronation Street*, followed by *Brookside*. It had only been a problem because the day fell on the Saturday of a Bank Holiday weekend, when she had little to do but wander around Portobello Market buying vegetables for the week ahead. On the anniversary of the 'proper' wedding, 2 June, a Sunday four weeks later, she'd hoped in vain Peter would remember and send her a card. For days afterwards, Kaisa had scanned the post, but nothing came. And why should it, she'd scolded herself. Her sister and mother remembered the date, and had phoned her, taking turns to speak. But it was difficult to talk in private in the hall downstairs, where the landlady and her slimy boyfriend could hear every word. Knowing how she'd felt on the anniversary in May, she had decided to go out for the day, and had walked from her bedsit in Notting Hill to Hyde Park. It had been a beautiful sunny day and she'd bought an ice cream and watched boys play football on the grass. She remembered how Peter had broken her heart in Hyde Park by telling her they should be free to see other people while Kaisa was finishing her studies and unable – and unwilling, it has to be said – to move to England to be with him.

She felt as if she'd seized up since Matti's death, as if everything had closed up down there. With those awful pictures, and what Vappu had told her about Matti's life after Kaisa had left him, she felt that she'd had too much sex in her life already. Thoughts of Duncan entered her mind, and she brushed his memory away. Men were bad news, all of them. This was her new life, working on a worthwhile feminist cause in London. Why was it so important to be sleeping with someone as well?

But in the end Kaisa agreed to go to Rose's party. She knew she would need to talk to other people eventually, people other than her colleagues, all of whom were women, except for the magazine delivery boy, Jack, who appeared once a month on the doorstep of the offices in Clerkenwell. He was an overconfident young lad, who joked with the women about lesbians and 'giving them all one'. Rose and the rest of the editorial staff put up with him, calling him a prat to his face, to which the boy laughed and said, 'You're gagging for it, admit it.'

The warehouse party was to celebrate someone's birthday. It was a friend of Rose's but Kaisa didn't know her. She was turning 30 and had a rich daddy, who was paying for it, Rose told Kaisa. 'Free booze, lots of good-looking men and women,' Rose said and grinned. 'Let your hair down for once, Kaisa.'

At home in her bedsit, which was damp and cold even in June, Kaisa spent a stupid amount of time deciding what to wear. Finally, after trying on several trousers, jeans and top combinations, she decided on a cotton dress, which she'd bought from Miss Selfridge, a heady moment after the last issue of *Adam's Apple* had come out. She'd written an article on the benefits of proportional representation, and how it would help women be better represented in parliament. It was her first long piece in the magazine, and she'd felt on such a high, she'd gone to Oxford Street and bought the dress and a pair of high-heeled shoes to go with it. For weeks, the dress and the shoes had stayed unworn in the small wardrobe in her bedsit. There didn't ever seem to be an occasion to wear them. Kaisa's daily uniform was what Peter would have called her 'boy clothes', jeans and checked shirt with a jumper if it was cold. The dress, in contrast, was very feminine; it had a gypsy-style ruched skirt and an off-the-shoulder top. The summer had arrived in London and the weather was warm. She couldn't wear a bra with the dress, but she'd lost nearly five kilos during her time in London, so that wouldn't be a problem. She just didn't have an appetite, and often skipped having an evening meal altogether. It wasn't so easy to cook in her small bedsit, especially when she had to sleep in the same room, with the smells of the cooking lingering into the night.

Kaisa added a narrow gold belt to the outfit, pulling it tightly across her waist. She put on some make-up, including eyeliner, and even wore lip gloss for once. When she gazed at herself in the mirror that she'd put against one wall of the bedsit, she approved of the way she looked. Perhaps it was time she trapped, she thought, and smiled at the memory of an expression Peter often used. Don't think about him, she reproached herself, and closed the door behind her.

EIGHTEEN

'C'mon it'll be fun,' Val said and pulled Peter's hand. They were in London, walking from Farringdon tube station towards an address that Val had written on a piece of paper. Peter had asked to see the address, so that he could plan their journey on the tube, but Val had pulled the piece of paper from his hand and laughed. 'I live here!' Peter had got hold of her tiny waist and tried to wrestle the paper out of her hand, but she'd not given it up. Instead, they'd ended up on her bed, making love for the second time that morning.

Peter had weekend leave and had come up to London to stay with Val in the house she shared with five other people in Earl's Court. It was a massive Victorian townhouse with the bedrooms arranged over four floors. Val's bedroom was on the top floor, in a former attic space, which had been turned into a room with two dormer windows overlooking the rooftops of West London. Val said she knew the girl whose party it was, and she insisted on going. Peter didn't like parties anymore, not since the court martial. There was just too much to explain when people asked him what he did. When they found out he was in the Navy, they wanted to know all about his career to date. He hadn't learned to lie properly yet, and often left a silence in the air, revealing that there was more to his past than he was saying.

Peter now felt almost equally uncomfortable walking along the London streets, not knowing where he was, or where they were going. He wasn't sure if Val deliberately put him in situations where he felt uneasy. Earlier that day, when he'd arrived on her doorstep, Val had introduced him to two of her fellow housemates as 'My bit on the side — or, no sorry, I'm his bit on the side!' When Peter had shaken hands with a lanky boy with long blond Duran Duran-style hair, and what Peter could have sworn was make-up around his eyes, she'd added, 'And he's in the Navy.' The inevitable questions had followed, which Peter had tried to put a stop to by saying he was a submariner, based in Plymouth.

'So you're not firing nukes as your job then,' the boy, who'd introduced himself as Josh, had said, giving Peter a hard stare. 'One of them,' Peter had thought and decided he needed to be careful about what he said.

The second person sitting at a long pine table in the dark kitchen accessed through a long corridor on the ground floor of the house, was a girl with spiky, mousey-coloured hair. She wore trousers that were too large, bunched up around the waist. Her oversized T-shirt was tucked into the trousers, making her look a bit like a clown. She was wearing no make-up, apart from very red lipstick. 'I'm Jenny, she said and shook Peter's hand, holding onto it for a bit longer than was comfortable. Peter thought the girl was a little older than Val or Josh, and it turned out she was the owner of the place, and occupied the entire first floor. 'I'm a nurse,' she informed Peter. Later, up in her room, Val told Peter Jenny had inherited the house from her parents, who'd been killed in a car accident a few years back. She was their only child and didn't know what to do with herself now she was on her own, so she put an ad in the paper to share her house with students.

Peter could hear the loud music of the party a few streets away before he saw the disused warehouse. The open windows on the second floor were flung open to the warm June evening, and the flickering lights of a disco ball gave the street below an unreal feel.

NINETEEN

The party was packed with people, all talking, laughing and dancing. Waiters carrying trays of drinks and canapés moved through the large space, which doubled as the dance floor, although many people swayed along to the music in small groups wherever they stood. There were fairy lights and pink balloons emblazoned with the number 30, and Kaisa wondered which one of the many women in expensive-looking satin dresses was the birthday girl.

Kaisa sought out Rose, who stood next to an older man with a huge moustache.

'You look lovely,' Rose said into Kaisa's ear. Smiling, she added, 'This is Roger.'

Roger took Kaisa by surprise by kissing her quickly on the mouth. The brittle blond hairs on his upper lip tickled Kaisa, and she laughed to hide her embarrassment.

The music was so loud, even at the far end of the room that you couldn't talk normally. Frankie Goes to Hollywood was playing, and Kaisa noticed how the space looked exactly like the one in the *Two Tribes* video. All that was needed was a boxing ring and sawdust on the floor. They were joined by staff from *Adam's Apple,* and Rose began a shouted-out conversation with them about the next issue. They were in disagreement about the cover, a discussion that had started in the office on Friday afternoon. Kaisa didn't want to take part, because she saw both sides of the argument. Besides, she was the newest member of the team, and didn't feel she had enough experience to know what would be best – a commercial cover that might pull in more readers, or a punchier one, conveying the message of feminism to readers and non-readers alike. On Friday, there'd been a lot of heated talk about what *Adam's Apple* really stood for versus concerns about the falling readership. Rose was in the latter camp; she'd been brought in to revive the magazine, Kaisa had learned, and wanted a more mainstream feel. Some of the older members of the editorial team felt she was going too far. Kaisa knew Rose would be looking for her support, but late on Friday afternoon Kaisa hadn't been able to decide which course was best. She'd said nothing and kept her head down, preparing her latest article.

Kaisa moved away from the group, and lit a cigarette. It was a warm June night, and she was glad she'd worn the new gypsy dress that left her shoulders bare. Still, she felt hot, so she moved towards the large windows to get some air and cool down. It was when she looked out onto the street below that she saw them. Or him.

It couldn't be him, surely. Kaisa's eyes must be playing tricks on her. Or could it? Kaisa leaned further over the open window and stretched her neck for a better view of the two people who stood in the spot below the streetlight. Kaisa froze when she saw it really was Peter. He was holding the hand of a slight, dark-haired girl. 'Jackie?' Kaisa thought with mounting horror. Peter was wearing jeans and a cotton shirt, and the girl wore a pretty little flower-patterned dress. It wasn't Jackie after all. My, the man moves fast, Kaisa thought, but she immediately reproached herself – hadn't she tried to have sex with Tom? And tonight, she was on the lookout, whether she admitted it or not. On her feet, the unknown girl wore cowboy boots. The look suited her. Although she couldn't fully see their faces, Kaisa could hear Peter and the girl laughing as they stepped inside the door.

What was Peter, a naval officer, doing in an artsy party in London? Kaisa panicked, and wanted to flee. But she knew Peter and the girl must now be coming up the stairs. Kaisa scanned the vast space for an exit sign, or another entrance. Suddenly she heard a group coming through a door behind her. She put her cigarette out, slipped past them and climbed a steel staircase onto the roof of the building. She was out of breath when she reached the roof. She'd been so flustered, she hadn't counted the number of floors. When she reached the roof, she noticed that someone had put cushions on the ledges to make temporary seats. Kaisa scanned the area, but couldn't see anyone there. The noise of traffic and the hum of people standing outside a pub a few streets away drifted towards Kaisa. Sighing with relief, she sat down on the nearest seat. She needed to think. For whatever reason, Peter was at the party, and whoever that pretty girl was, Kaisa didn't want to see either of them. At least it wasn't Jackie, Kaisa thought; still, she fought back tears when she thought about Peter and this new girl. Really she shouldn't have been surprised. Even before they were married, Kaisa had to fight off the girls vying for Peter's attention. She'd known that he'd moved on as Pammy's letter had indicated. His letters containing her allowance were as short as ever. Kaisa felt bad about continuing to accept Peter's money, but her salary was so small she needed the extra cash to survive in London. When she'd told Rose about Peter's allowance, Rose had said, 'You're still married, he has a duty to support you.' Kaisa felt that was a little hypocritical, but didn't want to say so to Rose; besides, she was sure her boss would come up with a perfectly well thought-out reason for Kaisa still being entitled to some of Peter's money. Something to do with the inequality in wages, Kaisa supposed. To her surprise, when Kaisa had told Peter about her new address, he hadn't commented on her move to London. She hadn't told him about *Adam's Apple,* just that she'd got a job working on a magazine. Peter hadn't even asked if she was working for *Sonia,* so he was obviously utterly uninterested in Kaisa's life. Kaisa realised she'd been hoping that he was simply still angry, and that with time he'd come around. How foolish she'd been! It was obvious he wasn't in the least bit concerned about Kaisa; as long as he paid her off each month, his conscience was clear. Kaisa could feel the familiar anger surge inside her. How was it possible even after all these months of not seeing him, and having a new, meaningful career (in London!), and after all they'd been through, that Peter could still ignite such emotion in her?

Kaisa shivered in the balmy air of the June night. She needed to think rationally. She would have to leave the party soon, but she needed to be sure she could slip out without being seen by Peter and his new girlfriend. Just thinking that thought made Kaisa feel short of breath. As she gasped for air, she told herself to calm down.

'What are you doing here?'

Kaisa hadn't noticed that the door to the roof space had opened, but she recognised his voice immediately. She got up and looked at Peter. He had put on some weight, she saw, but it suited him. His arms looked more muscular under his striped cotton shirt, and his face even more angular. He stood in the doorway, which made his hair and eyes look darker against the light coming from the stairwell below. He moved towards Kaisa and got a packet of cigarettes out of his jeans pocket.

'I could ask you the same thing,' Kaisa managed to say.

With shaking hands, she took a Marlboro Light out of the packet Peter offered her, and waited for him to find his zippo lighter. As if in a dream, she put the cigarette to her lips and bent down to catch the flame from the lighter between Peter's cupped hands. She saw the zippo had a ship's crest on it and guessed it must be that of HMS *Orion*. Kaisa pulled a drag and watched Peter light his own cigarette.

'How are you,' Peter asked, his face showing no emotion.

Suddenly Kaisa's knees felt weak, and she sat back down on the raised bit of the roof. 'I'm fine.'

Now Peter grinned at her, 'Fancy seeing you here.'

Kaisa looked at him in surprise; it was as if the old Peter was back. 'Yeah, I wasn't expecting you either.'

Peter took a seat next to Kaisa, and for a moment they sat side by side, smoking their cigarettes.

'So how is life in the big city?' Peter asked, turning his face towards Kaisa.

She told him about *Adam's Apple,* and about her bedsit in Notting Hill.

'A feminist magazine, eh? That must suit you down to the ground.' Kaisa could hear the bitterness in his voice.

Kaisa took a deep drag on the cigarette. 'Yeah, Rose got me the job. She's invested a lot of money in it and wanted me to help her.'

Peter's mouth was a straight line. 'That's cosy.' He got up and, with his back to her, gazed across the London skyline. Kaisa spoke to his back, 'Really, Peter, you must believe me, he's the last person in the world I want to see. And Rose has been very good to me. I haven't seen him and Rose isn't speaking to him either. She thinks what he did was despicable.'

Peter gazed down at her, and Kaisa noticed his eyes looked sad. 'He still writes to you, though, doesn't he?'

Kaisa's heart raced. So it had been Peter who had forwarded Duncan's letter to her in Helsinki. She could feel tears well up inside, but she controlled herself. 'I had nothing to do with that.'

Peter turned around and sat next to her again. 'Really?'

'Really. I tore it up, and wouldn't dream of writing back to him. I have no feelings – apart from anger – towards him.' Kaisa had placed her hand on Peter's arm. Looking down at it, Peter said, 'You and me both.' She quickly took her hand away and the two sat side by side, watching the view over nighttime London in silence. There was an office building opposite, all its windows dark apart from one.

'Someone's working overtime,' Kaisa said, and stubbed out her cigarette on the lead roof.

'Or having it off with the boss,' Peter said, flicking his cigarette over the edge of the roof.

Kaisa turned her head towards Peter. 'Sorry, bad joke, in the circumstances,' he said. He was smiling, and nudged Kaisa. She also laughed and they sat quietly for a few moments more, then spoke at the same time.

'I wanted to ...' said Kaisa. 'Perhaps I should ...' said Peter.

'You go first,' Kaisa laughed.

They argued for a while about who should speak first, and Kaisa felt the awkwardness diminish by the second. 'No, you go, no you ...' Eventually Peter spoke. 'Look Kaisa, I was wondering if we should talk about the future.'

'Yes, I was thinking the same.'

'Go on.' Peter's voice was soft and kind, and his eyes had the familiar tender look in them. She wanted to lean across and put her head on his shoulder and ask for his forgiveness. But the image of Peter with the unknown girl laughing on the street below reminded her that he was no longer hers.

'I am not earning as much as I'd like. The magazine isn't really making money yet, so,' she began.

'It's OK, you're still my wife. I'll carry on helping you as long as you want.'

'Thank you,' Kaisa said.

'It's OK.' Peter put his hand on Kaisa's knee. Kaisa looked up at him and before she could say anything, Peter had put his lips on hers. His kiss was urgent, and he placed his arms around Kaisa. She relaxed into his embrace. Her heart was pounding.

Kaisa wasn't sure if she saw the girl first, or felt her punch Peter in the back.

'What the hell is going on here?'

The dark-haired girl was standing in front of them, with her hands on her hips, staring at Peter and Kaisa, who'd detached herself from Peter and was staring back at the girl. Peter quickly stood up, 'Look Val, this is,'

'I don't care who the hell she is! I leave you alone for a minute, and you sneak up here and make out with a bloody ...' The girl gave Kaisa a look up and down, and continued, 'a bloody blonde bimbo!'

Kaisa couldn't help herself, and let out a short laugh, or more like a snort. A bimbo, her? She looked at Peter to see what he would say, or do. Surely he would tell the girl to F off? Surely the kiss meant they were back together, or at least they'd try to patch things up again? Or?

Peter took the girl into his arms, and even though she resisted at first, she soon gave in and listened to Peter's words: 'Look, it meant nothing. Kaisa is my ex, and one thing led to another ...'

Kaisa stared at the pair in front of her. Did she hear Peter correctly? It meant nothing! Kaisa got up and ran through the open door and down the stairs. When she reached the floor where the party was, she heard Peter's voice call out behind her, but she ignored it and ran through the room and down the stairs again. It wasn't until she was sitting at the back of a black cab that she let herself cry.

TWENTY

Peter got a first class ticket back to Plymouth because he just didn't have the patience to share a compartment with sailors he knew, as he had on the way up to London. He wanted to read the *Telegraph* and think how he could untangle himself from the web of women he'd become caught up in.

First there was Sam. Sex with the soft-skinned Wren was very satisfying, and she was always available. She was also kind, and cared for him, as he'd found out during an awful night when Peter had come back to the base from the GX alone. They'd bumped into each other in the corridor. He was very drunk, could hardly stand up, but Sam put his arm around her slender shoulders and quietly guided him into the correct cabin, undressed him and even brought him a glass of water and a bucket from the bathrooms, in case he was sick later. To be truthful, Peter didn't remember all that was said, but the next morning, when he woke up with the most awful hangover and tried to piece together the events of the previous night, he knew he'd poured his heart out to her. He remembered how he'd tried to take her clothes off for a quickie, and she'd just laughed and said, 'Another time, darling Peter.'

It was that word, 'Darling' that had unsettled him. Following that drunken night, he'd only been with her once or twice. He'd tried to play it cool with Sam, to show her that it wasn't serious. He'd told her from the start that his life was too complicated for a relationship, so she must know. But she was there, always around at the base. They still greeted each other in the wardroom, but he saw the yearning in her eyes, and as much as he liked the girl, he couldn't cope with that. It was difficult because the refit on HMS *Orion* kept overrunning; they should have sailed weeks ago. Now he was single again, he relished the time away at sea. It was different before, when it had meant leaving Kaisa.

Kaisa.

Thinking about Kaisa turned his thoughts immediately to Val. For some reason, he felt guilty about his affair with the young student. He was a little older than her, that was true, but only by a couple of years. It wasn't as if he was cradle snatching!

Sex with Val was a different thing altogether. Once, when they'd managed to sneak into her room at her parents' place in Plymouth (Peter hadn't met them and had no intention of doing so), Val had bitten his nipple during sex. Because they'd needed to be quiet, Peter couldn't cry out, even though the pain had seared through him, taking him by surprise. Somehow, that had made it better, though. There was plenty of passion with Val, and just thinking about her in the empty carriage, with the motion of the train gently rocking his body, Peter felt himself harden.

But she'd not let him back into her bed since she'd surprised him with Kaisa on the roof. Peter had to plead with her just to let him back into the house in Earl's Court, and then she'd made him sleep on the sofa in the lounge on the second floor. He'd had a disturbed night, with various residents of the house coming in at different times. Waking early, he had tried to call Kaisa on the number she'd given him in one of her long letters. He wanted to hear her voice, and was surprised to find she wasn't at home. Did she have someone else too? Someone she'd run to after kissing him? Peter waited for half an hour for her to ring back, but when the telephone in the hall remained silent, he snuck back into Val's bedroom upstairs and gathered his things. She was sprawled on her bed, wearing just her T-shirt. Her feet were protruding from under the blanket that covered the lower part of her body. From the contour of the thin covering, Peter could make out her feminine shape and remembered the small patch of dark hair between her legs. He could see her small breasts poking out from underneath her T-shirt. It took all his willpower to control himself and not take her into his arms. When he was at the door, he went back and kissed her forehead. Her lips were pink, and her eyelashes dark against her pale skin. He touched her cheek, but Val just murmured and turned her head away. He left the room on tiptoe and made his way to Paddington.

TWENTY-ONE

On the Sunday after the party, Kaisa stayed in bed as long as she could. By twelve o'clock she couldn't read anymore, and decided to go and get a newspaper and then telephone Rose to explain why she'd left without saying goodbye. There was a telephone fixed to the wall on the ground floor of the house, and as she lifted the heavy black receiver she saw her name, or a version of it, written on a folded piece of paper, stuck with a red pin on the noticeboard. It was the custom at the house, which contained five bedsits, to leave telephone messages on the board. Once again, whoever had taken the message hadn't bothered to come up the stairs to find her, nor could they spell her name correctly. Kaisa sighed and read the message.

'Keesi, someone posh called Peter left a message to call him back.' There was a London number below. On the spur of the moment, Kaisa lifted the receiver and dialled the number.

She had to wait five or six rings before anyone answered. 'Hello?'

Kaisa recognised the voice straight away. Surprising

herself with her gumption, she said, 'Can I speak with Peter, please?'

There was a short silence at the other end. 'Who's calling?' Val said.

'It's Peter's wife.'

'Just a minute.'

Kaisa held the receiver with both hands and waited.

After a while, Val came back to the telephone and said, 'Sorry, he's not in.'

'But ...' Kaisa began, but Val had already put the phone down at the other end, and all Kaisa could hear was the long tone of an empty line. He hadn't wanted to speak to her after all! Kaisa sat down on the rickety chair that the landlady had placed next to the phone, and thought for a moment. Had Peter's kiss been a reflex, a habit he'd not been able to shake off? Didn't it mean anything after all? Had it been a mistake, just as he'd told the girl, Val? Kaisa imagined the scene at the other end of the line: Val going to tell Peter that his wife was calling, and Peter shaking his head. Perhaps they were now in bed, laughing at Kaisa's eagerness to get back together with him? Kaisa shook her head. If that was the case, why had he phoned her in the first place?

Kaisa went back up to her bedsit and dug out a picture she had of Peter. She regretted she had no wedding photos of them together. In Finland, where they'd had the big wedding after the hasty registry office affair in Portsmouth, wedding photos were traditionally taken in a studio just before the ceremony. But Peter had said that was crazy; the groom wasn't supposed to see the bride in her wedding dress until she walked up the aisle. Instead, he wanted photos outside the church with all the guests and confetti flying above their heads. But the Finnish photographer wasn't used to taking wedding photos in the open air, and the resulting portraits were dark and terrible.

They'd decided not to develop many of the pictures, and had ended up just giving one to Peter's parents and another to her mother and Sirkka. The photo of Peter that Kaisa kept in her purse was taken a few months before they were married. It showed him sitting on the casing of a submarine, wearing a white uniform shirt, with the cuffs rolled up, and resting his arms on his knees. Wearing a cap, he looked relaxed, with his head turned towards the camera, laughing at whoever was taking the photo. The sun was behind him, and in the background you could see the dockyard, with a large crane just to the left of Peter. Kaisa always wondered who had taken the picture, and who Peter had been smiling at? When she'd asked him he said he couldn't remember.

On Monday morning, Kaisa came into the office of *Adam's Apple* early. She wanted to get a head start on the article she was preparing. She wasn't yet as confident in her English as a native speaker would have been, so it took her a lot longer to write the pieces Rose was now asking her to produce for every issue. This one was about what it was like to come and live in the UK as a foreign woman. Kaisa had interviewed three different people for the piece. In Brixton, in a council flat that smelled of strange spices, she'd interviewed Suni, an Indian lady, who wore a colourful sari and offered her home-made almond sweets. A lady from Jamaica had come into the offices, and spoken so heartrendingly about her first weeks in Britain, nearly twenty years ago, that the whole office had been in tears. Apart from Jenny, who'd balled her hands into fists and said, 'Those bastard skinheads, I could cut their fucking balls off.' But to Kaisa the tragedy of her story was the reaction – or lack of it – of ordinary people in England.

Imagining she'd be first in the office, Kaisa was surprised to see Rose sitting at her desk at the end of the room.

'Hi, Kaisa,' Rose said and looked up from the pile of papers in front of her. She'd recently started wearing a pair of reading glasses, with a golden string, which hung on her chest when she removed them, as she did now.

Leaving her handbag at her desk, Kaisa headed for the little kitchenette off the main office. She was holding a packet of her special coffee. Good coffee was the one thing she missed about Finland – the instant variety that everyone seemed to drink in England was more like muddy water – but about a month ago she'd made a discovery. In the streets around the office, she'd found several good coffee houses, mostly run by Italians, and she had recently found a new way to have proper coffee in the office, without having to buy an expensive perco-lator. Packets of single-cup ground coffee were stocked by a nearby shop. Every Monday she bought a packet of ten on her way to work and they just about lasted the five days. She could ill afford to offer them to others, but as everything was shared in the office she always asked around just in case.

'Would you like a cup of coffee?' she asked Rose from the doorway.

'Yes, please, but instant will do for me,' Rose said and smiled.

When Kaisa came back with two cups of hot, steaming coffee, Rose said, 'What happened to you on Saturday?'

Kaisa felt pang of guilt; after the unsettling call with Peter's girlfriend (just thinking about those two words made her chest fill with pain), she had completely forgotten to tele-phone Rose. She slumped down at her desk. 'Peter was there.'

'What?' Rose got up from her desk at the other end of the room and came to sit in front of Kaisa. She took Kaisa's hands in hers and said, 'Are you alright? What happened?'

Kaisa told Rose about seeing Peter, fleeing to the roof, how they'd talked and how it had seemed like old times. As if the past few months and the awful business with Duncan and

Peter's court martial hadn't happened. 'And then he kissed me.'

'Oh, Kaisa,' Rose said.

From her face, Kaisa couldn't determine whether she thought this was a good thing or a catastrophe.

'And then his girlfriend saw us and punched Peter.'

'Oh, my God, was he alright?'

Suddenly Kaisa began to giggle; the whole thing seemed like a scene from a very bad film. But Rose regarded her with a serious face. 'What happened then?'

Kaisa told Rose what Peter had said to the girl, that the kiss hadn't meant anything. 'Peter told the girl I was just his ex.' Kaisa said. 'And then I missed his call on Saturday morning. When I called the number he'd left, the girl said he wasn't there.'

'Oh, Kaisa,' Rose said again. She rubbed Kaisa's hands, and cocking her head, gazed at her face. 'You still want to get back together with him, don't you?'

Kaisa looked down at her lap. 'I do still love him, but I don't know if we can ever get back together. I love my job here, and I'd never be able to give that up.' Tears were running down Kaisa's face. 'So I don't think our marriage was ever going to work.'

Rose hugged Kaisa. 'Oh you poor, poor love.'

When they heard the door open at the bottom of the stairs, and the voices of the other women, Rose quickly fetched a small packet of tissues from her desk and handed them to Kaisa, who fled to the cold bathroom next to the kitchenette. There, looking at her puffy red eyes, she decided enough was enough. She needed to face facts. Peter had moved on, that was probably why he'd called her on Saturday morning. To tell her the kiss was a mistake, and that she should forget about it. And Kaisa decided she would. She, too, would move on. She would make an effort to find somebody too. She'd say 'Yes' to the after-work drinks at the pub, she'd even go to the clubs Jenny and Barbara were forever talking about. She would at last have some fun.

TWENTY-TWO

Three weeks after she'd seen Peter at the party, and the kiss, Kaisa still hadn't heard anything further from him. There was no letter, no phone call. Kaisa hadn't told Peter where the offices of *Adam's Apple* were, so the only phone number and address he had for her was the Notting Hill bedsit. After she'd missed the call on the Saturday, Kaisa had stuck a note next to the telephone asking everyone to PLEASE let her know about any calls. Of course, this was what was supposed to happen anyway, but the others in the house seemed to have nocturnal lives; Kaisa very rarely saw anyone else.

Kaisa knew Peter could have gone off to sea. Still, serving in a diesel boat, he'd have the opportunity to write and post a letter even at sea, unlike when he served on the nuclear subs, or the Polaris ones. Kaisa shivered when she thought about the awful, long weeks she'd spent alone in Helensburgh. It felt as if all of it, the friendship with Lyn at the peace camp outside the Faslane naval base, the brief, but life-changing affair with Duncan, the disapproval of the other Navy wives, which she'd felt so acutely during the whole of their time in Scotland, had happened to someone else. Out of all the other wives she'd got to know in Scotland, she'd only been in touch with Pammy since leaving Helensburgh for Helsinki. Pammy and Nigel now had a little baby girl. Kaisa had sent a long letter of congratulations and a parcel containing a pale pink teddy bear with the softest fur and a friendly face, which she'd found and fallen in love with at Hamley's on Regent Street. Pammy wrote back and begged Kaisa to visit; Nigel had gone on patrol the day after the baby was born and Pammy was desperate for company. She wrote to say how she still felt responsible for all that had happened between Kaisa and Peter, and for the fight with Duncan. Of course, it was true that had Pammy not told Kaisa's secret to Nigel, and he in turn hadn't told Peter, perhaps the fight in the pool at the base might never have happened. But Kaisa knew it was really nothing to do with Pammy; it was all her fault, and hers alone. She was the one who had let Duncan into her bed, and then gone and told Pammy about it. So it seemed strange how so many people around her felt guilty about the affair. Even Rose, her boss, felt bad about it, because she had encouraged the friendship between Duncan and Kaisa, not realising that her cousin had designs on her. But Kaisa had benefited from Rose's guilt, she was sure of it. Why else would Rose have invited her to London and given her such a crucial role in the magazine? It was true that *Adam's Apple* had no formal management structure, but everyone recognised that Rose was their editor, and Kaisa, as the newcomer, was the junior member of the team. Kaisa had also learned that when Rose had joined the magazine, she'd brought a substantial amount of money with her. It was these funds that had kept the magazine going, and before Rose had stepped in, there'd been talk of closing down the press. This made Kaisa feel even worse; in effect, Rose was funding her career. So Kaisa worked as hard as she could, helping Rose with research, writing articles whenever she was asked, even making cups of tea and coffee for everyone.

But the salary from *Adam's Apple* wasn't enough to sustain Kaisa, so she – to her shame – continued to accept the £200 from Peter, which he now paid directly into her bank account once a month. When Kaisa talked to Rose about taking the money, her boss was still adamant that she deserved it and she shouldn't feel bad.

After the party, Kaisa got into the habit of going to the pub with the rest of the girls after work. She'd have one pint of beer with them (all the women drank pints unlike the lady-like halves that the Navy wives ordered) in The Horseshoe pub at the end of Farringdon Close. The Horseshoe reminded Kaisa of The Palmerston Arms in Portsmouth; it had the same black paint outside, beneath a white-clad upper storey where she presumed the landlord lived, just like the publican parents of Jeff, Peter's best man. The bar filled half the pub, and there was even a snug at the back, around the far corner, just as there was at The Palmerston. There were no bunkettes, however, only round tables and chairs, in mock mahogany. The crowd in the pub mostly consisted of staff from other small publications around the area, and the team from *Adam's Apple* was often viewed with something alternating between fear and mockery. The other crowd, the working men, who came in their dirty overalls, splattered with paint, would nudge each other, make jokes under their breath, and grin in the women's direction. On occasion, the women, tired of the jibes, would go to the Three Kings at the other end of Clerkenwell Close. Or if they were celebrating a new issue, or a large donation, they'd cross the railway tracks and go into the Coach and Horses, which was frequented by reporters from the *Observer* or the *Guardian,* whose well-known offices were a few paces away from the large public house.

On a Thursday in late August, the staff of *Adam's Apple*

were celebrating their best distribution figures since Rose took over the editorial team. They'd sold over 1,500 copies of the summer issue, and Rose's latest cover, for which she'd again had to fight hard, was deemed a great success. When Rose had opened the envelope containing the sales report, she'd thrown the sheet of paper up in the air and declared that the drinks would be on her after work. They had their first pints at The Horseshoe and then made their way to the Coach and Horses. Usually nights at this larger, and a lot posher pub, where the lounge and the rowdier bar were separated by a half-glazed wall, would go on until closing time. Alternatively, they'd move south to the bars around Fleet Street. As it was a Thursday, when the women entered the bar it was already full to bursting. Rose knew many of the *Guardian* reporters who drank there, so there were a few whistles and loud clapping when they entered. Everyone there had read the same sales reports and knew of the success of Rose's new venture. Most of the men in the pubs of Clerkenwell were a lot older than Kaisa, but on this night her eyes met a tall man, leaning on the bar, next to a greying man in a waistcoat who was talking animatedly with Rose. Kaisa recognised Roger from the warehouse party; she wondered if Rose was having a relationship with him.

Kaisa was handed her drink – she'd switched to a G&T because too much beer made her feel bloated – and was standing alone, separated from her colleagues by the general commotion their entrance had caused. The man next to Roger was watching Kaisa, and when their eyes met, he lifted his pint to her in a greeting, his smile revealing the whitest teeth Kaisa had ever seen. Kaisa smiled back, feeling a warmth in her body, and a flutter in her stomach. The man wore a white shirt, the sleeves rolled up on account of a heatwave in London, and a waistcoat and matching trousers in dark grey stripes, which were obviously part of a suit. He had very dark features, a black, almost shiny, mop of hair, and brown eyes. Kaisa hadn't felt a flutter like this in months, even years. The man leaned over to say something to his shorter friend, and walked over to Kaisa.

'Hello, I'm Ravi.' He offered his hand and for a moment she just stood there, holding onto his warm, firm handshake and sinking deep into those dark eyes. Ravi had thick, almost feminine eyelashes, making it look as if he'd applied eyeliner under and above his eyes. 'What's your name?' he continued when Kaisa didn't say anything.

'Kaisa,' she breathed. She hardly had any air left in her lungs.

'And you are part of this women's magazine?'

'Yes,' Kaisa said, and managed to move her gaze away from the man's eyes.

'Well, for an *Adam's Apple* reporter, you don't have much to say for yourself!' Ravi laughed.

Kaisa laughed and took a sip of her G&T. The laughter had managed to break the spell, and she asked, 'Are you from the *Guardian*?'

'Oh, lord, no. I work in the City.' Kaisa now realised, listening to the man's voice, that he was a posh boy.

It transpired that Ravi's parents were Indian. They'd come over to Britain during the partition, and Ravi, the youngest of five had been born in the UK. He'd been a clever boy at school and had gone to Cambridge, where he'd studied law. He worked for a Swiss bank.

'What are you doing here on a Thursday night?'

'Oh, one of my friends from Cambridge works for the *Observer*, so we often meet after work.'

Kaisa and Ravi talked all evening about everything and anything. Ravi told her about his traditional Indian family, about how his mother cooked the best dahl and chapatis in the world. Kaisa knew nothing about Indian culture – she'd been to an Indian restaurant while in London, of course, but Ravi said that food in those places was nothing like his mother's. He said how different life had been in Cambridge after his grammar school just outside Birmingham, where he'd grown up.

'I was the only Indian boy at my college in Cambridge, and although everyone was friendly, I knew I wasn't one of them,' Ravi said. Kaisa was mesmerized and wanted to lean over and kiss those full lips. She realised she was a little tipsy.

Kaisa knew exactly what he meant. She told Ravi about her studies at Hanken, where the others had come from wealthy Swedish-speaking families, and she'd felt like an outsider. She also told him about her move from Finland to the UK, and about her failed marriage.

'You're married?' Ravi asked, his face displaying surprise. 'You seem hardly old enough to be out of school!'

Kaisa looked down at her hands. If only he knew the whole sorry story, she thought. They talked until last orders were announced at 11 pm, and then Ravi told Kaisa he was going home.

'But I've enjoyed talking to you,' he said and looked deeply into Kaisa's eyes.

'Me too,' she smiled.

Kaisa gave Ravi her telephone number, and he thanked her, bowing his head. Kaisa realised the reason she was attracted to him, apart from his looks, was his polite and attentive manner. In London, men were different, much direct with their advances. Kaisa had got so used to the politeness and chivalry displayed by naval officers that she was shocked by British men's rowdy and leery manners in the pubs around the office. Jenny had laughed when Kaisa had mentioned this to her.

'Why should men open doors and let women go first?' She

laughed, but growing serious, added, 'It's patronising and sexist.'

Kaisa could only agree; still in her unvoiced opinion it was equally sexist to shout out lewd remarks at a woman passing a building site, or to bother a woman in a pub when she obviously didn't want to talk, or to shut a door in a woman's face if she didn't reciprocate a man's advances. In Finland, men had to be quite drunk before they approached you in such a forthright manner.

Ravi telephoned her in the office the next day. 'I didn't give you this number,' she laughed.

'No,' he said, 'but I knew I'd get hold of you here. I wondered if I could take you out tonight?'

Kaisa was so surprised, that she didn't immediately reply.

'If you're free, that is?'

'I'd love to.'

Ravi said he'd pick her up from work, and Kaisa panicked; she was wearing her 'boy clothes' to work again, and remembering how smart Ravi had looked the previous evening, she wanted to wear something more feminine.

When Kaisa told Rose about her date, and asked if she could take a long lunch hour, Rose gave Kaisa a £50 note and said, 'Treat yourself.' Kaisa tried to refuse the money, but Rose was so insistent, it suddenly seemed impolite to say no. She ran down the stairs from the office and made her way to Miss Selfridge on Oxford Street. It was still hot in London, so Kaisa looked for a summer dress in the sales. She found a floaty Laura Ashley-type cotton dress. It fitted her nicely, making her look slim, with a small waist. She found a pair of strappy wedge sandals, too, and then took the tube home to make a quick change and collect some make-up to apply later. When she got inside the house, and picked up the pile of post on the mat, she saw a blue airmail envelope addressed to her in familiar handwriting. She tore open the letter and read the words inside.

Kaisa,

    I hope you are keeping well. I'm away at sea, but will be back end of August. I wonder if we could talk? I will be in London on 28th. Meet me at Café des Amis, 11 Hanover Place, Covent Garden at 7 o'clock.

    Peter

Kaisa sat down on the thinly carpeted stairs, and reread the short letter. What did this mean? After the kiss, and the missed phone call, she hadn't heard from Peter for two whole months; no nearly three months, because it was now nearly the end of August and the party had been in mid-June. The letter was dated two weeks earlier, and the postmark was somewhere in Scotland, so he must have posted it from one of the small villages they occasionally docked at. But why did he want to meet? To talk about what? And today! Kaisa thought for a moment, but she knew, had known as soon as she read the letter, that she had to meet up with Peter. There was no getting around it. But she didn't have Ravi's number.

Kaisa got up and dialled the office number, 'Rose, I've had a letter from Peter. He's in London tonight and wants to meet up.'

'You must go,' Rose sighed, 'What will you tell Ravi?'

'That I've taken ill. A tummy bug? Is it alright if I stay at home this afternoon? Just in case he comes early or something. And can you talk to him, please?'

'OK,' Rose said, adding, 'Look, if you want to meet afterwards, we'll be in The Horseshoe until closing time.'

THE CAFÉ DES Amis was on a side street off St Martin's Lane.

Kaisa didn't know Covent Garden very well, and got lost before she saw the red neon lights of the restaurant. When she got inside, she was led down a set of stairs into a cellar, which was lit by dimmed lights and candles on red-check tablecloths. Peter was already there, sitting at a table in the far corner of the room. He looked tanned, and his hair was a little longer, touching the collar of his shirt. He stood up when Kaisa approached, and kissed her lightly on the cheek.

'You look good,' he said as they both sat down, and then seeming to regret his words, he coughed and added, 'I mean, that's a nice dress.'

'Thank you, so do you.' Kaisa had decided to wear her new purchase. She needed to have the confidence of looking her best when seeing Peter. She now gazed up at Peter's face and saw he was smiling. 'I mean you look good, too, not that your dress is nice.'

They both laughed.

'You got my letter,' Peter said after the waiter had given them menus and Peter had ordered a bottle of red wine.

'Yes, today!' Kaisa told him how she'd gone home during her lunch hour (she didn't say why), and had she not happened to do that she would not be sitting opposite him now.

'Well that's lucky then,' Peter said, but he wasn't smiling. His eyes were sad, as if he wished Kaisa hadn't got the letter in time. 'What will you have?' he added quickly before Kaisa could say anything. 'My treat.'

Kaisa ordered *moules marinieres* to start and a steak for mains. She felt like eating meat tonight, even though during her time in London she'd become almost vegetarian. Most of the girls in the office were fierce non-meat eaters, so it was just easier not to bring in ham sandwiches. Besides, Kaisa liked the lentil stews and bean salads they ate, and it was cheaper. Her new diet must have been why she'd lost so much weight. She was a size 10 now, whereas when she was married she'd sometimes had to go up to 14 in jeans and trousers.

'You've lost weight,' Peter said and lifted his glass.

Kaisa wondered if he was reading her mind.

They tasted the wine, which was very good, and again neither spoke for a while.

Kaisa could sense that there was something Peter wanted to say, but he didn't know how to get around to it. Kaisa was surprised by her own reaction to him. She had been very nervous on the tube, which was probably why she had got so hopelessly lost, but now, facing him, her feelings had settled. It was nice to see him looking so well. The gaunt look he'd had in June had disappeared. Perhaps he'd put on some more weight, or perhaps it was the sea air. 'You've been away?' she asked.

'Yes, got back on Wednesday. I've been in Pompey with Jeff.'

'Oh, how is he?'

'He's getting married.'

"Finally!' Kaisa laughed, 'is this one going to go through with it?'

'I think so, she's a Wren, so there should be no problem career-wise.'

'That's good. Send him my love.'

Peter's eyes met Kaisa's and he nodded. 'The wedding's tomorrow.'

'And you're not out with him? Shouldn't he be having his stag night now?'

'No, Milly, that's his wife-to-be, forbade it.'

'Well, miracles never cease,' Kaisa said.

They both laughed again. Kaisa wondered if he was going to take Val to the wedding, but stopped herself before formulating the question. Who Peter decided to date was nothing to do with her.

With the wine, their conversation grew warmer, and they

began reminiscing about Jeff's various girlfriends, which led to talk about their married quarter in King's Terrace and the incident of the lost car. Although it was Duncan who had driven the car into next door's garage, making Kaisa believe that the vehicle had been stolen, his name was studiously avoided by both of them.

'I'm sure the policemen had a good laugh afterwards. I can't believe I told them the car had a heart on its bonnet!' Kaisa said, giggling, remembering how Jeff had drawn the shape of a heart on their small Ford Fiesta after the registry office marriage in Portsmouth. Because Kaisa had neglected to wash the car for weeks afterwards, the heart remained a special feature of the car.

'Bloody Jeff. I got less money for it because of the corrosion that shaving foam caused!'

'You sold the Fiesta!' Kaisa exclaimed and they both laughed again at the sentimental associations of that car.

Towards the end of the meal, when they were both tucking into their puddings – they'd both asked for a *creme brûlée*, almost simultaneously – Peter grew quiet.

'I've missed you,' Kaisa said. She was surprised by her boldness, but suddenly thought this was her chance, and if Peter was here to talk about a reconciliation, why shouldn't she help him out a little? She reached across the table and touched his fingers. 'You know I regret everything that happened.'

'Everything?' Peter said, and hearing the hostility in his voice, the coldness that had made her flee Helensburgh for Helsinki, she removed her hand and looked down at her dessert. The waiter appeared with coffee, and they both thanked him. Kaisa was grateful for the interruption, and when the waiter had gone, she lifted her eyes once more to gauge if Peter's mood had permanently changed.

'I am sorry,' Peter said, 'and of course I've missed you too.'

Peter took hold of Kaisa's hand and she had to fight back tears. 'But we have to make a decision about the future.'

'What do you mean?'

Peter gave Kaisa a long, kind look, as if to warn her, 'I want a divorce.'

TWENTY-THREE

'How did it go?' Jackie asked as soon as Peter walked through the entrance at the bottom of the stairs.

'Fine' he replied and gave her a light kiss on her mouth.

'C'mon, did she make a fuss?'

'Let me have a drink first.'

Jackie was wearing a very short leather skirt, and when she bent down to pick up a glass from the sideboard, Peter could see the tops of her stockings. 'Gin and tonic OK?'

'Sure.'

Jackie disappeared into the kitchen, which was just off the large living room in her Chelsea flat. Smiling, she brought in two drinks in heavy cut glass tumblers. Peter took one and swirled the ice cubes and the slice of lemon in the glass to buy some time. He was sitting on a dark burgundy Chesterfield sofa, and Jackie settled herself next to him. She pulled her legs up and curled herself like an attention-seeking cat in the crook of Peter's arm. Peter could see inside her bra, and enjoyed the view of a pink areola. Now the straps of her suspenders were visible too. Peter put his glass down and ran his fingers along Jackie's thigh.

'Not until you tell me everything,' Jackie said and gently brushed Peter's hand away. 'You naughty boy,' she purred and placed her hand on his groin. He felt himself harden even more.

They had sex on the sofa, fast, and afterwards Jackie said, 'Really, now you have to tell me.'

She'd been to her bedroom to change into a dressing gown, but she'd kept her stockings on. She knew exactly how to play him, Peter thought, and relaxed back into the sofa. 'Another drink?'

While Jackie went to fix them a second round of G&Ts, Peter thought how perfect she was for him. Their 'romance', as Jackie insisted on calling it, whenever she described their two-month old relationship, began at the Drake Summer Ball. Peter had just come back from London, where Val had practically thrown him out of her house, and he was in no mood for a party. He'd forgotten all about the event, and on the morning of the ball, he had to beg the laundry to clean and iron his Mess Undress shirt in double quick time. When he'd signed up for the ball, he'd decided not to ask Sam to accompany him, although she'd sent him woeful glances right up until the day of the ball. He'd had enough of women for one weekend, so he was going to fly solo for once. Besides, the taste of Kaisa's mouth was still lingering on his lips.

But he soon changed his mind. He'd spotted Jackie as he sat down at one of the long tables of the wardroom, below the wooden models of 17th-century sailing ships. She was sitting diagonally opposite him, wearing a low-cut dress with a pearl choker around her neck and long black gloves. The dress had no straps, and she was not wearing a bra. When she leaned over, Peter (and every other officer around the table with a view of her chest) could make out the loose, untethered shape of her breasts. When Peter caught her eye, she smiled and held his gaze for a moment longer than necessary. 'Game on,' Peter had thought and sought her out as soon she got up.

'Fancy seeing you here,' Jackie had said, taking his arm when he reached her at the end of the long table. Peter kissed her lightly on the cheek, and walked her to the ladies. He'd gone to pee himself quickly, and then waited outside the ladies for her. He'd been rewarded with a wide smile, and when they were back in the wardroom, Jackie had organised for Peter to sit next to her for the coffee and port. They'd talked all night, occasionally going for a dance in the disco set up downstairs. They were old friends, after all, Peter thought, but he knew he was really fooling himself. Jackie and he had had a short dalliance when he'd been at Dartmouth, well before Kaisa. She was a catch, everyone kept telling Peter then, but he wasn't interested. He wanted to be single and free of any ties. His career in the Navy was just beginning, and the stories older naval officers kept telling him about the 'runs ashore' when the ship docked at different ports, and skirt was easy to come by, excited him. His future didn't feature a wife sitting at home, waiting for him to come back from sea. Luckily, he'd already been appointed to his first ship at the time, and had sailed the next day. Jackie and Peter had exchanged a few letters, and had kept in touch even after he'd met Kaisa, but there had never again been more to it than friendship. Peter recalled the breakfast party Jackie had invited Peter and Kaisa to the year before. They'd been so happy and Kaisa had looked gorgeous in her strappy top, which she'd worn without a bra, showing off her lovely figure. All the men at the party had been jealous of him, and that bastard Ducan had been all over Kaisa. Peter brushed away any thoughts of *him*, and instead thought of how Jackie too had congratulated him on his beautiful new bride. She'd seemed genuinely happy for him then. But, of course, Kaisa had smelled a rat; she knew Peter too well, and on the way home they'd had another argument, this time about Jackie. Peter shook his head when he remembered all their bitter rows, then recalled the way they used to make up in bed afterwards, and sighed. It was no use thinking of Kaisa, she was history now.

At the ball, Jackie had initiated a kiss goodnight with Peter, and he held tightly onto her tiny waist. The trouble was, even though she was short, had dark hair and a large, wide breasts so different from Kaisa's blonde locks and small pointy breasts, there was something about the curve of her bottom and the smooth skin of her thighs that made Peter think of Kaisa. When they were doing it, he'd close his eyes and pretend he was with his soon-to-be ex-wife.

'So,' Jackie now said, handing Peter his second drink, 'please tell me how it went.'

'Actually, it was alright.' Peter said, taking a sip of out of the glass.

'Yeah?' Jackie narrowed her dark eyes, which were smudged with makeup, making her look more dirty, and sexy. Her hair was short and wavy, a sort of auburn version of Princess Di's. She had a very long, slender neck, and she held herself well, displaying her posh background, Peter supposed. It was her class that turned Peter on. For now, although she was from a very different world from his, she was only wearing stockings, suspenders, and expensive French knickers underneath her silk dressing gown, just for his benefit. He knew this posh girl was all his.

'So she agreed to the divorce?'

'Well ...'

Jackie moved herself away from him. 'Peter, you did tell her?'

Jackie had been the one to insist on the conversation with Kaisa. Her father was an admiral, and she knew a thing or two about how the Navy worked. She'd said that for his career, the best thing he could do was to get a divorce as soon as possible. 'You won't get anywhere if you don't deal with her,' she now said. 'You know that. I talked to Daddy only yesterday ...'

Peter sat up on the sofa. 'What, you talked to your father about me?'

Jackie was playing with the belt of her dressing gown, rolling it up to a tight ball. She wasn't looking at Peter. 'I just wanted to hear it from him, you know, to see what his advice would be.' Jackie lifted her eyes to Peter. 'He has a lot of experience and has chaired a lot of court martials. He really knows what's best, so why wouldn't I ask him?'

Peter slumped back down on the sofa and took a long pull out of his glass. He didn't want to think back to the court martial, to that awful chilly morning last January. To how unhappy Kaisa had been, to her hopeless tears, to his inability to comfort her. He lit a cigarette and offered Jackie one.

'No thanks,' she said.

Peter took a few drags out of his cigarette before he spoke. 'So, go on, tell me what he said.'

Jackie's dad had confirmed what Peter already knew. Everyone felt that, though Duncan had behaved despicably in seducing another officer's wife (here Jackie looked down at her hands, and not at Peter. She knew Peter didn't like talking about the detail of the events in Helensburgh), Kaisa had also been to blame. There had also been talk in Faslane about Kaisa befriending one of the peace campers, but these rumours were just that, rumours. 'Still, rumours can bring down a career,' Jackie's father had said. He'd concluded that if, as his daughter had told him, Peter was already estranged from his foreign wife, the best thing he could do was to make the state permanent. 'Forget all about her, put the whole saga down to the hotheadedness of youth and move on,' was his advice.

When Jackie had finished, the two were silent. Peter lit another cigarette, and listened to the distant noises of the city.

Jackie's flat was in a cul-de-sac of mews houses, and the main thoroughfare was several streets away, so the far-away sound of police sirens reached the flat only occasionally. But now, some poor bugger must be in trouble, Peter thought, as he listened to the wail of sirens disappear into the London night.

'Well, I told her I want a divorce and she seemed OK about it,' Peter finally said. He got up and yawned. 'Bed?' he said and Jackie nodded.

TWENTY-FOUR

Ravi telephoned Kaisa the next day. She was still in bed when she heard the knock on the door. An older man, Colin, who Kaisa knew lived in the ground floor flat with the landlady, Mrs Carter, stood in his pyjamas and a stripey dressing gown outside her door. 'Phone for you.' He seemed angry in his worn out slippers, his grey hair sticking out in all directions. Kaisa suspected it was Colin who hadn't told her about Peter's phone call earlier in the summer, and was now annoyed with her because he'd seen her note on the pinboard. She thanked him, put on a jumper over her pyjamas and flip-flops that she wore to go to the bathroom, and hurried down the two floors to the entrance hall.

'Hello.' Kaisa was a little out of breath, but she was afraid Peter would give up if she made him wait for too long.

'Hi, Kaisa. It's Ravi, I just wanted to phone and see if you are feeling better.'

Kaisa held on to the receiver, trying to think what to say. 'Hi, Ravi.'

'Rose told me you weren't very well?'

'I'm fine now, feeling a bit weak, that's all.'

'I'm glad.'

Kaisa cleared her throat. 'Thank you for calling,' she found it difficult to lie, so she said simply, 'and I'm sorry I couldn't make it yesterday.'

'That's alright. But, I really wanted to see if you'd be up to doing something tonight. Or perhaps on Sunday?'

Kaisa sighed.

'But don't worry, if ...'

'Ravi, I'm not feeling quite up to going out yet,' she said, interrupting him. Now she wasn't lying. She'd not had a tummy bug, but she wasn't feeling well after last night.

'Oh, OK. Take my telephone number in case you change your mind.'

Kaisa hung up and stood in the hall for a moment. Should she have bucked herself up and agreed to see Ravi after all? But she just couldn't. She needed to be on her own and think. Kaisa walked slowly up the stairs and, once in her room, flung herself on the bed and let the tears flow.

She spent the rest of Saturday morning in Notting Hill Gate Library, a large white-clad stucco building just off Portobello Road, where the market was in full swing. She was helped with her research by an older woman wearing half-moon glasses. 'I think you might need to consult a lawyer, dear,' she said to Kaisa after they'd spent more than an hour going through various government information papers.

Kaisa walked home through the throng of people wandering slowly along Portobello Road, browsing the rickety stalls that sold anything from silverware to fresh vegetables. They looked happy and free, talking and laughing with each other. Kaisa couldn't concentrate on the colourful scene. She felt as if she was in a trance. Just as she had got herself a job, almost a new boyfriend, and had finally accepted during the hour or so spent crying her eyes out that her marriage to Peter was over, her life in London was to be served a final, fatal blow by the British government.

It had occurred to her, as she had lingered in bed that morning, trying to get used to the idea of a divorce from Peter, that if he really wanted to sever their relationship for good, she probably could live with it. She had a new life now, living in London with a job that was worthwhile. Isn't that what she'd always wanted? The job may not pay as well as it should, but Kaisa was sure she could ask Rose for a pay rise to cover at least some of the money she'd lose from Peter's monthly allowance. She'd felt bad about taking the money for so long, and it would be a sort of relief for it to stop. They hadn't discussed money at the restaurant the night before, but it was obvious to her that a divorce meant the allowance would end. She was certain that wasn't the reason for Peter's wanting a divorce, but she'd been too shocked to ask him. If she was truthful to herself, she hadn't wanted to be told he was going to marry the leggy dark-haired girl from the party. But now, thinking about their marriage and how it all came about, Kaisa had remembered that the only reason she had 'leave to stay in the United Kingdom', as the stamp on her passport said, was because she was married to an Englishman. What if they divorced? Would her 'leave to stay' be removed? The answer from her research at the library was that this was most probably the case.

Kaisa cursed herself. She should have been braver. If this was true, she needed to stay married for at least seven years to be able to say and work in England. Otherwise she'd have to apply for a work permit, which she knew she wouldn't get for her job at *Adam's Apple*. Every week they got a letter or two asking if there were any jobs going at the magazine from school leavers, and even graduates in journalism. Most of the letters were written in terrible English, but some of them were good, and these were kept in a special file on the shelf behind Rose's desk. Any one of those girls could replace Kaisa in the blink of an eye.

When she got back to Colville Terrace, Kaisa took out the scrap of paper on which she'd written Ravi's number.

'Hi Ravi, I'm feeling better.'

Kaisa didn't come clean to Ravi about why she wanted to see him until they were sitting opposite each other in a Chinese restaurant. She'd planned to tell him on the phone, but he had sounded so elated about her change of heart that she couldn't bring herself to spoil it. When she saw his wide smile outside Tottenham Court Road tube station, she walked up to him and let him kiss her on the cheek. He suggested going to see a film, *Letter to Brezhnev*, at nearby Leicester Square Odeon. When they were out of the cinema, sitting in a restaurant in China Town, Ravi said, 'That wasn't very diplomatic of me, was it?'

Kaisa smiled, 'Actually, the theme sort of touched upon the reason I wanted to see you.'

'Oh?'

'Yes, finding, and, in my case, losing love during the Cold War. My husband wants a divorce.'

Ravi's beautiful face was suddenly serious. There was also a look of disappointment in the line of his mouth. Kaisa wanted to tell him that she also really liked his company, but that she just wasn't ready for a relationship yet. She might have been, had she not seen Peter again. But she couldn't tell him the truth about last night, not yet. 'I'm sorry, but I've come out with you under false pretences. I need your help,' Kaisa said.

Ravi gazed at Kaisa for a long time. 'I'm not a divorce lawyer,' he said finally.

'I know, and that's not what I meant.' Kaisa told Ravi about what she'd found out in the library. The man sat opposite her and listened. The restaurant was a large room, where round tables, covered in crisp white linen, were set out in the middle of the room. Small Chinese women walked in and out of a set of swing door at the far end, pushing a trolley filled with bamboo steamers and bowls covered with small silver domes. Each time they moved through the doors, smells of cooking wafted into the dining room. Ravi had ordered for them both, because Kaisa had never been to a Chinese restaurant before, and the menu didn't have an English translation. They'd been given bowls of rice and a sticky vegetable dish, but they hadn't touched them yet. Kaisa hoped Ravi wouldn't be angry with her. She didn't know him at all, but she was desperate. Ravi was the only lawyer she knew.

When Kaisa had finished speaking, Ravi picked up a set of chopsticks and smartly moved a piece of courgette from the dish into his mouth. Kaisa watched him and waited.

'OK,' Ravi said and carefully set down his chopsticks on a side plate. Absentmindedly, Kaisa noticed how slender his fingers were.

'This is not my area of expertise. I'm a commercial lawyer, but I have dealt with a few work permits for Swiss residents in the bank.' He lifted his eyes up to Kaisa and continued. 'You are correct in that you will lose your right to stay in Britain, and your work permit, if you divorce. If you had had a child with your husband, that would be a different matter. In that case, you'd be able to stay as you are now. Another issue is the length of marriage. Here there are two problems. Firstly, since the marriage has been so short, less than seven years, as you correctly found out, you will simply lose your leave to stay. Secondly, and here I need to give a word of caution, if it is deemed that your marriage was a sham, in other words, you married under false pretences, both of you could be charged with an offence against the Immigration Act. It will normally only result in a fine, so there's no danger of a custodial sentence. However, if you were to stay after your divorce, then you may be detained under the Immigration Act, until you are deported back to Finland.'

Kaisa noticed how he avoided saying Peter's name and couldn't help but smile, which she suppressed as soon as she saw Ravi's serious expression. 'I see,' she said, and added, 'What do you think I should do?'

Their conversation was interrupted by the delivery of more food. A smiling lady placed a steaming bamboo dish from her trolley in front of them and bowed. 'Please,' she said and carried on towards the next table.

Kaisa picked up a hot dumpling. 'This is delicious!' she said, and now Ravi smiled.

'Look, you really need to go and see a family lawyer, or someone who specialises in immigration law. You could try the Citizens Advice Bureau.' Ravi lifted his dark eyes at Kaisa. 'But I think the best option is to stay married.'

ON MONDAY, when Kaisa got to the office, Rose was already there.

'So, how did it go on Friday?'

Kaisa slumped down in her chair and said, 'He wants a divorce.'

Rose came over and perched herself on Kaisa's desk, 'Oh, my dearest. But, you know, this might be for the best.'

'Yes,' Kaisa said and added, 'so I went out with Ravi on Saturday.'

Rose smiled, 'Good girl!'

Kaisa didn't tell Rose why she'd met up with Ravi. She didn't want Rose to think she might lose her permit to stay in England, so she just smiled and picked up the list of companies Rose had given her the previous week. With the increased reader figures, the magazine was writing to as many potential advertisers as possible. Rose had told Kaisa that the magazine was still losing money. The letters all said the same, but Rose didn't want to send photocopies. 'Not personal enough,' she said, so Kaisa's job was to write fifty letters that were identical apart from the person's name and address. It was boring work, but Kaisa didn't mind it. As long as she could stay in London and work for *Adam's Apple*, she'd be happy. The idea of asking Peter to forget about a divorce and stay married to her for another six years so that she'd be able to stay in the UK sent a chill down her spine. How would she be able to ask Peter that? She decided she'd just have to get in touch with him and explain the situation. At the end of their unusually unromantic evening, Ravi had asked her if she wanted to see him again. His eyes were so very brown and his mouth so very full that Kaisa couldn't resist him and had said, 'Yes, but I am a bit confused, so ...'

Ravi had taken her hands into his over the table and said, 'I understand.'

He was such a gentleman, and so good-looking, but Kaisa had noticed how they'd received sideways glances by people on the street. When they'd queued up to buy their tickets at Tottenham Court Road tube station, an older man had stared at them so intently that Kaisa thought he would say something. Not letting go of Kaisa, Ravi had straightened himself up and looked back at the man. Eventually the man had muttered something under his breath and turned towards the woman behind the glass. Ravi lived in north London, so they'd parted ways at the bottom of the escalator. 'May I kiss you,' Ravi had said, causing Kaisa to smile. After a moment's hesitation she replied, 'Yes.'

Ravi took hold of Kaisa's waist, and pulled her close to him. His lips were soft, and when they met Kaisa's mouth, she relaxed into Ravi's arms. The kiss lasted just for a few seconds, but it was so gentle that Kaisa had an odd dreamy sensation all the way to Notting Hill Gate. In bed that night, she half wished she'd asked Ravi to come home with her, but she knew she couldn't have gone through with anything. It was just lovely to be kissed by a man after such a long time. Kaisa tried to brush away the memory of Peter's lips against hers in June. She must forget all romantic ideas she had of their continued relationship and move on. It was obvious he had. All she needed was for him to postpone the divorce. She hoped he'd agree to stay married for the sake of her work permit – and career.

During her lunch hour, Kaisa used the telephone box on the street corner and telephoned the wardroom at Devonport. 'Can I speak with Lieutenant Peter Williams, please?'

'Just a moment, madam,' came the reply from a man at the other end. Kaisa had half expected them to tell her he wasn't available. Still, he probably didn't know and had to check. Kaisa hoped that Peter hadn't sailed yet; at the same time, she was nervous about having to speak with him. But she couldn't risk him talking to a lawyer, and starting the divorce proceedings, before she'd told him what the consequences would be for her. Or perhaps he knew? No, that couldn't be. Kaisa remembered how friendly their dinner had been – or more than friendly. It had been like old times until he'd dropped the bombshell.

'Yes,' the voice at the other end of the line said.

'Peter?' Kaisa found she was suddenly breathless.

'Kaisa?' Peter's voice was full of surprise. 'Is something wrong?'

'No, no,' Kaisa heard the concern in his voice. She was touched; he still cared for her! 'But I need to speak to you about what we discussed on Friday.'

'Oh?'

'Yes, it's a bit difficult on the phone. I'm in a telephone box outside my office, and, well, there's a guy waiting to use the phone.' Kaisa looked at the man through the dirty glass of the phone box. He was wearing a suit, watching her every move and listening to her every word. 'It's not very private,' she added, giving the man a look, but he continued to stand there, close to the door.

'Right,' Peter said. He was quiet for a moment, thinking.

Kaisa didn't dare say anything, and just waited.

'Look, we're sailing on Friday, and I don't have any leave before that.'

'I see.'

'But, if you can get yourself here, I'm off till tomorrow evening.'

'To Plymouth?'

'Yes, unless it can wait six weeks?'

Kaisa was thinking hard. A return ticket to Plymouth would be expensive, but she could manage it. She'd have to leave work early, and come back with the last train of the day. Or perhaps with the milk train that ran through the night.

'Ok,' she said and Peter told her the train she needed to catch. He'd come and meet her at the station.

IT TOOK NEARLY four hours to get to Plymouth, so on the long journey she practised what she would say to Peter. She first thought she'd ask him why he wanted a divorce, but then realised that she didn't want to hear his reasons. No, the best thing was just to come out and say it. Explain how much she loved working for *Adam's Apple,* and that she needed to be married to continue working in the UK.

TWENTY-FIVE

PLYMOUTH

Peter was standing on the platform in Plymouth, wearing a pair of cords and a light blue cotton shirt. He'd tied a jumper around his shoulders. It was early September, but the weather was still warm, even with the sun just setting behind the drab-looking 1960s railway building. Kaisa walked nervously towards him, but couldn't help but smile and quicken her step when she saw the grin on his face. For a moment, she felt as if everything that had happened during the past year was forgotten. As if any moment now, Peter would open up his arms and welcome her into his embrace. But when she got close to him, he continued to stand motionless, looking at her. She was conscious of the clothes she'd chosen for the journey. She was wearing a skirt for once, instead of her 'boy clothes', and her beige boots that she knew Peter liked. She wore a mohair jumper over a strappy vest, and had taken a small overnight case with make-up and a change of underwear in case she needed to go straight to the office from the train the next morning.

'Hi,' Kaisa said and stopped in front of him.

'Am I allowed to hug you?' Peter said, after they'd stood facing each other for a while. The train had emptied of people, most of whom had walked past them, some giving them odd looks for standing in the middle of the concourse, in their way. Now the platform was empty.

Kaisa didn't say anything but nodded and moved closer to Peter. He put his arms around her, first tentatively, then firmly, and hugged her hard.

Kaisa breathed in Peter's scent. He'd used his familiar coconut scented aftershave, and the smell of it made Kaisa feel faint. She'd dropped her bag on the platform, and now lifted her hands and wrapped them around him. His body felt taut, as he squeezed her hard. Quickly, he let go of her and took hold of her bag. 'This way,' Peter said and guided her through the low-slung building towards the car park. His new car was another sports model, but this time it was red and a lot bigger than the Fiesta, or the yellow Spitfire he'd had when Kaisa first visited him in Portsmouth five years ago.

'Nice car,' she said while Peter busied himself with getting the roof down. 'A Golf GTI,' he said with some pride. 'Get in,' he added and put on a pair of aviator sunglasses.

They drove through the city, which was a combination of old white-clad buildings and new high-rises. After the crowded streets of London, Plymouth seemed to be deserted. With the roof down, Kaisa could sense the presence of the sea, even though she hadn't yet glimpsed it. There were the familiar calls of the seagulls and the unmistakable smell of seaweed. The place reminded Kaisa of Portsmouth, and also of Helensburgh. They drove through a street that had grey cement buildings set onto a hillside, just like the Scottish naval quarter estate. Kaisa looked away – she didn't want to be reminded of that place. The sounds and smells of the sea did make her miss Portsmouth, however, and she wanted to share this with Peter, but she remained quiet. She didn't want to start an argument, which reminiscing about old times might bring about. But she could still feel his strong arms around her, and if that wasn't going back to old times, what was? She glanced at Peter's profile. His mouth was set into a half-smile, as it always used to be, before Helensburgh. She couldn't make out the expression in his eyes because of the sunglasses. She suddenly remembered that they hadn't really argued properly since before Peter's fight with Duncan.

Peter parked the car near the seafront, in an area he said was called the Barbican. 'There's a decent French restaurant here.' They walked side by side down a narrow street, with stone-clad houses on either side and the dark blue sea beyond. The restaurant was called Chez Marie and Peter and Kaisa were shown to a table in the corner of a small room. It was covered with pink linen and set with long candles. Peter ordered himself a beer and Kaisa a G&T.

'You look good,' Peter said and grinned.

'Thank you,' Kaisa replied, and added, 'so do you.' Peter's eyes looked intensely dark. He continued to smile at Kaisa, and she wondered if he knew what she was about to ask him. Or had he had a change of heart? The place was nearly full; only one other table was unoccupied, and there was a pleasant low murmur of other people's conversations, which made Kaisa feel more comfortable about what she needed to talk to Peter about.

Kaisa turned her eyes towards the menu and asked if Peter had been there before.

'Yes,' he said.

Kaisa tried to look at his face, but he too had his head bent over the menu, a black folder in which the first two pages listed the choice of wines. Kaisa looked around the room. All the other tables were occupied by couples; this restaurant was obviously where you took a girlfriend, or your wife. So, who had Peter brought here? The dark-haired girl from the party?

'I think I'll have the Dover sole,' Kaisa said.

'You not having a starter?'

Kaisa glanced back at the menu and made a snap decision. 'OK, I'll have the moules marinieres.'

Peter looked up at her and grinned. 'Good girl, I'll have it too, and the steak with chips.'

As soon as they'd put down their menus, the waiter came to the table and took their order in heavily accented English. He nodded at Kaisa when she told him her choices, and looked deeply in her eyes when he said, 'Very good, madam, the Dover sole is delicious.' Peter placed his order and asked for a bottle of white wine and a glass of red to have with his steak later.

When they were alone, Peter lifted his beer glass. 'The food is very good here, so I hope you like it.'

'I'm sure I will.' Kaisa felt dizzy, the way Peter had told her she was a good girl reminded her of all the other times they'd eaten out. He knew she didn't usually have starters, and only ordered one so that Peter could have one too. Peter was always hungry, whereas Kaisa's appetite was much smaller. It was as if, since meeting at the station, they'd gone back in time, and were back in Portsmouth having a celebratory meal in one of the French places there.

The waiter brought the wine and there was the silly tasting bit, when Peter smiled at Kaisa as he sipped the wine and nodded his approval.

'I have no idea if it's any good or not!' he said when the waiter had disappeared, and they both laughed.

'We came here to celebrate one of the guys getting his Dolphins,' Peter said, as if he'd known she was wondering about the girl.

'Oh,' Kaisa said.

'Yes, he's become a mate. Looks up to me a bit. Not that there's much to look up to.'

'Of course there is!' Kaisa said. 'Everyone was always telling me how good you are at your job,' she added, before she could help herself.

Peter looked at her, and now his eyes had grown sad and serious. Kaisa knew she'd upset him with talk of past. They were quiet for a while, both draining their glasses.

'How's Jeff?' Kaisa said after another awkward silence.

Peter told Kaisa about Jeff's wedding in Portsmouth Cathedral, and about the reception afterwards. 'He asks after you,' Peter said, and he lifted his eyes towards Kaisa.

'Really?' Kaisa wondered again if Peter had gone alone to the wedding. 'Tell him I miss him.'

Peter opened his mouth to say something, but changed his mind. After a while, having fiddled with the stem of his wine glass, he said, 'I will.'

Kaisa asked Peter about Jeff's new wife, and Peter told her how practical Milly was, 'a no-nonsense kind of girl'. Kaisa laughed; they both agreed this was exactly what Jeff needed. Peter said how much in love with her he seemed, and how she could wrap his parents around her little finger. 'Milly lost both of her parents when she was young, so she's had to look after herself from an early age,' Peter said, and added, 'Saying that, she's really, really lovely.'

'What's she going to do now?' Kaisa knew that Wrens had to resign their commission once they became married, something that seemed Victorian to her. At the same time, how could two Navy careers ever be compatible with children? It would be worse than having a civilian wife who worked in one place. Wrens didn't go to sea but they got sent to different bases and even abroad if they were appointed to work for Nato.

'I'm not sure, but no doubt she'll think of something practical that'll fall in line with Jeff's career.'

'That's good,' Kaisa said. 'Unlike me,' she thought but didn't say anything. Anyway, it was different for an English girl, she thought. And Milly was in the Navy herself, so she knew the drill better than anyone.

TWENTY-SIX

The sight of Kaisa stepping off the train took Peter's breath away. When he'd suggested she came down to Plymouth, he hadn't for a second thought that she would. He knew, of course, she wanted to talk about the divorce, but he didn't know why she was so against it, because that's what her trip down to him must have meant, surely? But here she now was, wearing those boots that looked so good on her, with a skirt pulled tightly around her small waist. She'd lost weight and a slimmer frame suited her. It made her legs look even longer and her face more slender and fragile-looking. The outline of her small, perky breasts was visible underneath her thin jumper and Peter couldn't take his eyes off her as she walked towards him. She was so stunning, that all the men leaving the train couldn't help but give her a glance. It made Peter wonder how many men in London had asked her out.

When Peter had booked the French place, which was the only decent restaurant in Plymouth, he hadn't realised it was so obviously the number one romantic spot. When he'd been there for Simon's celebration dinner, after he'd finally got his Dolphins, and become a submariner, there was a group of twenty officers, some with their wives or girlfriends, and they nearly filled the small dining room. But tonight, when he stepped inside the restaurant with Kaisa, Peter felt a little embarrassed when he saw all the other tables occupied by couples leaning in and whispering sweet nothings in each other's ears. He glanced at her, and hoped she wasn't getting the wrong idea. 'This is the best restaurant in Plymouth,' he said, but immediately regretted his words. That, too, sounded as if he'd planned to make a special occasion out of this evening.

But everything was so easy with Kaisa; the ordering of drinks, wine, food. They knew each other so well, and talking about old times, about Jeff and his new wife, made the evening go quickly. It wasn't until Peter noticed it was past ten, and the tall dark-haired waiter, who couldn't take his eyes of Kaisa either, had brought them coffees that she eventually told him why she was there.

'Look, Peter, I know you want to move on.' Kaisa leaned closer to him and her piercing blue eyes fixed their beautiful gaze on him. Whether it was all the wine he'd drunk, or whether it was the false naturalness of the situation (him out with his pretty wife; what could be more normal than that?), or whether it was the candlelight that made Kaisa's face glow and her lips look soft and inviting, he wasn't listening to what she had to say. Instead, Peter put his hand on hers, picked it up and kissed her palm.

'I love you,' he said.

Kaisa pulled her hand away and stared at him. Peter, too, was shocked at what he had said. 'I mean, I still love you,' he muttered. 'You're still my wife.'

'Yes, yes, of course,' Kaisa said. 'But you said you wanted a divorce.' She leaned over and whispered the last words. While they'd eaten, drank, talked and laughed, the place had emptied, and they were now the last people sitting down at a table. They'd suddenly both become aware that the two waiters standing at the back of the room, seemingly waiting for them to leave, were now intently listening to their every word.

Peter looked up and nodded towards their waiter, to show he wanted the bill. 'We can't talk here,' he said to Kaisa.

Outside, it had started raining. Large drops were rapidly falling down, as if someone was emptying a bucket of water over them. Kaisa had no coat, so Peter gave her his jumper. They ran to Peter's car and once inside, started giggling. They were both absolutely drenched. Peter's shirt was sticking to his chest and when Kaisa pulled his jumper over her head, Peter could see her hard nipples poking through her thin jumper. He leaned across the gearbox and took Kaisa into his arms. They kissed with an urgency he couldn't remember ever feeling with anyone. Peter slipped his hand under Kaisa's jumper, and she gave a moan when his fingers touched her breasts. He was so hard he thought he might pass out.

When Kaisa put her hand on Peter's crotch, he whispered, 'Back seat?' The carpark was deserted and with the torrential rain outside, the streets around the Barbican were empty. Kaisa nodded her assent and climbed between the seats. Peter dashed in and out of the car, locked the doors and joined Kaisa on the back seat. As soon as the light inside the car went out, Peter reached underneath Kaisa's skirt. He pulled her tights and knickers down and hurriedly undid his fly.

They held each other's gaze, and when Peter entered her, Kaisa moaned softly and arched her back. He could feel her grip on him and kissed her small, pink nipples, her mouth and finally her slender neck as, with a loud groan, they both climaxed.

Afterwards they held each other and listened to the rain pelting onto the roof of the car. Peter stroked Kaisa's blonde hair, which had gone curly in the rain during their passionate lovemaking. She was half-sitting, half-lying down in the crook of his arm, with her legs across the back seat of the car. Peter thought he'd never forget this moment, and stared at the snowy mountain scene that formed the pattern of her skirt. Had she worn the outfit, which she'd often worn when she met him off the train during their marriage, to trap him, he wondered briefly, but brushed aside such thoughts. That was what Jackie or Sam might do, but not Kaisa.

'You OK?' he now asked her.

The head underneath his hand moved and Kaisa sat up. Her make-up was smeared and she looked as if she'd been sobbing. Peter was shocked, he hadn't realised she was crying. 'What are the tears for?'

Kaisa put her head in her hands, 'Oh Peter, what are we going to do?'

TWENTY-SEVEN

Peter drove Kaisa to the train station and waited with her until the night train pulled up to the platform. He'd held her all evening after the love-making in the car, and had told her over and over how much he loved her. She too, had told Peter how much she loved him, and promised to write to him. Peter was going to go away in two days' time, but this time he'd be on a diesel submarine, which meant correspondence would be easier, as the boat would be docking at several ports during its time at sea.

'As long as you write to me too,' Kaisa had said to Peter, looking into his dark eyes.

After Peter had climbed back into the driver's seat, with Kaisa next to him, they hadn't discussed the future any more. Peter told Kaisa, 'We'll work something out,' and at the time Kaisa had believed him. He held her hand and only removed it to change gears, grabbing hold of her again when they were driving along the main thoroughfare towards the station. It felt so good, this familiar feeling of his fingers around hers. She wanted the drive to go on forever, and very nearly asked Peter to drive her all the way to London, just so she could carry on being close, inhaling his scent and feeling his warm hand around hers.

When the train pulled up Peter found Kaisa an empty compartment, where she could lie down across three seats. They hugged and kissed each other for so long, he nearly missed the whistle and got stranded on the train. Hurrying out, he took hold of Kaisa's hands once more, and said, 'We'll be together again, I promise.' He stayed on the platform to wave goodbye. As she stared at his diminishing figure, she let the tears run freely down her face. No one was there to see her smudged make-up or hear her sniffling.

Kaisa had a fitful night's sleep on the train. She was restless because of everything that had happened during the evening, but she was also disturbed by the train stopping at each and every station on the journey to London. When she arrived at Paddington at just past 5.30 am, she could still feel Peter's kisses on her lips. But then she found out she had to wait for the tube to start running at 6am. Sitting at the end of a bench, just a few centimetres away from a drunk fast asleep and covered with old newspapers, she shivered in her skirt and thin jumper and began to think about the future with Peter. How would they be able to make things work? And how could Peter go from wanting a divorce to wanting them to try again in the space of three days? What was the real reason for the final separation, and his desire for a divorce? Another woman? That girl from the party? Kaisa put her head in her hands, but that made the man next to her shift, and an awful smell of sweat, combined with urine, hit Kaisa's nostrils. She stood up and began walking along the empty platforms, thinking.

Even if Peter really did want to make a go of things and wasn't just 'thinking with his dick' as he sometimes said of the sailors and their love lives (or 'lust lives' as he put it too), what was he going to do about the woman he was seeing? Supposing there was another woman. A huge problem with a future life together was money. Peter's salary was just enough to live on if they were in a married quarter, and Kaisa's salary hardly covered her living costs. Even together they wouldn't be able to afford to rent a flat in London. Besides, what would be the point if Peter couldn't afford train fares back and forth to London each time he was ashore and on leave? Then there was Kaisa's career, which she'd fought so hard to get off the ground. The problems that had always existed between them would still be there. Unless Kaisa gave up her job in London, and moved down to a married quarter in Plymouth, they'd never see each other. But there was no telling how long Peter's appointment in HMS *Orion* would last; Kaisa knew that it was highly likely his next sub would be based in Helensburgh. And Kaisa just couldn't go back to that life. Perhaps she really didn't love Peter enough? Kaisa fought tears. When a thin man with long, dirty blond hair approached her for money she quickly wiped her tears away and began walking up the road from the station. She found an open café with steamed up windows opposite the station. It was full of construction workers in overalls, but a girl in a pink apron showed her to an empty table at the back.

'What can I get you?' she said, looking Kaisa up and down. There were a few sneers from the men, and one shouted, 'Walk of shame, is it love?'

The waitress turned around and said, 'Shut up or I'll throw you out.' Returning to Kaisa, her pen still poised over her notebook, she said in a hushed voice, 'Don't mind the animals here.'

Kaisa smiled a 'thank you' to the girl and ordered a coffee and a cheese roll. The watery liquid warmed her a little, and although she had to scrape a thick layer of butter from inside the bun, eating it made her feel better. How she wished Peter was with her to protect her from the men, who were still leering and shouting the occasional comment on her appearance in spite of the telling off from the waitress. It felt as if they knew she'd been fucked in the backseat of a car only hours before, and she felt dirty and vulnerable. Kaisa nodded to the waitress, who was leaning across a small bar at the back of the café, smoking a cigarette. Kaisa paid and returned to the station, where the early morning rush-hour had begun. Kaisa took the tube to Ladbroke Grove, and tried not to think about Peter or the future.

AFTER A QUICK SHOWER and a change of clothing in her bedsit, Kaisa got to work just after eight. Rose, as usual, was already there.

'Hi Kaisa,' she said but only looked up from her desk quickly. Kaisa was glad Rose had forgotten about her trip down to Plymouth; she didn't have the energy, or desire, to tell her about her wonderful but confusing evening.

About an hour later, when all the other women had settled themselves behind their desks, Rose stood up and said, 'I need to talk to you all. I'm afraid I have some very bad, and sad, news.'

Kaisa and the other members of *Adam's Apple* editorial office listened in quiet shock as Rose told them that the paper was folding. 'We have enough funds to complete this forthcoming issue, but after that, I'm afraid it's over.' Her voice trembled and Kaisa could tell her boss was fighting tears. 'So let's make this issue the best yet!' she said and left the room.

The women looked at each other in shock, then their gazes turned to Rachel, who had been at the magazine the longest and often accompanied Rose to meetings with 'the money men'.

'But I thought the increased sales figures this summer meant we were OK,' Jenny said. She wore her usual uniform of a white shirt, buttoned up to her neck, and high-waisted black trousers. She had her hands buried deep inside her pockets.

Rachel shook her head. 'They've been telling Rose to put up the price, but she won't because she says it's vital all women, especially those struggling with money, can afford to buy a copy.'

Everyone around the room nodded. 'What are we going to do?' Jenny said.

'We'll make the next issue the best yet!' Rachel said, and at that moment Rose came in. The little make-up she wore had gone, and Kaisa suspected she'd been crying. Kaisa had never seen her face look so white and gaunt.

She moved her gaze from one face to the next and said, 'You have been, are, all amazing women, and I am so grateful for all your support over the last six months. But we have to face facts. I have sunk all my money into this project because I firmly believe women need a voice, a sensible voice amongst the glossy magazines advocating traditional values. But there is no more, and it seems my last backers have had enough. But I believe *Adam's Apple* has made a difference both in the past, and during my short stewardship, and it has influenced the rest of the women's press to cover stories that are relevant to the woman of today. All we can now do is make this last issue of *Adam's Apple* count, make it into something that will be looked upon as a shining example of modern, feminist journalism.'

Kaisa and the rest of the staff clapped.

'So, my good women, let's get back to work!' Rose said.

Kaisa went back to her desk, following the example of the others. She tried not to think about the future, because she believed in the magazine and its power to change the lives of women in Britain for the better. And she wanted to do just as Rose had said: help make the last issue the best yet. But she couldn't help but think about her own situation. She looked around the room. All the other women were seasoned journalists, or editors. They would get work without any problems. Although *Adam's Apple* was a radical paper, sneered at by some of the other (male) journalists in the Coach and Horses, she understood from the way the women talked in the office that most people in the industry had a secret admiration for the magazine. It was progressive, left-wing and often challenged the status quo of British society. 'It's what every reporter dreams of doing when they're at journalism school,' Jenny had once told Kaisa.

Kaisa sighed. She hadn't been to journalism school. She looked down at the list of companies she was asking to advertise in the magazine, and saw she was about halfway through. She got up from her desk and went over to Rose.

'Are we still sending these out,' she asked, holding up one of the letters.

Rose leaned back in her chair and thought for a moment. 'Why not, send them all as usual. We might as well try up till the very last.' She smiled at Kaisa and then her expression changed. 'Oh my God, I'd forgotten, how did it go yesterday?'

Kaisa shrugged her shoulders. 'Fine, a bit confusing, but fine.' She couldn't help herself. A wide, happy smile spread over her face.

Rose's eyes were on Kaisa, 'Oh yes?' she said. Her voice was full of meaning, and she was grinning.

Kaisa looked down at her hands. How could Rose know what had happened in Plymouth between her and Peter. Suddenly she felt angry at her boss. It was her life, not Rose's. If she wanted to sleep with her ex, that was her business.

'I'll finish these today,' she said, not looking at Rose. 'I'm sorry it's taken so long.' Kaisa turned on her heels and returned to her desk. She could feel her face redden and knew Rose was still looking at her.

At one o'clock Kaisa got up and said she was going to get a

sandwich. Rose looked up from her papers. 'Wait, I'll come with you.' The other women around the office were still hard at work, with their heads bent over typewriters, but Rachel glanced up and gave Rose a questioning look. She shook her head, as if to answer an unposed question. Kaisa wondered what the two women had said about her. Rachel knew Kaisa was the only one in the office who wouldn't be able to get a job when the magazine folded, or had Rose told Rachel about her private life? As far as Kaisa knew, Rose hadn't told anyone about how they'd met, that Kaisa knew Duncan, her cousin, or what had happened between Kaisa and Duncan. The anger surged again; Rose had no right to tell anyone about her life!

'OK,' Kaisa said, but she gathered her things and walked quickly out of the office and onto the street without waiting for Rose.

'Wait Kaisa!' Rose shouted.

Kaisa sighed. Perhaps it was the sleepless night after such an incredibly wonderful, but unsettling evening that was making Kaisa so ratty and sensitive. Or maybe it was the knowledge that she'd be jobless soon. She had a month's notice on the bedsit, but she could pay the rent with Peter's allowance, which he was still paying into her account every month. She had no idea how he could afford to do it, but presumed living in the wardroom was cheaper. But without any other income, that left no money whatsoever for food. At worst, she'd have to go back home, to Helsinki, and sleep on her sister's sofa bed again, but after everything that had happened, with Matti's death, the disastrous date with Tom, and her sister's new relationship, she didn't even know if the sofa bed was still available to her. Besides, she had no money for the journey. She'd have to call her mother and ask her for the fare.

'Let's go to Terroni's – I'll buy you a proper coffee and a

sarni. I know how much you like your coffee!' Rose took hold of Kaisa's arm, and Kaisa couldn't help but smile at her.

'Hello, Toni,' Rose said. A tall dark-haired man came out from behind a counter laden with Italian meats, fresh salads and cheese. At a further section, Kaisa saw cream filled cones and small cakes. Behind the counter were two large coffee-making machines, where another man pulled leavers amid plumes of steam.

'How is my favourite lady?' the Italian man said as soon as Kaisa and Rose walked in. 'Please, please sit down and tell me what you want.'

'Thank you, Toni, we'll have two caffe americanos – yes?' Rose looked over to Kaisa. 'Black coffee, that's right, isn't it? No milk?'

Kaisa nodded. Rose had never taken her to this place before; it was like being abroad with the hustle and bustle of diners, staff hurrying between tables, and the steam rising from the coffee machines. The sweet scent of real coffee made Kaisa's spirit rise. Kaisa remembered the Italian restaurants in Stockholm; they'd had the same aromas of cooking and coffee.

'And who is your beautiful young friend, Rosa?'

'This is Kaisa. She's come all the way from Finland to work with me.'

The man took Kaisa's hand and kissed the back of it. Kaisa was reminded of how Duncan had done the same when she'd first met him at Jackie's party. 'Finland! A beautiful woman from a beautiful country.' Toni was a slim man, with a mop of dark hair, a little older than her, Kaisa supposed. His eyes were dark and he was shamelessly flirtatious. Kaisa noticed a ring on his left finger.

An older, shorter man, with a round belly, shouted something in Italian to Toni, and he sighed theatrically. Letting go of Kaisa's hand, he went back to the counter. 'I will bring you coffee.'

'I keep telling him my name is Rose, but he says that Rosa is the same name in Italian, so he insists on calling me that.'

Toni made a fuss of the two women, bringing them toasted bread called bruschetta, topped with tomatoes, olive paste and strong smelling cheese.

As soon as they had a moment to themselves, Rose looked at her. 'I know you must be worried about your job.'

'I am,' Kaisa said.

'Which is why I brought you here.'

'Oh?'

'I know it may be difficult for you to find something similar to *Adam's Apple*, but I will recommend you to a couple of people. However, I've been thinking about it, and I think it would best if you enrol on a journalism course. I can write you a letter of recommendation, and it'll just be for one year, but it'll open doors for you.'

'But, I haven't got the money,' Kaisa said. Suddenly she felt huge affection towards Rose. How wrong she'd been; instead of gossiping about Kaisa's love life, Rose had been worrying about her future.

'Yes, this is why I brought you here.'

Kaisa said nothing; she was confused.

'I know it's not what you want, but hear me out.' Rose took a deep intake of breath and continued. 'Toni here is always looking for someone to help out, and I know if I ask him, he'll give you a job as a waitress. I know it shouldn't count, but your looks will bring in customers.'

Kaisa stared at Rose. This was completely against what they both believed in.

'Don't look at me like that. Sometimes when the chips are down, we have to take advantage of what we have.' Rose grinned. 'While working, I think you should enrol on the jour-nalism course. There's an evening programme, so you can work during the day here, and attend lessons afterwards. It'll be very hard work for a year, but I know you'll manage.'

Kaisa looked around the café. It was busy with men in suits. Some were queuing up at the counter, and some were sitting at tables eating their lunch and drinking coffee. Toni smiled at her from the other side of the counter. Even though he'd been flirty before, his smile now was friendly. Had Rose already spoken to him about her? To her surprise, Kaisa could imagine working here. She nodded to Rose.

The older woman put her hand on Kaisa's and said, 'Think about it.'

TWENTY-EIGHT

LONDON

The phone began ringing when Kaisa was still outside, looking for the keys to the front door. She hurried to open up and ran down the few steps to the back of the hall.

'Hello?'

'Hi, it's me,' Peter's voice sounded low.

Kaisa hugged the receiver. 'Hello.'

'You got back OK?'

'Yes, the train stopped at every station, so I didn't get much sleep.' Kaisa said.

'I couldn't sleep because I was thinking of you,' Peter said. 'I miss you,' he added.

Kaisa didn't know what to reply to Peter. Did his words mean that they were back together now? But surely he didn't think that she would come back to him, and the life of a Navy wife, after everything that had happened? 'Peter,' she began.

'Yes, I know, Kaisa. I'm going away tomorrow, and you're up in London with your career. But I just wanted to tell you how much I love you.' Peter paused for a short moment. 'I wanted to tell you that before we sail.'

Kaisa could hardly breathe. Did he know how she'd longed to hear those words? All those months in Helensburgh, first when the bomber was on its long patrol, then after the fight, when they'd both been so unhappy and Peter had drifted further and further away from her. And all the time in Helsinki, when she'd written to Peter and he'd replied in short, official-sounding communications. But what, she suddenly thought, about that girl he was seeing?

'Kaisa, are you there?'

'Yes,' Kaisa tried to disguise her sniffles.

'Please don't cry. I promise I will sort something out. If we love each other, we can make this work, I promise.'

'The magazine is folding,' Kaisa managed to say between sobs.

'Oh.'

'Yes, we have about six weeks until we are out of the office and I'm out of a job. I don't know what I'm going to do.' Kaisa found a tissue in her handbag. She heard a door open and the man who lived with the landlady passed her on his way to the kitchen in the back of the house. He gave her a look of utter disapproval. Was crying against some sort of house rule? Kaisa turned her head towards the wall and away from the man's gaze.

'Kaisa, you know you can always go and stay with my parents, don't you?' Peter said. 'I'll write to them tonight and tell them you'll be in touch.'

'No, Peter.' The thought of having to face Peter's mum's disapproving gaze, or worse still a sad one, filled her with dread. And his father, who'd been so kind to Kaisa, how would she ever be able to meet him after everything that had happened? Having to see Peter's family again hadn't crossed her mind before. She knew for certain she couldn't face them alone.

'What will you do then?'

'Rose has organised a job for me in an Italian café, and she thinks I should go to night school to take a journalism qualification.'

'I see,' Peter's voice was dry. Kaisa remembered how Peter had reacted when she told him about working for Rose, Duncan's cousin. He hadn't believed that Kaisa no longer had anything to do with Duncan. 'It's one alternative. She has also recommended me to other magazines, but without a journalism qualification, she thinks it'll be difficult.'

Peter was quiet at the other end of the line.

'I haven't decided what I'm going to do yet, but if nothing works out, I might go back to Helsinki.' Kaisa was surprised at her own words, at her confidence. Suddenly, she knew what her options were after the most confusing twenty-four hours of her life. She realised she couldn't go back to being dependent on Peter again. And the thought of seeing Peter's parents scared her. Her only alternative was to go back home to Finland. Her hands holding the receiver became clammy just at the thought of facing Peter's parents, let alone his brother and sister-in-law, or lovely Nancy, his sister. She felt sure that his family would think everything that had happened was her fault. And they were right, of course. It was all her doing. She had ruined Peter's career and she had no right to him, she saw that clearly now. She didn't want to spoil his life any further.

'Well, I just wanted to hear you'd got back to London, OK,' Peter now said. His voice had cooled.

'Thank you, that was very kind of you.' After a short pause, she added, 'I really enjoyed last night.' She wanted to tell him how much she loved him, but she knew that by doing so she would give him false hope.

'Yes, so did I.' Peter's voice was dry. 'I've got to go,' he said and put down the receiver.

Kaisa listened to the long tone on the line. She was rooted to the spot, looking at the scribbled notes on the wall before her. Half-covered by another, newer communication to someone called Tracy was a piece of paper in Kaisa's own handwriting asking to be told of any phone calls for her. How long ago it seemed since she'd missed Peter's call. And now, today, after the most wonderful reunion, she was the one who'd decided there was no future for them.

TWENTY-NINE

Kaisa fell in love with Italian food and culture. Had she not been on her feet all day long, she was sure she would have put on tons of weight and become the shape of the 'Mama' who cooked in the kitchen. Mama was as tall as she was wide, but as soon as Kaisa started at the café, two months previously, Mama had taken Kaisa under her wing. She even taught Kaisa Italian, though in truth all the family members who worked at the Farringdon Road café corrected her pronunciation of the dishes and words like 'prego', which meant please, and 'grazie', which meant thank you. Kaisa found it easy to pick up the language, and she began to feel like one of the family.

When she'd phoned her mother to tell her she was working in an Italian café, her mother had said, 'You have Italian blood, of course you like it. And you'll learn the language fast.' Kaisa had laughed She didn't quite believe the stories about her Italian roots. There was no evidence, just some tale, told by an old aunt, that the family name, Flori, on her maternal grandmother's side, hailed from a small village in Northern Italy. Kaisa didn't think her mother would have approved of her graduate daughter working in a café if it hadn't been Italian.

Kaisa still lived in the bedsit in Notting Hill and took the tube to Farringdon each day, but instead of turning right towards Clerkenwell Close, she walked for ten or so minutes to the café on Farringdon Road.

She'd even started calling Rose, 'Rosa', during her daily visits to Terroni's. Kaisa knew the older woman was checking up on her, making sure she was OK. She also helped Kaisa with her English. The course at London School of Journalism was demanding, and her assignments were becoming more and more difficult, so Kaisa needed all the help she could get. Rose was now working for the *Observer* where she'd become the editor of a supplement aimed at women. 'Back to fashion, make-up and trouble with men,' Rose had laughed, but Kaisa had heard from Ravi, whose friend worked at the paper, that Rose had been taken on to revamp the supplement and make it 'more current and relevant to women of today'. He also told her that Rose was doing a brilliant job and that she was highly regarded by everyone in the industry.

'You're lucky to have such a prestigious woman as your friend,' Ravi said.

Something good had come out of all the bad that her affair with Duncan had caused, Kaisa thought, but she didn't say anything to Ravi. Although she was seeing him regularly, she didn't consider that she was in a relationship with him. They'd had sex a few times, but she didn't feel the same about him as she had about Peter. She'd discussed Ravi at length with Rose; in fact, she'd discussed her whole life at length with Rose. They'd become firm friends in spite of their ten-year age difference. Kaisa felt much older than her 25 years, because of all that had happened to her.

'It's OK to have sex with someone who you're not madly in love with,' Rose had advised her. 'It's a lot easier, and less painful. Just enjoy it! Men don't worry about being in love with women they fuck!'

Kaisa had laughed nervously and looked around to see if anyone had heard what they were talking about, or Rose's language. They'd been sitting at a restaurant in Maida Vale, where Rose often took Kaisa after her course finished in the evening. She refused to let Kaisa pay for anything. She said she still felt responsible for what Duncan had done, however much Kaisa protested that she'd been a willing partner. In the early days of Kaisa's course, which had started in September, Rose had surprised Kaisa by waiting outside the Victorian red-brick building where her classes were held. She'd hugged Kaisa warmly and suggested they go and eat something. When they'd sat down, she'd put her hand on Kaisa's arm and said, 'Let me treat you. I don't have any children of my own to look after.'

'I'm too old to be your child!' Kaisa had protested, but Rose had just laughed and said, 'OK, a younger sister then!'

Soon it had become a regular event, that once a week, on a Thursday, Rose would turn up at the school and they'd walk arm in arm to their favourite place by the canal in Little Venice, where the Maitre D' knew Rose and Kaisa and gave them their favourite table at the end of the glass-walled room.

It was now late November. Terroni's café in Farringdon was filled with elaborate Christmas chocolates, beautiful glacé fruits and piles and piles of tall Italian cakes called *panettone* in cardboard boxes. Kaisa was desperately home-sick and really wanted to go home to Helsinki for the holidays – she had three weeks off from the School of Journalism – but she couldn't afford the airfare. So she'd decided to work in the café on the days it was open, but she still had the whole of Christmas week to fill, when Terroni's would be shut. Rose had asked her to come to the family farm in Dorset, but Kaisa didn't want to risk seeing Duncan, nor did she wish to meet any of Rose's other cousins. They were bound to know about the affair and how it had caused Duncan's dismissal from the Navy, and the break-up of Kaisa's marriage.

'Duncan would behave, you know that, don't you?' Rose said with concern in her eyes.

But Kaisa shook her head, and Rose didn't mention the matter again.

Even Ravi, who didn't celebrate Christmas because he was a Hindu, was going to his parents' home outside Birmingham. He hadn't invited Kaisa to come with him, and she suspected his mother wouldn't approve of their relationship.

On the last Thursday in November, two weeks before her classes were due to finish for the year, Rose and Kaisa were sitting at their favourite table in the restaurant in Maida Vale when, smiling widely, Rose said, 'I've got some great news!' She brought a newspaper cutting out of her handbag. 'Look at this!'

Kaisa read the notice: 'Finnish radio journalist for BBC World Service.'

'But I've never worked for radio, and I'm not even a journalist yet.'

'Yes, but read on, they say they can train you! How many Finnish speakers do you think there are in London?' Rose said. 'Holding a valid work permit, that is!'

Kaisa hung her head; the work permit and her marriage to Peter were still unsolved issues. She hadn't spoken to him since that awful telephone conversation after returning from Plymouth. He hadn't contacted her about a divorce, so in theory she was still married to him and had the right to work in England. And the monthly allowance was still going into her bank account. But a national broadcaster like the BBC would surely check her living arrangements and see that she was separated from her husband? She looked at Rose.

'You know, Rose, if I'm separated from Peter, I am not entitled to a work permit, so I'm actually illegally employed by Terroni's at the moment.'

'Who says?'

'Ravi.'

Rose leaned back in her chair and said, 'I see.'

'Sorry, I didn't want to tell you before.'

'Oh, I'm sure no one will check,' Rose said. She was quiet and suddenly Kaisa got the feeling that something else was worrying her.

'Are you OK?' Kaisa asked.

Rose looked up, startled. 'Yes, I'm just thinking about Christmas.'

'What about it?'

Rose gazed at Kaisa and hesitated, 'Oh, it's nothing.'

Kaisa leaned over and took hold of the older woman's hand, 'Something's bothering you, I can tell.'

Rose lifted her pale eyes to Kaisa's. 'Roger's asked me to marry him!'

'That's wonderful news!' Kaisa got up and went to hug Rose, but before she could put her arms around her friend, Rose said, 'I haven't said yes yet.'

Kaisa sat back down. 'Why not? Don't you love him?'

Rose sighed, 'Well, I just never thought I'd marry. You know, with my career, there's just not been time for a serious relationship.' And then she smiled, 'But I really, really like being with Roger. He has his own career at the *Guardian*, and we are quite grown-up, both of us, so ...'

'So, why not marry him?'

'He's coming to the country with me for Christmas, to meet my uncle and the rest of the family.'

Kaisa smiled. Tactfully, Rose hadn't mentioned Duncan. 'That'll be nice.'

'Yeah,' Rose replied.

'So, did he give you a ring?' Kaisa asked.

Rose smiled and dug out a small container from her handbag. Inside was a huge emerald ring, the kind that Princess Diana had.

'It's beautiful!' Kaisa said. She knew Roger was quite high up at the newspaper, but she had no idea he was rich enough to afford a ring like that.

Rose gazed down at the ring, but didn't put it on. 'Isn't it a bit too much?' she said, but her smile had grown so wide that Kaisa knew she'd say yes to Roger.

'It's perfect. I'm so happy for you.' Kaisa got up again and hugged her friend. Rose's body seemed slight in her embrace and Kaisa felt quite protective towards her. 'Why don't we all go out and celebrate in the New Year?' Kaisa said. Although she'd met Roger several times in the pub, she didn't know what kind of man he was. Kaisa suddenly felt responsible for her friend and wanted to make sure she wasn't making a mistake.

Rose nodded and put the ring back inside its tiny box.

THIRTY

Peter got off the train in Westbury and saw his sister standing beside her car outside the small station. It was the day before Christmas Eve and it was raining when he emerged from the station building. Peter's mum had begged him to come home for the holidays, now he wasn't at sea, and Peter had eventually agreed. Christmas on the deserted base would have been depressing, and the alternative, to go and stay with Jackie in London, didn't appeal to him. He was trying to cool things with her after she'd thrown a strop about Kaisa. He knew she thought he would propose to her as soon as he divorced Kaisa, but that was the last thing on his mind. And he couldn't bring himself to send Kaisa the papers a lawyer had prepared for him, not yet.

Nancy looked flustered, something he wasn't used to seeing in his older sister. As he sat down in the passenger seat of her her brand-new silver Volvo Estate, he glanced behind at the two Moses baskets strapped head to head in the back seat. While he'd been away at sea, Nancy had given birth to twins, a boy and a girl. They were now about two months old, and both had the Williams' hallmark mop of dark hair. One of them, the boy, Peter assumed, judging by his powder-blue romper suit, began crying as soon as his sister sat down in the driver's seat.

'Shh, Oliver,' Nancy said and quickly started the engine.

His sister lived in a large Bath stone house in Trowbridge, only a couple of streets from where Peter and Nancy had grown up with their older brother, who now lived in London. Her sister's magnificent, detached house was a lot grander than their old family terraced house, but that was explained by the man his sister lived with (scandalously unmarried, even though Nigel kept asking Nancy to tie the knot). Nigel owned his own estate agency, which took on properties over a certain price. Nancy had known Nigel since school, and they'd been going out forever, so neither Peter, nor his mother, understood why she wouldn't marry. Nancy just smiled, and said, 'There's no hurry, is there?' The twins had obviously made it more urgent, as Peter's mother had pointed out in one of her many letters to Peter, but Nancy had simply said that she wasn't going to walk down the aisle with a huge bump under her dress.

When she parked the car outside a green garage door, Nancy asked Peter to carry one of the babies inside. As soon as Peter lifted Oliver's basket, he opened his large blue eyes, lifted his little arms up and began to whinge.

'Just let him cry,' Nancy said in an exasperated voice as she led the way into the house. She placed Beth, the baby girl, on the kitchen table and told Peter to place the other basket next to it. The kitchen, like the hall they'd walked through, was wide and filled with light from the French windows over-looking the garden. Everything looked new; since Peter's last visit they'd fitted out the kitchen with light-coloured cabinets and a breakfast bar with dark leather stools.

'Do you want me to do anything?' Peter asked over the noise of the babies. Beth had joined Oliver in his protests.

Nancy looked at Peter, as if considering whether he could

be trusted to carry out any kind of task relating to the twins. 'Sit down at the table and hold Beth while I give Oliver his bottle. 'Wash your hands first,' she ordered, and Peter visited the small cloakroom off the hall. When he came back, Nancy had both babies in her arms. The scene was so unfamiliar to Peter that he stood in the doorway, unseen, for a moment. Without realising it, in his mind he replaced his sister's face with Kaisa's, and the overwhelming sensation of tenderness and pride he suddenly felt towards the crying babies took him by surprise. He had to swallow a lump in his throat.

Holding Beth was even worse. Her little fingers were perfect, and her little feet, moving anxiously in the arms of a total stranger, melted Peter's heart. 'She's beautiful,' he said and smiled at his sister, who was feeding the now quiet Oliver from a bottle half-filled with milk.

'Do you want to feed her?' Nancy asked and showed Peter how to tip the bottle so that Beth could drink without getting air inside her tummy. The little sucking noises Beth made, while still eyeing him suspiciously, brought a smile to Peter's lips. 'You've done well,' he said to Nancy, and her sister returned his smile. Gazing down at this little wonder suddenly made all his problems with the court martial and Kaisa's rejection fade away. Peter realised he was an uncle now, an uncle to these wonderful, new human beings. They were his flesh and blood, if only by a fraction. Inhaling the new baby scent, he vowed to be there for the twins, his little niece and nephew. He would look after them if need be.

Nigel found the sister and brother feeding the babies in the kitchen. 'You've got a job there if you want it,' Nigel joked. He was wearing a smart business suit and was carrying a large leather briefcase, which he plonked onto the breakfast bar. He gave Nancy a peck on her cheek and said, 'Fix me a G&T while I make a couple of calls.'

Nancy just nodded, but Peter said, 'I'll do that while you

see to these two.' Beth had fallen asleep in his arms, so Nancy placed her back into the Moses basket.

'So, how's the life of a sailor?' Nigel said when Peter handed him the drink. He was sitting, still in his suit, in an armchair in the corner of the lounge, next to a green pot plant. His round face was a little flustered, as if the effort of walking from his car to the house was taking a toll on him. Peter noticed he'd put on weight; the striped shirt underneath his suit jacket was straining at the buttons. His fair hair was thinning, and he looked every bit the prosperous estate agent he was.

'OK,' Peter replied. He dreaded these moments with Nigel because, unlike his sister, Nigel didn't evade any subject. Peter suddenly realised that Nigel completely lacked tact. That must be why he was so successful in business, Peter thought, and took a large gulp of his own G&T. The embodiment of Thatcher's Britain, Nigel made money out of the rich who wanted bigger and better homes. His company, Hammond's, didn't let anyone who wasn't wearing designer clothes, or at least a smart suit, even walk into their office. 'I wouldn't know, we don't sell council flats,' Nigel had once sniffed when Peter had asked if there was any money to be made in Thatcher's new policy of letting council residents buy up their properties.

'You've got over that thing, the court martial, now?'

Peter lifted his eyes to Nigel. He was looking at Peter squarely, inquisitively. Peter saw no malice in his plump face, and wondered how he'd convey to his common-law brother-in-law that this was one subject he really didn't want to discuss.

'Yeah,' he said, hoping that would do the trick.

'Saw it in the papers. Not too bad, as far as I'm concerned, brought a lot of interest and even a few house sales my way. People love a scandal, and as far as I could see you were well within your rights to give him what's for.' Nigel lifted his glass towards Peter. 'So, well done, I say.'

'Thanks,' Peter said and downed the rest of his drink.

'And that Scandinavian girl, you still married to her?' Nigel continued.

There he goes, Peter thought, the second subject he'd rather not talk about. Classic Nigel.

Peter was rescued by his sister, who'd changed out of the tracksuit she'd been wearing earlier and into a neat little dress that suited her slight frame. 'Is he boring you with talk of his house deals?' she said, sitting on the arm of Peter's chair.

'No, not at all,' Peter said, and gave Nigel a look that he hoped conveyed his unwillingness to discuss things any further. 'You look nice,' he added.

'Well, we thought we'd take you out. One of Nigel's friends has taken over a pub in Hilperton, and the food's really good, so we thought we'd go there if that's OK with you? Nigel's niece is babysitting. Do you want to have a shower and change before we go?'

During the meal, when the nice-looking barmaid, who kept giving Peter the eye, took their plates away, Nigel leaned back in his chair. Sending Nancy a quick glance, he said, 'The reason we wanted to see you before you go to your parents is that I have a proposition for you.'

Lying in bed in Nancy's pink guest bedroom later that evening, Peter thought about what Nigel had said to him. 'My customers would love you, ex-naval officer, good manners, looks and charming personality.' Peter knew the job would be that of a salesman, but the starting salary Nigel had suggested (without commission) was more than he was earning. But was he ready for the civvy lifestyle? If he was truthful, his last time away with HMS *Orion* had been the most boring yet. Nothing had happened. They hadn't got a sniff of a Russian sub, or a destroyer, and the only thing they'd done was endlessly repeat the workouts they'd already completed before going away. And the cramped quarters onboard the diesel submarine had got on his nerves too; as had the jibes about being a 'Bomber Queen', the Navy's slur for the submariners who'd served on the much more spacious Polaris vessels, if he even hinted that he didn't enjoy living in someone else's armpit. He hadn't dared complain about the way they had to sleep and eat their meals in the minuscule wardroom.

But could he cope with civilian life back in Wiltshire so soon after articles about him had appeared in the local and national newspapers?

'Everyone will have forgotten about it already, the papers will be fish and chip wrappers by now,' Nancy had said, taking his arm between her hands. 'We just want you to be happy, Peter,' she'd added, and it made him realise that she worried about him. Had Nancy and her mother put Nigel up to this?

Peter promised he'd think about it. Nigel shook his hand as if he'd already agreed to the whole deal.

THE NEXT DAY, Christmas Eve, Nancy drove Peter and the babies, plus a great deal of baby equipment, to his parents' house.

For a while Peter stood outside his parents' house. He'd only been to see his family once since the court martial, a short visit mainly spent holed up in the blue bedroom. The same bedroom in which he'd spent many nights making love to Kaisa, trying not to be noisy. Once he had to hold his hand over her mouth for the duration, and they'd giggled afterwards, realising too late that his parents would hear and think they were still doing it. During his last visit, only days after the court martial, he had cried for the first time since his childhood, remembering how happy he'd been there with Kaisa. He couldn't remember ever feeling more sorry for himself. It just wasn't the way he was made.

His mother and father had been gentle with him, not

mentioning the fight, Kaisa's infidelity, or the court martial. But Peter had seen the disappointment in his father's eyes. His father had said, without looking at him, 'You'll put this behind you. Just work hard, lad, and they'll forget all about it.' His father had been in the Navy himself during the war, and although Peter didn't know much about his time at sea, he could guess that his father had seen and heard far worse than the tale of his pathetic fight with Duncan. His parents had even hidden the papers in which the story appeared, placing them underneath a pile of magazines next to the fireplace in the lounge. Of course, on the second morning in his parents' house, when they'd been at work, he'd found the papers. Disgusted by what they said, he had fled Wiltshire, leaving a note to his mother. 'Sorry, Mum, couldn't stay. I'll write to you. Love Peter.'

He'd travelled back to Helensburgh and found the flat in Smuggler's Way cold and empty. There was a letter from Kaisa on the mat, in which she said she'd arrived in Helsinki OK.' There'd been no mention of when she was going to return. That night Peter had gone to the Ardencaple with Nigel and drunk himself silly.

Now, as he opened the door to the pink painted bungalow, Peter could still see pain around his mother's eyes. She hugged him, 'I am so glad you are home and safe.'

Peter returned the hug. He was reminded that here were the people who truly loved him. His long and boring time at sea had given him time to think and to put his misadventure into perspective. He had come to realise that he wanted to work hard and make something of himself. He'd thought that something would be his career in the Navy, and that, as his father had told him, he just needed to get his head down and work hard. Which he had. His Captain on HMS *Orion* had told him he'd done well just before he set off on leave. 'I had misgivings about you Peter, I can't lie. But you've worked hard and I'm glad to have you as one of my officers.' That had meant a lot to Peter. He had crossed his fingers and hoped that he'd soon get a call from the Appointer with a better job. But now, for the first time since he'd applied for the Royal Navy at the age of seventeen, he was thinking that perhaps a civilian life might be a better option after all.

Peter, Nancy and his mother sat around the small kitchen table while the twins slept. 'We all worry about you, you know,' his mother said. She placed her wrinkly warm hand over Peter's on the table and squeezed it hard.

'I know mum, but I'm OK now.'

'Glad to hear it, son.'

'Nigel offered him a job last night,' Nancy said, and their mother immediately, too soon, replied, 'Oh really, well that's something, isn't it, Peter?'

Peter smiled but didn't tell the two women that he'd realised their ruse. He went along with it. 'I have to think about it, mum. I can't just leave the Navy like that anyway. I have to give at least one year's notice, or longer, if they can't replace me in HMS *Orion*.' Peter looked from his sister to his mum, and they both nodded.

'Of course, dear, of course. But it's worth thinking about, don't you agree? Nigel is doing very well, and he needs help from someone he can trust. Family, that is.'

Nancy gave her mother a look of warning, and she got up and put the kettle on. Peter nearly laughed. How did his mother know so much about it if she'd just heard about the job offer now? It was so evident that the two women had plotted this. If he was going to consider the job, he'd need to get Nigel on his own. Peter resolved to swing by his agency on his way back to Plymouth during one of the days between Christmas and New Year.

THIRTY-ONE

K aisa's Christmas was saved at the last minute by Toni, her boss at Terroni's. The day before Christmas Eve, he asked what she was doing for the holidays and when he heard she would be alone, he invited her to the restaurant for both Christmas Eve and Christmas Day. At first, Kaisa refused, but Toni roped in Mama, who in the end convinced Kaisa she was 'part of the family' anyway, so she must join them. They had a tradition to close the restaurant and have a big family party, setting all the tables together and closing the curtains to the outside world.

In the end, Kaisa spent Christmas Eve with her friends from the *Adam's Apple* – Rachel, who was now working for the *Guardian* together with Rose, called in at the café and invited her for drinks at the Coach and Horses. Rose had already left for Dorset, but both Jenny and Rachel were there. Kaisa enjoyed the evening; in London, everyone seemed to be up for a party on Christmas Eve, and Kaisa met and flirted with several good-looking men.

On Christmas Day, Kaisa was treated to the best food she'd ever had at Terroni's. There were fresh griddled fish, delicious salads, ham, pasta and the most fantastic cakes, moistened with coffee and filled with Italian cream cheese and fruits. It wasn't quite like the quiet Christmases in Finland, but it was better than the one she'd shared with Pammy in Helensburgh, which ended in Kaisa confessing to her affair with Duncan, and led to all that followed. With the Terroni family on Christmas morning, when her glass was refilled over and over again, first with Prosecco then with white and red wines, those dark days in Scotland felt like light years away.

Kaisa spent New Year with Ravi, again in the Coach and Horses, and then on the morning of 2nd January she got a letter from the BBC asking her to attend an interview. She was so delighted she told Mama and Toni about it. They both looked sad, and made her promise to come back and see them often when she was 'a famous BBC reporter'.

'I haven't got the job yet,' Kaisa had laughed.

'But you will, Bella,' Toni had replied and hugged her.

BUSH HOUSE, the headquarters of BBC World Service, was on Aldwych. Kaisa took the tube to Holborn and, because she was early, took a slight detour through the gardens of Lincoln's Inn Fields. The trees were bare and sad-looking, but the grass behind the iron fence was green, unlike in Finland, where, according to her sister, there was still snow on the ground. When she came to the impressive-looking building, which dominated Aldwych with its tall pillars and inscription reading BVSH HOVSE, Kaisa felt intimidated. Was the incomprehensible lettering Latin? The lobby, too, was high-ceilinged and clad in cream marble. Kaisa had never been inside a place like it. Her voice shook when she asked the lady behind a round desk where she should go. After scanning a list, she gave Kaisa a name badge and told her to wait on a leather sofa.

An older Finnish woman, who introduced herself as Annikki Sands and had a very stern manner, came to fetch her. When they were going up in the lift, Kaisa could make out at least three languages being spoken around her. At Terroni's she'd become used to hearing Italian, but this was different; it was as if she'd suddenly stepped into the most international and sophisticated world. These people even dressed differently; one man in the lift had a dark moustache and wore a spotted bowtie with a matching handkerchief in his jacket pocket. When he saw Kaisa looking at his attire, he made a slight nod and smiled. Kaisa turned her head towards Annikki, who luckily had her back to Kaisa and so hadn't seen her fraternising with the locals already. Somehow Kaisa knew the older Finnish woman wouldn't approve. When they reached the fourth floor, Annikki Sands walked in front of her, past a vast central lobby, where five different red clocks displayed the time in different parts of the world. People were milling around and Kaisa saw two doors surmounted by red lights saying, 'Quiet: Recording.'

The interview was conducted in a small, messy office, with piles of Finnish newspapers and magazines stacked high against the walls. The smell of newspaper ink made Kaisa recall her days at *Adam's Apple*, but otherwise it couldn't have been more different. For one thing, everyone spoke Finnish. Kaisa had been in London for such a long time that her Finnish faltered at first and she had to look for words, but she soon got used to it and spoke fluently. The woman, Annikki, didn't smile once for the duration of the interview. Kaisa assumed she was about the same age as her mother, in her late forties. The man next to her was a little younger and had a very quiet voice and manner. When Kaisa shook his hand, their palms barely touched before he pulled away. 'My name is Juha Helin,' he said. Juha was short, with soft sandy coloured hair. He looked kindly, and Kaisa was glad she had had at least one friendly face in the room, especially when Juha seemed impressed by Kaisa's degree from Hanken, as well as her short career in journalism.

'And you are taking a diploma at the moment in London?' Annikki Sands asked. Her tone was so level, that it almost dipped at the end of the question.

'Yes,' Kaisa replied, and when her words were followed by a silence, she realised she should elaborate. She described the subjects she'd covered to date, and told them how much she enjoyed studying at the School of Journalism. Kaisa had noticed that, once again, she was the most highly qualified on her course; none of the others in her class of about twenty people even had a university degree, let alone a Masters from a school of economics. Still, she was studying in a foreign language, which meant that she wasn't any faster at learning the techniques than her classmates.

After she'd finished, they both nodded, and then looked at each other.

'Your CV is very impressive. Have you applied for other jobs?' Annikki Sands asked.

Kaisa was quiet for a moment, then said, truthfully, 'No, but my previous employer at *Adam's Apple* has suggested a few places, such as the *Guardian* or the *Observer*, where she works.'

Annikki and Juha exchanged glances.

'You'll need to do a voice test,' Annikki Sands said. 'We all broadcast as well as write the programmes, so you will need a voice that is strong enough. I'll organise that, and send the appointment date and time to you.' She looked down at her notes and Kaisa confirmed that they had the correct address.

When Kaisa was walking back to Holborn tube station, she realised she'd not even asked how many other applicants there were. The advert had given the salary, which was far more than she'd ever earned, twice what Rose had been able to pay her at *Adam's Apple*. The start date, too, was stated in the newspaper – 3 February 1986 – though Annikki had hinted that they might have to move that forward. Kaisa cursed her nerves; it had taken all her concentration during the interview not to let her voice quiver, or her hands shake, but she should have been more inquisitive; she feared she might have come across as someone who didn't care whether she got the job or not. That said, when she'd left, the man, Juha, had smiled at her and nodded as if to say that she'd done well. But then, he might have done the same to everyone they interviewed. Plus, she had only nodded when they'd asked if she was married to an Englishman. There had been no mention of their living arrangements, or what her husband's profession was, so Kaisa didn't volunteer the information.

THE BBC LETTER offering her a job as a 'Junior Reporter, World Service, Finnish Section' arrived exactly two weeks after Kaisa had attended the interview at Bush House. It appeared that the voice test had just been a formality; they told her that her pronunciation needed to be worked on, that her 's' was a little too soft, but that with training she could become better. Even the interview with a slim, carefully made-up lady from the Personnel Department, who told Kaisa she was a former air hostess with British Airways, hadn't brought up Peter's profession. When Kaisa had told the woman her address she hadn't asked if she lived alone or with her husband. Kaisa decided she'd assumed they lived together, and Kaisa hadn't volunteered any other information. She had spoken with Rose on the telephone the night before the interview, and she had been adamant that she was within her right to work in the UK.

'Besides, once you're there, even if the divorce comes

through, they'll have to get you a work permit, because by then I bet they'll be counting on you, my dear,' she'd said.

Rose was staying with her uncle for an extra two days, in addition to the two weeks she'd taken off for Christmas and New Year. 'I've not taken a long holiday like this for ages,' she'd said on the phone. Rose had seemed very relaxed and Kaisa wondered if this was a long celebration of the engagement, because she kept postponing her return.

As it was, the personnel manager, who, with her slim figure and blonde hair pulled into a chignon, had reminded Kaisa of the wife of one of Peter's former captains (who had also worked as an air hostess for the national airline), hadn't asked a thing about Peter, apart from his name.

THIRTY-TWO

On Kaisa's first day, in early February, she found out that she'd been the only applicant with the relevant qualifications and a work permit. They had interviewed a couple of reporters from Finland but 'their English language skills weren't as good as yours,' Annikki told her. 'Besides, it's easier with someone who already lives here in London. And your Swedish language knowledge will come in useful too,' she added. Her face was still stern, but Kaisa could see a smile hovering at the corners of her eyes. Kaisa decided not to worry about her work permit, but reminded herself that she needed to let Peter know about her new status, just in case some eager civil servant somewhere in the great machinery of the Royal Navy and the British Broadcasting Corporation decided to check her credentials. She'd have to contact Peter, but she had no time to worry about that while Annikki showed her around her new workplace and introduced her to the new work colleagues.

That same evening, after an exhausting day spent meeting the Finnish team and being told she'd start a course in radio broadcasting on 10th February, she decided to try to call Peter.

She had no idea if he was still based in Plymouth, nor if he was away at sea. But she wanted to tell him the good news about the new job at the BBC. The magnitude of this hadn't really hit Kaisa yet. She'd been so worried about the work permit, and then about her ability to do the job. Now she just needed to make sure Peter wouldn't do anything, such as file for a divorce, for the next few months.

Kaisa dialled the number for the Devonport wardroom. She was nervous; what would she say to him? How would she formulate what she needed to ask him? She was standing in the hallway of the house at Colville Terrace, and prayed that the slovenly boyfriend of her landlady wouldn't suddenly decide he needed something from the kitchen. That had happened more and more often, but tonight the whole house seemed empty; keeping her fingers crossed, Kaisa listened to the rings on the other end of the line.

'Hello, I wonder if I could speak with Lieutenant Peter Williams.'

The gruff voice at the other end said, 'Who's calling?'

'It's Kaisa Williams,' Kaisa hesitated for a moment and added, 'his wife.'

'Just one moment, please,' the man said. He betrayed no emotion, or recognition of the name. Perhaps Peter's court martial and the events leading up to it had already been forgotten, Kaisa thought. Or perhaps this man was new and didn't know Peter's infamous history.

Kaisa could hear the echo of steps, then a door being closed at the other end, and then more steps. The receiver was picked up.

'Hello?'

Hearing Peter's voice took Kaisa's breath away. She was reminded of all those times when they'd been apart, her still living in Finland and him in Britain, when phone calls had been so precious. And then when they were living in the married quarter in Portsmouth, and he'd been away. She remembered the delight she'd taken in listening to him say he missed her, and the relief in realising he was safe, that the submarine hadn't sunk somewhere in the middle of the ocean, only to be reported missing weeks later. The horror of what the men onboard would have gone through would play on Kaisa's mind when she couldn't get to sleep. She always imagined the worst.

'Hello,' Peter said again. This time his voice displayed irritation.

'Hi, it's me,' Kaisa said quickly. She didn't want to lose him now. She held tightly onto the heavy black receiver.

'Kaisa,' Peter's voice was warm. 'How are you?'

'I'm well, and you?'

'Good.' There was a brief silence. 'We came back a few hours ago.'

Kaisa could hear that Peter had had a beer (or two) and she smiled without thinking. The crew wouldn't have had a drop to drink during all their weeks away, so sometimes just one beer could make them sound drunk. 'Really?'

'You didn't know?' Peter said.

How could she have known, Kaisa thought. 'No.'

'Oh.'

'Listen, I have a bit of news: I've got a job with the BBC!'

'Really,' Peter said. 'Congratulations.'

But Kaisa could hear disappointment in his voice, and she suddenly felt annoyed. This is what it always came down to with Peter. He didn't care what kind of job she had. All he wanted was to have sex with her, to have her at home when he came back from sea. She realised he must think she was calling to arrange a date. He thought nothing had changed; that she was desperate to see him again and to have him in her bed. But surely Kaisa had made it clear how she felt during their last conversation? Besides, the lack of letters over the months when they hadn't seen each other must have told him it was over? Of course, Kaisa had thought about him. Each time she was with Ravi, she thought about Peter. But she forced herself to forget all about him, for the sake of her career. However, it was evident from his reaction now, that to him, her career didn't matter.

'I'm only letting you know so that you needn't pay me any more money,' she said, trying to sound matter-of-fact. But she could hear the note of irritation in her voice. So what, she thought, serves him right.

'Oh, right,' Peter began, then stopped and said nothing more.

'We also need to decide about the divorce,' Kaisa continued. She was now so angry, she thought to hell with everything. She was the best candidate for the BBC job after all, and the others would have needed work permits anyway, so the BBC must be prepared to apply for one. Besides, now she had a contract, she was sure the BBC wouldn't get rid of her that easily. She had skills that no one else had, so she was sure she'd get a work permit now. She didn't need this selfish, arrogant, naval officer of an ex-husband anymore!

Again Peter started to say something, but then the doorbell to the house rang. Kaisa listened for a moment, but there was no movement in the whole place. The doorbell rang again and she said, 'Hold on a minute.'

Kaisa placed the receiver on the small table, and went to open the door. She was glad of the distraction, to control her temper. How was it possible that Peter could make her so angry so quickly when she didn't even live with him anymore, and hadn't talked to him since the brief phone call after that stupid, stupid, loss of self-control she'd had in Plymouth?

On the doorstep stood Ravi, holding a vast bunch of flowers in one hand, and in the other a bottle of champagne. He was grinning widely, showing his incredible white teeth. 'I thought we should celebrate your brilliant new career!' Ravi looked more handsome to Kaisa than he had for a long time. He was wearing a pair of smart trousers and a striped shirt under a double-breasted jacket with gold buttons. His pitch-black hair was just touching the collar of his shirt and his lips looked full and inviting. Kaisa smelled the flowers and in a loud voice said, 'Thank you, darling, come in, I just need to finish this telephone call.' She took hold of Ravi's arm, and pulled him inside.

Ravi stepped in and, looking puzzled, gave Kaisa a quick kiss on her lips. 'Who is it?' he whispered.

'Oh, it's no one important,' Kaisa said, again loud enough for Peter to hear, and she picked up the receiver.

'Sorry, I need to go. I just wanted to let you know about the money,' Kaisa took a deep breath, and continued, 'and the divorce. You can go ahead with it now.'

'Right,' Peter said. Kaisa could hear emotion in his voice now. Was it anger, or something else? She hesitated for a moment, but then thought, I'm glad I've upset him. Bloody man!

'Good,' she said.

'Yes, good.' Peter said.

'Bye,' Kaisa said and put down the receiver.

Ravi was standing in the hall, looking uncomfortable. They didn't often meet in the house, and if they did, they tried to sneak upstairs unnoticed. Kaisa's landlady, or the unpleasant boyfriend, didn't approve of Ravi. The landlady had once asked Kaisa, when Ravi had been waiting for her outside the house, what she was doing with a 'Paki'. Surely Kaisa, a good-looking girl, even if she was foreign, could do better than that? At the time, Kaisa had been going through a bit of a crisis of conscience with Ravi and had decided to finish it with him, perhaps because it was only a week after she'd slept with Peter, or because she realised she didn't love him and never would. They hadn't yet had sex, and Kaisa knew that she would have to let it happen soon, so it was only fair to end it. But the landlady's racism had made Kaisa defiant. She'd got drunk that evening and had invited Ravi to her bed. At the same time, Kaisa couldn't afford to be thrown out of the bedsit, so they'd been careful not to be seen in the house together again.

'Come on, let's go upstairs and open this!' Kaisa said. 'The house is empty!' she grinned, taking the flowers from him. She led him up the stairs and into her room. She didn't have any proper champagne glasses and they had to drink it out of water tumblers.

When they'd settled on the bed, sitting side by side, Kaisa began kissing Ravi, and undoing his buttons. Ravi put his hand on Kaisa's fingers, stopping her midway. 'Was that your husband on the phone?'

Kaisa looked at Ravi's dark eyes. 'Yes, why?'

Ravi stood up, and placing his glass on the small kitchen worktop opposite Kaisa's bed, said, 'Look, I like you a lot.' He rubbed the dark stubble on his chin and gazed at Kaisa for a while. 'As a matter of fact, I think I might be falling for you.'

Kaisa sat on the bed, looking at her hands. She didn't dare to look at Ravi.

'But I cannot be part of a game you are playing with your husband.'

Kaisa looked up, 'What do you mean, a game?'

Ravi came over to her, crouching opposite her, and took her hands in his. 'Our relationship is not an easy one. Already we have to sneak around this place.'

'But I don't care about them!' Kaisa looked at his sad eyes.

'I know you don't, and believe me, I don't give a shit about people like that either. I meet them every day, so I'm used to it. But my community, they would be, and are, the same. I'm constantly fighting a battle against my mother.' Ravi lifted

Kaisa's chin up and looked deep into her eyes. 'She wants to find a suitable wife for me. She's relentless.' Ravi gave a small laugh. 'So, what I'm saying is that if we were to get more serious, it will be difficult and we will need to be sure of our feelings for each other.'

Kaisa nodded. She moved away from Ravi, and went to stand by the sink. She couldn't face him.

'And I'm not sure you are over Peter,' Ravi said to her back.

Tears began running down Kaisa's face. The whole awfulness of the conversation with Peter just dawned on her, at the same time as the realisation that she was also losing Ravi. He stood up and put his arms round her. He rocked her back and forth for a while. Kaisa turned around in his arms, and put her head on his shoulder. 'I'm getting make-up on your smart shirt,' she said.

'That's alright.'

They stood there for a moment, until Kaisa finished crying. Ravi let go, and gave Kaisa a peck on her wet cheek. 'If you need any help with anything, call me, eh?'

Kaisa nodded. When the door closed behind Ravi, Kaisa sat down on the bed, sipping the champagne. She sat like that for at least an hour, watching the lights of the houses opposite go out and the street quieten. The room grew darker, and Kaisa got up. She put the half-full bottle of champagne in her little fridge and found the pint glass Ravi had once stolen for her from the Horse and Coaches, when she'd told him she only owned a pair of tumblers to put his flowers in. Kaisa sighed. Ravi was right, she knew. She cared for him. But she still had feelings for Peter. What kind of feelings, apart from the anger and annoyance she felt for him, she didn't know. But because she felt those emotions so strongly, it was obvious she needed more time to get over him. Had she been selfish to have sex with Ravi? Had she led him on? Not according to Rose, but then Rose wouldn't have predicted that Ravi would leave her.

Suddenly Kaisa laughed; she'd been dumped! This was how it felt. Served her right for everything she'd done to the men in her life; still, she couldn't help but feel sorry for herself. She pulled her legs up on the small comfy chair in her room, poured some more champagne, and settled down to watch an old American black-and-white film on TV.

THIRTY-THREE

Peter put the phone down and stood gazing at the door to the wardroom for a moment. Then he turned back to the phone and dialled a number. 'Are you doing anything this weekend?'

Jackie shrieked. 'You're back! No, what are you planning?'

Peter made a date to go up to London on Friday evening. Jackie's delight at the other end of the phone was palpable; Peter almost felt embarrassed on her behalf.

Peter hadn't seen Jackie since Kaisa's visit to Plymouth. They had sailed a few days later, and had not got back until just before Christmas. The next trip had come as a surprise; they'd sailed immediately after Peter got back to Plymouth after the New Year. Jackie had written to Peter, and he'd even managed to reply, but he'd kept his letters cool on purpose. He didn't want a repetition of the discussion – or rather argument – about his divorce and the possibility of marrying Jackie. Peter shook his head; she must be completely mad to think he would enter headlong into another serious relationship like that. 'Women!' he thought a few days later as he drove along the motorway towards London. He decided that if Jackie started that kind of talk again, this would be the last time he'd see her.

But when Jackie opened the door to her flat in Chelsea, and flung herself around his neck, he regretted his decision to drive all the way up to London to see her. He felt bad, because he knew he was taking all his anger for Kaisa, all his jealousy, out on Jackie. He was using her.

'Darling Peter, I knew you'd come around!' Jackie cooed.

'Look, this was a mistake,' Peter said, forcing Jackie's hands from his neck. He was holding onto her wrists, and realised too late that he was squeezing them a lot harder than he'd intended.

'Kinky!' Jackie laughed, 'You want to tie me up?' she said and wriggled her bum. She was wearing just a thin dress and high-heeled shoes. It was a cold evening, and he could see her hard nipples through the gathered material of the dress. Peter could guess what, if anything, was underneath, and felt himself harden. 'Come in!' Jackie said and pulled him inside.

Why the hell not, Peter thought, but afterwards when they were lying on Jackie's satin sheets, smoking cigarettes, Peter said, 'Look, we can't do this anymore.'

'What?' Jackie sat up in bed, revealing her full, naked breasts.

Peter sighed, 'Sorry, Jackie, but I ...'

'Shh,' Jackie said and kissed Peter. 'Don't worry, I'm not going to mention the 'M' word,' she gave Peter a grin, 'or the 'D' word for that matter. Let's just have fun, eh?'

'OK,' Peter said, but he knew that wouldn't be the end of it with Jackie. However, if she didn't want to spell it out, if she said she wanted just to have fun, that meant no ties, right? But this woman scared him and Peter resolved that this was the last weekend he would spend with her.

On Sunday, when it was time for Peter to return to Plymouth, he told Jackie at the door, 'I'm sorry, but this is it.'

Jackie's face fell, 'What do you mean?'

'I'm not going to be back.'

Jackie stared at Peter. She tried to pull her mouth up into a smile, but managed just a lopsided grin. Peter shifted his weight from one foot to another. He wanted to be away, but he also wanted to make sure Jackie was clear on his decision. Her father was an Admiral after all, and goodness knew what weight he still carried in the Navy.

'Look, I'm sorry. I just can't.' He took Jackie's hand in his. 'It's my career, and who knows what my next appointment is going to be.'

'But I do!' Jackie said.

'What?'

'But if you don't want me ...'

Peter gazed down at Jackie. She was standing in her stockinged feet, shivering inside her dressing gown. Was she bluffing? 'Have you done something, organised something to do with my career?'

'Oh, Peter,' Jackie came and put her hands around his waist. 'I just asked Daddy if there was any chance you might get a job nearer London, you know a shore job for a change, and he said he'd see what he could do.'

PETER DROVE BACK to Plymouth with his head whirling with different ideas. A shore job in London would change everything. But, of course, nothing was certain yet; Jackie's dad could be bluffing; why would he want his daughter anywhere near Peter? Perhaps once upon a time, but not now when his career was doing a nose dive. 'A submariner in a nose dive is never a good thing,' Peter thought and grinned at his own joke. All the same, if he was given this fantastic opportunity to be ashore for a while, he'd make use of it. Poor Jackie, she'd well and truly shot herself in the foot this time.

THIRTY-FOUR

When she got home to her bedsit, there was a cream-coloured letter waiting for Kaisa. Even before she turned the envelope in her hands, she guessed who it was from. She could recognise Peter's handwriting in a darkened room by touch alone, she was sure of it. She smelled the envelope before opening it, but there was no hint of his coconut aftershave. It wasn't what he normally did, anyway, it was the other way around; Kaisa was the one who was supposed to drown her correspondence in perfume.

Dear Kaisa,

I hope you are well, and still living in the same address in London and that this letter reaches you.

I wasn't sure if you wanted to hear from me, but after so many weeks at sea, I felt I should at least let you know I'm back in port and not likely to go away again soon. And I have some news.

I am visiting my family in Wiltshire at the moment, and this is one of the reasons I wanted to write. I thought you'd like to know that Nancy and Nigel have had two little babies,

twins, Oliver and Beth. They're now three months old, and
very beautiful, although the boy, Oliver, cries a lot, especially
at night. Nancy is very well too, as is Nigel. My mum and
dad send their regards, and wish you well.

Love,
Peter x

Kaisa reread the letter three times, standing in the hall. She was rooted to the spot, mulling over what Peter's words might mean. The tone of the letter was like old times; he'd even put an x after his name. Suddenly a door opened and Mrs Carter peered at her.

'Everything alright?'

Her landlady was wearing a faded housecoat and had rollers in her artificially bleached hair. She looked annoyed.

'Yes, sorry, I just got a letter and ...'

'The hall's not for lounging in,' Mrs Carter said.

'Who is it?' Kaisa heard Colin's shout from inside the room.

'No one,' Mrs Carter said and banged the door shut. Kaisa put the letter back into the envelope and fled upstairs. Kaisa's landlady had been particularly unfriendly to her in the past few weeks. She'd told Kaisa that she was going to marry the brute Colin, who'd been staying there ever since Kaisa moved in. He didn't seem to get dressed, and was always wearing his long johns, or boxer shorts in summer, whenever Kaisa saw him in the stairwell. Mrs Carter had told her that they were going to be making changes to the house. 'Colin thinks we should turn this place into luxury flats,' she'd said. There was no timetable for this, of course, and Kaisa doubted the two of them would ever get round to it, but it seemed obvious they wanted her out. In any case, Kaisa didn't want to rock the boat by making a nuisance of herself and give Mrs Carter and the horrible boyfriend any cause to ask her to leave sooner than they were planning. Although, with her new BBC job, she'd be able to rent a whole flat, Kaisa didn't want to count her chickens. Not yet.

Thinking about her living arrangements calmed Kaisa and she could now go back to wondering what the letter meant. She looked at the envelope. It was dated more than a month ago, 2nd January 1986. Why had it taken so long to reach her? And why had Peter written to her in the first place? Before he went away in November, she thought they'd made it clear to each other that they had no future together. Perhaps he had suddenly felt nostalgic for her, and the happy times they'd had in his parents' house in Wiltshire. Kaisa looked at the postmark on the envelope, it had 'BFPO Ships' on it, which meant he'd sent it while away at sea, or from the wardroom before he went away. Still, that meant it had taken a month to reach her. Another thought entered her mind. Because she'd had no communication from Peter, she'd assumed he was away at sea for Christmas. Although she'd not wanted to spend the holiday with Peter, in her desperation during the days leading up to the holidays, when she was facing a long weekend alone in the bedsit, she might have considered meeting up with him if she'd known he was ashore.

Kaisa looked at Peter's letter again. She thought about those mysterious words, 'not likely to go away again soon'. What did they mean? Kaisa's heart skipped a beat when she thought the unthinkable. No, that could not be what he meant? Peter would never even think about leaving the Navy – or would he?

Then there were the babies, twins! Kaisa wondered if the gene ran in Nigel's family. She'd certainly never heard of any twins in the Williams family. Finally, the mention of Peter's parents made her shiver. Even after all these months, and after everything she'd done, the life she'd forged for herself in London (with the help of Rose, of course), she still feared seeing Peter's parents the most. Of course, there was no chance she'd suddenly bump into them in Terroni's in Farringdon, or at the BBC in Aldwych, or on the street in Notting Hill. Still, just the thought of facing them after what she had done to their son made her palms damp. No, she would never be able to see his mother or father ever again.

Kaisa put the letter away and went to make herself a cup of coffee. While she sipped it, she thought how nice it would be to see Nancy and the twins. Then she imagined herself holding hands with Peter, looking down at two babies in their separate cots. There was no stopping her mind now. She immediately imagined herself in Peter's arms, kissing his lips, held firmly in his embrace, running her fingers through his thick black hair. 'Stop,' she told herself. 'Stop. That'll never happen, so just stop it now.' But she couldn't help herself, and she reread Peter's letter. She realised the sentence about not going away soon could mean anything. It could be that the submarine was in refit, that he'd joined another submarine that was being built, or that he was on a lengthy course in Portsmouth, or even London. The most unlikely alternative, that he'd decided to leave the Navy, was ludicrous. It wasn't even worth thinking about.

THE REST of her first week at the BBC, Kaisa existed in a haze of learning new things and meeting new people. She'd even been invited to the pub on Friday night, and she'd got to know the other Finns who worked at Bush House. She realised that the work was going to be hard, because it involved a lot of translation. News stories from the main bulletins at the BBC needed to be translated quickly into Finnish, edited into a suitably short bulletin, and broadcast, often on the same day. Her Finnish language skills had suffered during her time in the UK, but Juha, who had been assigned as her supervisor, told Kaisa she'd soon learn the ropes.

'There are people working here who've lived in England for ten, twenty years. It was much harder for them to relearn Finnish. You'll be fine,' he said in his understated way as they were queuing up for food in the canteen.

On Saturday evening, after her first weekend duty at the BBC, Kaisa sat down and wrote a letter to Peter. She'd learned that they would work four days on and then have four days off, but that would include any day of the week. Bank holidays were treated as any other day of the week. 'But we have Christmas off,' Juha had told her. She'd been to the pub with Juha after they'd completed that day's short weekend bulletin (Kaisa helped, but Juha did most of the work and read out the news in Finnish). There they'd met a couple of male reporters from Italy who'd been impressed by the little Italian Kaisa had learned at Terroni's. They also knew the café, and Mama Terroni, and said they recognised Kaisa from their visits there. It felt strange to have her different lives collide, but no one seemed to think it odd that a woman with her qualifications should have worked as a waitress for a time. London was truly different, Kaisa thought, and she smiled at the handsome Italians.

Dear Peter,

When we spoke I didn't get to say how happy I am for Nancy and Nigel. (I only got your letter last week.) They must be delighted with the new additions to their family, as must you and your parents be. And you are now an uncle! Please send my congratulations to Nancy and Nigel.

I'm sorry our conversation on Wednesday was cut short, it is difficult to talk when living in somebody else's house. This bedsit living is a bit like the wardroom, I'm sure. You can never be alone on the telephone without someone listening in.

The reason I phoned, was that I wanted to tell you that you can go ahead with the divorce. As you, I am sure, understand, my issue has been with a work permit. I found out some time ago that if you divorced me, as a foreign subject I wouldn't be allowed to stay in the UK. Now, however, with my new job at the BBC, I think I might be able to get a work permit after all. Also, as I said on the telephone, you don't need to support me financially any more. So you can be rid of me at last.

Best,

Kaisa

Kaisa reread what she had written and sighed. She'd decided not to put an 'x' for a kiss at the end of her name. That decision had taken at least ten minutes. She thought back to that crazy night in Plymouth and how wonderful it had felt to once again be held in Peter's arms. And the act of sex, how wonderful it had been, how good it had felt with Peter. She shivered when she thought about it now. She couldn't help it, but she longed for his touch, for the taste of his lips. But it could, would, never work, so Kaisa folded the paper, put it inside an envelope and, licking the glue, sealed it. She now had four days off, and on Monday she resolved to go and look for a flat of her own. Then she could give notice to her landlady and be able to have a bit of privacy at last. Perhaps then she could meet someone new.

THIRTY-FIVE

A week and a bit later, after Kaisa had done two four-hour shifts at the BBC, and had started her formal BBC journalism course, held in the top floor conference rooms at Bush House, she was getting ready to go out. She'd had to pull out of the course at the School of Journalism, but the lady in the personnel department had told Kaisa that BBC training was more prestigious. 'This will stand you in good stead worldwide,' she'd said smiling. Kaisa had been sad not to finish her course in Maida Vale, but the tutor had given her a letter, explaining to any prospective employer why she had dropped out. 'A job at the BBC!' he'd said. 'That's a job for life! Well done!'

Some of the other students had looked at her differently when they heard her news. Kaisa hadn't told them that she'd been the only proper applicant, or at least the only one with relevant education, experience, and language skills living in the UK.

Not working at Terroni's and dropping out of the course meant that she saw less of Rose, and so they'd decided to meet up on the Monday evening after her second four-day shift at the BBC. On the phone, Rose had told her that she'd accepted Roger's offer of marriage, and Kaisa had congratulated her. Rose had invited Kaisa to an engagement party at Roger's place in a couple of weeks' time. Kaisa hadn't been to the Coach and Horses since Ravi had broken up with her, and sitting on the tube on her way to Farringdon, she wondered if he'd be there. When she dug into her handbag to reapply her lip gloss, she noticed at the bottom of the bag the unsent letter to Peter. She'd been meaning to send it every day, but hadn't had time even to buy a stamp. She felt the thin envelope in her hands, and wondered if she should rip it up, when the train pulled into Farringdon.

The Coach and Horses wasn't full on a Monday evening in late February, and Kaisa quickly realised that she was about fifteen minutes early. The first person she set eyes on was Ravi. He was talking to a man, whom Kaisa recognised as one of his friends from the *Observer*. It was too late for Kaisa to back away – they had both seen her, and Ravi's friend had even waved. Kaisa took a deep intake of breath and walked towards the two men.

Ravi gave her a kiss on her cheek, and asked if she wanted a drink. Kaisa looked around; there was no sign of Rose.

'OK, she said, I'll have a glass of white wine.'

She suddenly thought Ravi must be thinking she was here to look for him. 'I'm meeting Rose later,' she said as he handed her the drink.

'Oh, OK.' Ravi said. Exchanging some silent message, with Ravi, his friend excused himself to Kaisa, saying he needed to read through something, and went to sit at a table in the corner of the pub. With his head bent, he started shifting through a pile of papers. Both Kaisa and Ravi looked at him for a while. Kaisa wished Rose would turn up soon; she didn't know what to say to Ravi.

'How have you been?' Ravi looked at Kaisa, his black eyes full of emotion.

'Good, the new job is tiring, but I like it there.' Kaisa moved her eyes away from his; she didn't want to sink into those deep pools of liquid black.

'Good, good,' Ravi said.

They stood quietly for a moment, sipping their drinks. Kaisa thought what a good-looking man Ravi was, and wondered if he'd succumbed to seeing any of the girls his mother had suggested for him. But those dark eyes, and the floppy black hair, and his muscular build didn't have any effect on her anymore. She was now glad he'd broken it off; he'd been right, she had no romantic feelings for him.

'Look, Kaisa,' Ravi looked around him to make sure their conversation remained private. He put his hand on Kaisa's arm and said, 'I've missed you.'

'Oh, Ravi,' Kaisa said. She didn't want to lead him on, but didn't know what to say.

At that moment she saw from the corner of her eye the door to the pub open and a man walk in. Afterwards, Kaisa was sure she'd felt his presence even before she'd turned to face him.

'Peter,' she said. Ravi still had his hand on Kaisa's arm, and suddenly she realised that anyone seeing the two of them like that would think they were a couple. She quickly pulled her hand away and moved towards Peter, who stood glued to the spot near the door of the pub. When Kaisa got to him, she saw his eyes were dark and serious. She wanted to explain to him that there was nothing going on between her and Ravi; that she kept thinking about the exciting, thrilling and completely mad lovemaking in the car in Plymouth; and that she couldn't forget about him. Instead, she said, 'What are you doing here?'

Peter brushed past her to the bar. 'It's a free country,

isn't it?'

He was now standing next to Ravi, who, taken aback at hearing the name, stepped away from Peter, and glanced questioningly at Kaisa. She just shrugged her shoulders and stood next to Peter.

When he'd got his drink, Kaisa said, 'Shall we go and sit down?'

Peter took a long pull out of his pint, and nodded. He gave Ravi a long look, turned away and walked to a table at the other side of the bar. 'Sorry,' Kaisa mouthed to Ravi as she followed Peter.

'So, you've moved on, then?' Peter said as soon as he'd sat down.

His voice was loud, and Kaisa could see he was angry. His tone of voice took her by surprise. She couldn't believe it. What right did he have to lecture her on moving on! She remembered the party in the summer, when they'd only been apart for a few months. He had kissed Kaisa, then immediately told the girl he'd come to the party with that the kiss hadn't meant anything. And when they'd gone out for a meal in Covent Garden a few months later, at the end of a wonderful evening, which had made Kaisa believe they were going to be reconciled, he'd told her that he wanted a divorce. True enough, after Plymouth, he seemed to want to get back together again, but by then Kaisa had known it wouldn't work.

Kaisa tried to suppress her anger. She took a deep breath in and sat down opposite Peter.

'It's not what you think.'

'Really?' Peter said.

'Not that it has anything to do with you.' Kaisa said, looking squarely at him. She was trying to keep her voice level, but she could hear her own words faltering.

Peter stared at Kaisa. He lowered his eyes to his pint, took a swig and said, 'No, I didn't say it was.'

They were quiet for a moment, not looking at each other. Kaisa could feel the eyes of Ravi and his friend, and a few other regulars in the pub, as well as the bar staff, burning holes in her back.

'So, how come you are here?' Kaisa asked, trying to find out if he'd come in search of her, or if it was another of those crazy coincidences that littered their lives.

Peter, who had been drinking his pint in large gulps, put down his empty glass. Finally, he met her eyes. 'You want another one?' he asked and got up.

Kaisa sighed, 'Please.'

He was doing what he did best, buying time and not talking. But Kaisa had got wise to his tactics and would get the reason for his visit out of him. She would have to be firm and brave. But when she glanced over her shoulder, checking that Peter hadn't gone to challenge Ravi, she was shocked to see that was exactly what he was doing. The two men were talking close to one another, seemingly in a civilised manner. When Peter returned to the table, Kaisa gazed at him, trying to gauge what he'd said to her ex-boyfriend. At that moment Rose walked in.

'Hello, darling,' she exclaimed and came to kiss Kaisa on the cheek. Directing her head towards Ravi, and lifting her eyebrows at Kaisa and Peter, whom she'd never met, Rose said, 'Everything alright?'

Kaisa spoke first, 'Rose, this is Peter, my ...' she hesitated and looked from Peter's face to Rose's. But Rose came to her rescue. She stretched her hand towards Peter and said, 'How lovely to meet you at last. I've heard so much about you.'

'I bet,' Peter said drily.

Rose gave a short laugh, 'Well, I should let you talk.'

'Rose,' Kaisa began again, only to be interrupted by Peter. 'Can I get you a drink, Rose?'

'That's very kind of you, Peter.' Rose smiled and said she'd love a gin and tonic.

When Peter had gone back to the bar, Rose sat down next to Kaisa. 'Look, if you want to spend the evening talking things over, we can reschedule.'

Kaisa looked at Rose's kind face. She was so overwhelmed by the situation that she could hardly speak. 'Thank you,' was all she managed to say.

'Just take a breath, darling.' Rose put her hand on Kaisa's arm and glanced at the bar, which had now filled up, forcing Peter to queue. 'Just listen to him, see what he has to say; find out why he's here to see you. Which is why he must be here, right? But don't promise anything. You have the world at your feet now, girl, so be strong and only do what you want to do. OK?' Rose was looking into Kaisa's eyes, and Kaisa nodded. 'OK,' she said.

When Peter came back Rose had managed to lighten the mood by telling Kaisa a story about a talking pig that the *Daily Mail* had carried as their headline that day. 'A slow news day!' She got up and said, 'Thanks for the drink, but I'm afraid I'm here to meet someone else.'

When Rose had gone, Peter said, 'Was that *the* Rose?'

'Yes,' Kaisa replied. 'She's been a very good friend to me, well more than a friend. She found the ad in the paper for this BBC job, and she helped me get the job at the café when *Adam's Apple* folded, and she wrote a letter of recommendation to the School of Journalism.' Kaisa saw Peter's eyebrows lift at the mention of the café and the journalism course. She realised he knew nothing of her life now. Suddenly she remembered the letter, still unposted, in her handbag. She'd thought it best to leave Peter to get on with his life, she now reminded herself.

Peter lifted his eyes to Kaisa, 'Yeah, I went to your old offices today, after Notting Hill.'

'You went to Colville Terrace?' Kaisa interrupted him. She

was astonished that he'd tried so hard to find her.

'Yeah,' Peter wasn't looking at her. 'Anyway there was just some caretaker at *Adam's Apple*, a young guy.'

'Jack?' Kaisa said, puzzled. What would the delivery guy be doing in the empty magazine offices?

'Yeah, I think that was his name. He was clearing out the place. Anyway, he knew you, and said there were a couple of pubs you used to go to nearby, so I took my chance and I found you here.' Peter paused for a moment, then added, 'With your boyfriend.'

'He's not my boyfriend.'

Peter gazed at Kaisa with his dark eyes. 'You sure about that?' He shifted in his seat so that he could look over to the bar past Kaisa. 'For a not-boyfriend, he seems to be keeping a very close eye on you.'

Kaisa turned around and saw Ravi looking at them. He lifted his pint at Kaisa and smiled. Kaisa smiled back, and nodded in what she hoped was a reassuring gesture. 'We used to see each other,' she said and faced Peter again. 'But we were never an item as such.'

'*Not an item as such*,' Peter repeated Kaisa's words. 'You've become very English,' he said, again with a kind of dry sarcasm.

Anger surged inside Kaisa and she snorted. 'And you can talk! What about the girl at the warehouse party? The one you told I was your ex, and didn't mean anything?'

Peter leaned back in his chair and said, 'That's over.'

'Oh.'

'That was over before it began. And it had just started when I saw you, so she was the one who didn't mean anything.'

'But you said ...' Kaisa was looking at her hands, trying to make sense of what Peter was telling her.

Peter bent over towards Kaisa and said, 'Look, it's really difficult to talk here with all these people.'

'I know.' Kaisa laughed. 'I suppose this is my local, sort of, so they all know me. Just like in Portsmouth.'

Peter laughed too, 'Yeah, I know.' He shifted in his seat, 'But we could go and have something to eat?'

Kaisa looked up at Peter. His eyes were kind now, and she could see he really did want to sort out their situation. Since starting her job, Kaisa had felt her life shifting, and settling into place, as if something at last was going right. One unsolved matter was Peter. Kaisa knew she needed to move on, so that she could concentrate on her career, and to do that she needed to sort out everything with Peter, once and for all.

'OK.' Kaisa emptied her glass of wine and got up. 'I'm just going to say goodbye.' She left Peter at the table and went over to tell Rose and Ravi, who were now standing next to each other talking at the bar, that she was going to have something to eat with Peter. She nodded to Ravi, whose eyes were still like deep, dark wells, and hugged Rose. 'Take care and remember what I said,' she whispered in Kaisa's ear.

Outside, Peter hailed a taxi and told the driver to take them to Covent Garden. 'You don't mind if we go to the same place as before, do you?'

'No,' Kaisa said. It felt luxurious to just step inside a black cab and be driven straight to one's destination, instead of walking into the dirty tube station. She watched the darkening city flash past as the driver ducked and dived through small streets that Kaisa didn't recognise. She'd sometimes seen Rose expertly hail a cab, and had on occasion accompanied her, but Kaisa couldn't afford to take them on her own. She always used buses and the tube to get around London. Or more often than not, if it wasn't raining, she'd walk. Perhaps now that she was on a much higher salary she could afford a cab or two, but then again, not if she was going to rent a place of her own. She'd been to see an agent, a thin young man in a shiny grey suit, and was surprised at the high cost of renting a one-bedroom flat. 'You'd be better off buying one,' the estate agent had said. He'd told her that she could get a 100 per cent mortgage on a flat. 'Think about it, if you have a steady income, it's worth buying now, mark my words,' he'd said and grinned.

THIRTY-SIX

Peter was quiet in the taxi, but Kaisa could feel his presence intensely. Their thighs were just touching, and she could feel the tension in his leg muscles through the thin fabric of her dress. He'd been watching the streets flash past on the other side of the cab, but now he turned towards her. 'Look, I've missed you.'

Kaisa was taken aback by Peter's words. It seemed absurd that those same words had been uttered just a few moments before by Ravi. Was she wearing some kind of perfume that attracted men like the rats in that children's tale? Kaisa held her breath when she saw Peter lean towards her, bringing his lips close to hers.

She put her hand on Peter's chest and said, 'Look, we need to talk.' She wasn't going to fall into that same trap of sexual attraction with him again.

'Oh, right.' Peter said, and giving her a searching look, he turned towards the window again. They sat through the rest of the journey in silence, and when they arrived at St Martin's Lane, Peter paid the driver.

'You still want to have dinner with me?' he asked when

they were both standing on the pavement outside the Café des Amis. While they'd been in the cab, the sky above London had darkened, and the lights from the passing cars and the neon signs of the restaurant gave Covent Garden a more sinister feel. Against this backdrop, Peter no longer looked so assured.

'We need to talk properly, don't you think?' Kaisa said. She felt like the grown-up, and for the first time in their relationship sensed that she had some control over the situation with Peter.

The restaurant was almost empty; it was Monday night after all. They were shown to a table by the window and ordered their food and wine. Kaisa could tell Peter was a little drunk by now and smiled to herself when he ordered a bottle of water, and then drank a glassful before even touching his wine. He was taking this meeting seriously and wanted to stay clear-headed. For some strange reason, even though she'd had three glasses of wine, Kaisa felt stone cold sober.

Again, she remembered her unsent letter and said, 'Thank you for your letter. And congratulations on becoming an uncle.'

Peter's face lit up, 'Yeah, thanks, I saw them over Christmas, they're beautiful babies. Both have a mop of black hair, and the baby boy, Oliver, he's got a pair of strong lungs on him! Cries a lot. The baby girl is beautiful.'

'Oliver and Beth are lovely names.'

'Yes,' Peter leaned closer to Kaisa and took her hands into his. 'Look, can we start this evening again?'

'Sure,' Kaisa smiled. 'Start by telling me why you wanted to see me?'

Peter sighed and said he'd been worried about her. Not getting a letter in reply to the one he'd sent (again Kaisa felt a pang of guilt over the unsent envelope in her handbag) had made him wonder if she was OK. He said he'd tried to call the house a couple of times, but he'd just been told Kaisa wasn't there. The man at the other end had offered no explanation, refusing to say if Kaisa even lived in the bedsit anymore. Peter had still gone over to the house, but no one had come to the door when he rang the bell.

That bastard landlady's boyfriend can't even be bothered to answer the door anymore, Kaisa thought.

'So, the pub was the final place where I thought I might find you.'

'I'm sorry, I should have replied to your letter.' Kaisa said.

'That's OK, we're here now and you're OK, which I'm glad to see.' Peter told Kaisa that he was now working up in Northwood. 'I'll be up here for a year at least.'

'Where's that?' Kaisa asked.

'Oh, North London, quite a way up. There's a train,' Peter said. He looked at his watch.

'Are you working tomorrow?' Kaisa said, looking at her watch herself. It was only just past 8 pm.

Peter shook his head.

They were both quiet for a moment, and then their food arrived. Kaisa wasn't at all hungry, but she forced herself to pick at the fish that she'd ordered. Peter attacked his steak with his usual enthusiasm; Kaisa smiled when she remembered his constant hunger. Hunger for food, and hunger for her.

While he ate, Kaisa told Peter about her new job, how she'd enjoyed her journalism course, and how she'd had to drop out in order to work for the BBC. She told him about Bush House, and how still, after two weeks, she couldn't quite believe she worked there when she walked through the magnificent pillars flanking the entrance and looked at the oddly spelled name.

'Well, I'm very glad for you. I knew you'd make it,' Peter said between mouthfuls. When he'd finished he put down his knife and fork and said, 'And making it obviously suits you. You look gorgeous.' Peter's face was intense, and his dark eyes made Kaisa's spine tingle. She looked down at her uneaten plateful of food and felt her cheeks redden.

For the rest of the meal they talked about their mutual friends. Kaisa told Peter about Sirkka and her mother in Helsinki, and about her sister's new more serious relationship. Peter told Kaisa about Stef and Tom, how they, too, had had a second baby. And that Pammy was pregnant again. Kaisa felt a quick pang of guilt; she'd not written to her friend since she'd had a 'Thank you' letter back for the pink bear she'd sent. She thought about the letter concerning Peter and Jackie that she'd received in Helsinki. Kaisa now wondered if there'd been any truth in it.

'There's a lot of it about,' Peter laughed, 'must be the water in Helensburgh.'

The mention of that place made them both grow serious and quiet for a while.

'Look, Kaisa,' Peter began, and at the same time Kaisa said, 'What do you want?'

'I want to see you again.'

Kaisa gazed at Peter. He'd stretched his hands out and knitted his fingers with hers. 'Let's start again; let's go out a few times and see how it goes?'

'But, Peter, you're still in the Navy, and one day, in one, or two, or three years' time, you'll be sent back to that awful place.' Kaisa sighed and squeezed Peter's hands, 'And I cannot be a Navy wife, who follows you everywhere you are posted. My life is here in London now. You know that.'

'Yes, I do, but haven't we always made it work, somehow?'

Kaisa laughed, 'Not really!'

Peter also laughed, and Kaisa wanted to touch the small creases that the laughter formed around his eyes.

'No, I know what you mean. But don't we deserve to give each other one last chance?' He squeezed Kaisa's hands. 'Just one more?'

Kaisa looked at Peter. She knew she loved him, but could she afford to take the risk of hurting him again?

'I'm afraid.'

Peter leaned closer to her, 'So am I. But let's not think! Let's just start dating. As if the past hadn't happened and we'd just met each other?' Peter's eyes were playful now, and the pressure of his hands had increased.

Kaisa was thinking hard. 'What if I hurt you again?' she said.

'I'm a big boy, I can take it,' Peter said and he leaned over the table to kiss her. Kaisa's heart filled with such emotion, such love, gentle and passionate at the same time, that she knew he was right.

But she forced herself to pull away from him, and looked deeply into his eyes. 'Are you sure you've forgiven me?'

Peter put his palm on her cheek and replied, 'My darling, there is nothing to forgive. We have no past, remember? We've just met!' He smiled and lowered his voice. 'I want to make love to you for the first time.'

Kaisa returned his smile. It was impossible! This man was impossible! But she knew in her heart that Peter was right.

They deserved to give each other one more chance.

THE TRUE HEART

Helena's next novel, the long-awaited fourth book in *The Nordic Heart* Romance Series is now out and available from good bookshops and online.

London 1990. When Kaisa suffers a third miscarriage, her submarine officer husband Peter is devastated. Kaisa, who has chosen a job with the BBC over the traditional life of a Navy wife, feels guilty. Has living apart from her husband to pursue a demanding career, contributed to her inability to keep hold of a baby?

But childlessness pales into insignificance when her old friend Rose tells Kaisa about a former lover's serious illness. The consequences of Duncan's condition could wreck Kaisa and Peter's future. Until life takes another heartbreaking twist …

Turn over to read the first chapter from *The True Heart*.

ONE

K aisa was trying to concentrate on the news bulletin she was preparing for broadcast later that afternoon when the phone on her desk rang.

'Hello, darling!' It was Rose.

Kaisa tried to hide her disappointment. 'How lovely to hear from you,' she said, lifting her voice higher than it normally was. She stifled a sigh in her hand and decided not to think about Peter. He was due home from a long patrol any moment, so when a phone call was put through to her at work, Kaisa immediately thought it must be her husband. He usually called from somewhere in Scotland as soon as he could, to tell her he was safe. Kaisa hadn't spoken to Peter for over six weeks and she was desperate to hear his voice.

'I'm up in town and wondered if I could see you after work?' Rose said, unaware of Kaisa's disappointment.

Rose met Kaisa outside Bush House, the headquarters of the BBC's World Service in Aldwych, central London, where Kaisa had been working for over three years.

'You look good!' Kaisa said, hugging her friend hard. She felt bad for wishing it hadn't been Rose on the phone. She rarely saw her good friend these days, not since she'd retired to the country.

'How's Peter?' Rose asked, letting go of Kaisa.

'On patrol,' she said, trying not to sound too miserable.

'You poor darling, I don't know how you do it!' Rose suggested they hop into a cab. 'Terroni's, yes?' she said. Kaisa nodded.

Kaisa loved the Italian café where she'd worked a few years ago, even if she had to cross town to visit it. During the months she'd been a waitress there, Kaisa had become one of the family and had even learned some Italian. She'd spent one potentially lonely Christmas Day with the Terroni family, and after that the Farringdon café, with its large steaming coffee machine, small round tables and curved chairs, and the best coffee in London, had been like home to her. Kaisa had got to know Rose, who had introduced her to Toni, the head of the Terroni family, through Duncan, a former friend of Peter's.

Rose had been instrumental in Kaisa's career. She'd first employed Kaisa at the feminist magazine *Adam's Apple*, which she'd run in the mid-eighties, then encouraged her to attend journalism school, and eventually to apply for a job in the BBC's Finnish section. Without Rose, Kaisa would still be living in Helsinki, miserable and divorced from Peter, and probably working for a bank like her university friend Tuuli. Not that Tuuli was unhappy, but work in finance suited her, whereas Kaisa knew it would have made her miserable.

When she'd first met Rose, Duncan's cousin, during a trip to London from Portsmouth, she'd thought her the most glamorous person she'd ever met. Her hair, clothes and manner had reminded Kaisa of Princess Diana.

Kaisa had been newly married and had only lived in the UK for a matter of months, but Rose had offered Kaisa a job as her assistant during a boozy meeting in one of the city's fashionable wine bars.

Peter's career had taken the couple to Scotland, so Kaisa hadn't been able to accept the job in London. Sometimes she wondered what would have happened if she'd refused to move up to Faslane, and had accepted the London job at that point in her life instead of later.

Kaisa grinned as she sat down opposite Rose. It was the life they had now, so why couldn't they have tried it sooner?

'What's so funny?' Rose asked.

'Nothing, just thinking of the past,' Kaisa replied. She gazed at her friend. Rose was quite a few years older than her, and since her move away from London and marriage to Roger, she'd put on a little weight. The added roundness suited her. Her face, framed by dark unruly curls, now mixed with grey, looked softer, and the few lines around her pale eyes just made her look friendlier.

'You look very happy,' Kaisa said and put her hand on Rose's as it rested on the table.

They'd been through the obligatory hugs and kisses from the café owner, Toni, and his wife, and 'Mamma', and were now facing each other at one of the corner tables by the window, their favourite, which Toni – miraculously – was always able to reserve for them.

'No point in dwelling,' Rose said.

'I guess not,' Kaisa said and thought about her own present condition, which wasn't a condition anymore. She was just about to tell Rose about it, when her friend said quickly, as if to get something out of the way, 'But talking of the past, I saw Duncan last weekend.'

'Oh,' Kaisa said and watched her friend as she lowered her eyes and fiddled with her large emerald engagement ring, now next to a gold wedding band on the ring finger of her left hand. Kaisa knew Rose felt guilty and responsible for the affair between Kaisa and her cousin Duncan. Rose believed that

Duncan had used her in order to impress Kaisa, and in a way that was right.

On the very night that Duncan had first introduced Kaisa to Rose, who had scheduled a date for a job interview with her, Duncan had tried to seduce Kaisa in his house in Chelsea. That had been the first time. Kaisa had barricaded herself in the guest bedroom, and the next morning had believed Duncan's profuse apologies and promises never to try anything like that with her ever again.

Yet Kaisa knew she had gone to bed with Duncan willingly months later in Faslane; it was her unhappiness at being so far away from home, frustration at not being able to find a job, and her loneliness without her new husband that had contributed to the events of that awful night.

In a way, Kaisa had also benefited from the guilt Rose had felt; she'd done so much for Kaisa that Kaisa herself often felt bad. They had discussed these feelings many times over the years, often without mentioning Duncan's name. Kaisa didn't want to think back to her awful mistake, and she also understood that Rose had severed all ties to him and didn't want to talk about her cousin. Kaisa was surprised that her friend mentioned Duncan now.

Rose lifted her cup of coffee up to her lips and gazed at Kaisa over the rim. 'He's not very well.'

Kaisa swallowed a mouthful of the strong black coffee and put her cup down.

Rose told her that Duncan had been unwell with a severe flu during the winter. A week ago he'd been to see a specialist and been diagnosed with AIDS. Rose whispered the last word, and looked around the café to see if anyone was listening to their conversation.

'AIDS!' Kaisa exclaimed.

'Shh, keep your voice down,' Rose said and leaned over the

table to take hold of Kaisa's hand. 'I'm only telling you so that you go and get tested.'

Kaisa stared at her friend, 'Tested, me?'

'And if you have it, Peter may have it too. And all his – and your – sexual partners for the past five years.'

'Oh, my God,' Kaisa felt her heartbeat quicken. The thought of having to tell Peter he had to go for an HIV test was beyond Kaisa. And for Peter to have to tell the two women he'd had affairs with while she and Peter had been separated would be unthinkable.

'And Ravi?' Kaisa gasped.

Rose nodded.

Kaisa felt sick. She took another sip of her coffee, but it suddenly tasted vile. 'But we're trying for a baby.'

'I know, that's why I wanted to tell you so that you can get tested in case ...'

Kaisa was quiet. Her mind was full of ifs and buts.

'Look, it's highly unlikely you have it. Duncan, as I understand it, has been more active sexually since you two, were, you know, together. I'm sure he was fine before.'

Kaisa sat with her hand over her mouth. She caught sight of Toni, who was watching the two women from his usual post behind the glass counter. Kaisa took her hand away and attempted to smile at him. The café owner nodded and waved a cup in his hand, asking if they needed a fill-up. Kaisa shook her head vigorously; the last person she wanted to tell Rose's news to was Toni. That would mean half of London would know it by supper time.

'But I thought he was living in the country?' Kaisa remembered a letter she'd received from Duncan, and immediately destroyed, when she was staying in Helsinki after the separation from Peter. He'd complained about the lack of female company in the countryside. Suddenly, Kaisa realised. Duncan must be gay! Or bisexual.

Rose raised her eyebrows. 'It only takes one sexual partner to be infected.'

Kaisa nodded. 'Of course,' then added carefully, 'But I thought you could only get it from gay sex?'

'No, that's not true!' Rose said emphatically. 'Anyone can get it.'

'Oh,' Kaisa said. Suddenly a picture she'd seen of a family somewhere in America, where a father was hugging his dying son with AIDS, came to her mind. In the photo the son had sunken cheeks and eyes, and his father's face was twisted in anguish as he embraced his son. And she thought about Freddie Mercury. There had been reports that he had AIDS. He'd looked thin and gaunt in the pictures Kaisa had seen in the papers.

Kaisa's thoughts returned to Duncan.

'How is he?'

Suddenly, Rose burst into tears, and before Kaisa could do or say anything, Toni and Mamma had come over and were making a scene, talking loudly and asking what the matter was.

Kaisa managed to calm her adoptive Italian family down, and eventually after they had made sure 'Rosa', as Toni insisted on calling Rose, was fine, Rose and Kaisa left the café and walked along the Clerkenwell Road towards Holborn. While they waited to cross the busy Grays Inn Road, walking arm in arm, Rose told Kaisa how Duncan had pneumonia, and the doctors were concerned about him. 'He's just not getting better, Kaisa,' Rose said. Her eyes filled with tears again and Kaisa pulled her into The Yorkshire Grey, a large pub on the corner of Theobalds Road.

'I think we need something a bit stronger than coffee,' Kaisa said.

Rose nodded and settled herself into a corner table. The pub was quickly filling up with post-work drinkers, but it wasn't yet crowded. It was a few minutes past five o'clock on a

Friday evening after all, Kaisa thought. The sun streamed into the dark space, making the interior feel stuffy.

Rose took a large gulp of her glass of wine and said, 'Look, I know it's unfair of me to say so, but he's been asking after you.'

'What?'

'Actually, he's been talking about both you and Peter.'

Kaisa looked at Rose. Seeing her friend so upset and the news about AIDS were affecting Kaisa's head. The room began to sway in front of her eyes. Suddenly all the memories of the first year of her marriage came into her mind. After the months she and Peter had spent apart, when Kaisa had forged her own career, finally getting the coveted job as a reporter at the World Service, she had tried to forget about Duncan, and her infidelity. When she and Peter had eventually reunited after several false starts and misunderstandings, they had vowed to forgive each other and forget the past. Since then, they had rarely spoken about the events leading up to their separation, or about the other relationships they both had had during that time.

'He needs to see that you've forgiven him.' Rose said, placing a hand over Kaisa's arm. Her pale blue eyes were pleading with Kaisa.

Kaisa said, with hesitation, 'You can tell him there are no hard feelings.'

Rose tilted her head sideways, and took another large gulp of wine. 'You don't understand.'

It was Kaisa's turn to take hold of Rose's hands, resting on the small, grubby mock teak table. 'What, tell me!'

'He is staying with us, Roger and I, and I wondered, well, we wondered ...' Rose began to dig inside her handbag for a tissue. She blew her nose, soliciting sideways glances from a group of men in pinstripe suits who were drinking pints of beer at the bar. When Rose had recovered a little, she finished her wine and Kaisa said, 'Want another?'

'Yes, let me,' Rose went back to her handbag, but Kaisa replied, 'No this is on me. You've bought enough drinks for me in the past.' She smiled, and got a nod from Rose.

Back at the table, when Kaisa was again facing Rose over their glasses of wine, Rose took a deep breath. 'I wondered if you might be able to come and see him.'

Kaisa stared at her friend. 'I, I don't know ...' she hadn't set eyes on Duncan since the awful fight between him and Peter in the pool. Duncan hadn't even turned up at Peter's Court Martial a few weeks later. He'd been dismissed his ship immediately after the fight, when his actions, 'unbecoming an officer of Her Majesty's Service' against a fellow naval officer, had come to light, and he'd left Faslane by all accounts that same night.

'Please, do this for me. I know his behaviour has been despicable, but he is a dying man.' Now tears were running down Rose's cheeks.

Kaisa glanced at the men behind her, and put her hands over Rose's on the sticky table.

'Of course I'll come,' she heard herself say, even though she had no idea how she would be able to face Duncan. Or how she would tell Peter any of it: her planned visit to see her former lover, or the AIDS tests they may both have to take. Or the consequences for their plans to start a family. *What a mess she had created.*

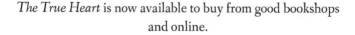

The True Heart is now available to buy from good bookshops and online.

THE YOUNG HEART

Why not sign up for the Readers' Group mailing list and get exclusive, unpublished bonus chapters from *The Nordic Heart* Romance Series? You will also get a free copy of the first book in the series, *The Young Heart*, a prequel novella to *The English Heart*.

> *'Wonderfully intimate and honest.'* – Pauliina Ståhlberg, Director of The Finnish Institute in London.

Is she too young to fall in love? A standalone read, *The Young Heart* is a prequel to the acclaimed 1980s romance series, *The Nordic Heart*.

Go to www.helenahalme.com to find out more!

COFFEE AND VODKA

Eeva doesn't want to remember. But now she's forced to return to Finland and confront her past.

'In Stockholm everything is bigger and better.'

When Pappa announces the family is to leave Finland for a new life in Sweden, 11-year-old Eeva is elated. But in Stockholm Mamma finds feminism, Eeva's sister, Anja, pretends to be Swedish and Pappa struggles to adapt.

And one night, Eeva's world falls apart.

Fast forward 30 years. Now teaching Swedish to foreigners, Eeva travels back to Finland when her beloved grandmother becomes ill. On the overnight ferry, a chance meeting with her married ex-lover, Yri, prompts family secrets to unravel and buried memories to come flooding back.

It's time for Eeva to find out what really happened all those years ago …

Coffee and Vodka has it all: family drama, mystery, romance and sisterly love.

If you like Nordic Noir, you'll love this rich Nordic family drama by the Finnish author Helena Halme.

'Coffee and Vodka *is a rich story that stays with us....with moments of brilliance.'* – Dr Mimi Thebo, Bath Spa University.

'Like the television series The Bridge, Coffee and Vodka *opens our eyes to facets of a Scandinavian culture that most of us would lump together into one. I loved the way the narrative wove together the viewpoint of Eeva the child and her shock at arriving in a new country, with Eeva the sophisticated adult, returning for the first time to the country of her birth, and finding it both familiar and irretrievably strange.'* – Catriona Troth, Triskele Books.

Pick up *Coffee and Vodka* to discover this brilliant, heart-warming Nordic family drama today!

ABOUT THE AUTHOR

Helena Halme grew up in Tampere, central Finland, and moved to the UK via Stockholm and Helsinki at the age of 22. She is a former BBC journalist and has also worked as a magazine editor, a bookseller and, until recently, ran a Finnish/British cultural association in London.

Since gaining an MA in Creative Writing at Bath Spa University, Helena has published seven fiction titles, including five in *The Nordic Heart* Romance Series.

Helena lives in North London with her ex-Navy husband and an old stubborn terrier, called Jerry. She loves Nordic Noir and sings along to Abba songs when no one is around.

You can read Helena's blog at www.helenahalme.com, where you can also sign up for her *Readers' Group*.

Find Helena Halme online
www.helenahalme.com
hello@helenahalme.com